THE

COLD

DISTANCE

NEIL COLEY

CRANTHORPE
—MILLNER—
PUBLISHERS

First published by Cranthorpe Millner Publishers (2023)

ISBN 978-1-80378-102-0 (Paperback)

www.cranthorpemillner.com

Cranthorpe Millner Publishers

Prologue: *Bad Moon Rising*

Sunday, June 1973

She stood in the dark silent kitchen, desolation and despair drawn on her face. Out of the window she could see the blurred lights of the nearby town and just beyond that the lake, a sliver of silver-white illuminated by the brightness of the bulbous full moon. Tears tracked down her cheeks just as they had done all the way back to the tenth floor of the tower block where her bedroom was located. Suddenly aware of how smudged and dirty the kitchen windows were, she opened the sliding door and stepped out onto the small balcony. She immediately felt the chill of the night-time breeze that ruffled her long blonde hair. She shivered and huddled into her thick jumper before dragging a sleeve across her face to wipe away the tears. The scratches on the left side of her face still felt sore and she touched them, feeling the raised lines that were red and livid against her pale skin. Leaning over the balcony's parapet she looked down to the flagstones of The Square below, which was deserted

1

and lit only by a few dim lights. Everywhere was still; only the wind whistling softly around The Tower disturbed the late night quiet of the university campus. She looked up at the dark blue-black sky. Not many stars were visible on this night. 'The moon's too bright,' she said out loud in a voice reedy with emotion.

There was a noise behind her from the kitchen. She didn't turn around; explaining why she was standing on the cold balcony crying was not something she wanted to go into at this time. She guessed it was one of the other girls making a late-night cup of coffee or tea. Perhaps they wouldn't notice her out here? Or if they did, they would choose to leave her alone with her thoughts. Then she heard someone step out onto the balcony, someone who was breathing heavily as if they had just run up all of The Tower's many flights of stairs. She felt a hand on her shoulder, gently squeezing. She turned around.

'Oh, it's you,' she said, sounding surprised.

The hand on her shoulder squeezed again. This time the touch was much firmer and gradually turned into a hard, remorseless and painful grip. She was shocked at the eyes that stared back at her: wide and enraged and pitiless, boring into her head. She felt a hand reach out and grab the large metal buckle of her belt. Her arms flailed uselessly as her body was quickly lifted upwards. A wave of terror swept through her as she realised what was going to happen. Her back scuffed against the rusted iron rail of the parapet as she vainly sought, but failed, to grab onto something that would stop this horror from happening. She wanted to scream but nothing emerged from her dry mouth as the balcony began to fly away from her. Her final thought, just before her head came into cruel contact with the unforgiving concrete and all thoughts in it ceased forever, was the simple question: "why?"

Chapter 1: *Something in the Air*

September, the present day

It all began with a letter; if I had known the trouble it would bring me, I would have chucked it straight in the bin and never opened the damned thing.

I still receive quite a lot of letters even though the art of writing them seems to have disappeared as far as most of the general population is concerned. On the whole I would rather deal with so-called "snail mail" than spend my time reading the half-baked opinions you tend to find on social media. Usually the letters I get are from elderly readers of my crime fiction and they generally come to me via my publisher. Invariably they are from fans of my books and are often just requesting a signed photograph, but some are keen to know when my next novel is due out and what it's going to be about. Poor deluded fools! If only they knew that when I sit down to begin a new book I have no real notion (apart from a few basic ideas) of what the plot's actually going to entail. Such is the perpetual plight of the murder mystery writer. I'm sure that it was the same even for the adored Dame Agatha.

Until very recently I would deal with my letters early in the morning, along with my emails, before I began the day's drudge sitting in front of a computer screen. I would tell myself that it is important to communicate with my readers, my fan-base, but really it was just a way of putting off that inevitable moment when I had to think and (God help me) be clever and creative. However, this particular letter on this particular day was very different from the usual sort of fan guff. There was no return address or date. It was postmarked a few days before I received it. It read:

Dear Mr Cross,

My name is Sarah Webb. You don't know me so I hope you don't mind me writing to you.

Recently my mother, Margaret Harman, sadly passed away. I believe you knew her when you were both at university. One of her final requests was that I should contact you and pass on a letter that she wrote in her final days, along with a particular item she wanted you to have. I do not want to specify the nature of the item in this letter, so I thought the best thing to do would be for us to meet up so I could hand it to you personally.

I am based in London, as I believe are you, so a meeting somewhere in central London would probably be best. I would like to suggest therefore that we meet in the lounge bar of the Russell Hotel in Russell Square on the 22nd of next month (October) at twelve noon. I will recognise you from your picture on the back cover of your recent novel. I will be wearing a yellow mac. I look forward to meeting you – or at least I hope I will.

Yours sincerely,

Sarah Webb (Mrs)

It was an odd letter. I read the final sentence several times; it seemed a strange comment for someone to make. After a good deal of thought I eventually decided that, as I knew no more about the matter than what was contained in the letter, it was pointless trying to speculate about what it all might mean. However, it did get me thinking. I certainly remembered Margaret Harman. She was part of the large circle of people I hung out with at the University of the North in the early 1970s. However, it was fifty years ago and my memory of those times is more than a little cloudy (age and the sacrifice of my 'little grey cells' on the altar of beer, wine and whisky, not to mention the occasional illicit substance, having taken their toll no doubt).

Margaret Harman. I trawled my memory. What did I remember about her? I had in my mind's eye a dark-haired, very attractive-looking girl known as Maggie by everyone, who wore purple or black clothes most of the time. For a while we had worked on the university newspaper together. At parties and discos she had a tendency to get very drunk and dance wildly and barefoot about the place in true hippy style. I recalled that we had slept together on more than a few occasions but there was never anything really serious between us, just frantic encounters, probably when we were off our heads on alcohol or pot. It was the 1970s after all.

Gradually I pieced together some other memories I thought I had forgotten about – vague monochrome spectral shadows that had been pushed to the back of my mind; grey ghosts that suddenly popped up out of the mental clutter accrued by fifty years of my subsequent life experiences. For example, there was an occasion on one Saturday evening when I was in my campus bedroom busily working at my desk. I think I must have been writing an essay that I was due to hand in on the Monday morning (that was how I used to work in those days in the mistaken belief that my brain functioned better under pressure). Anyway, there I was tapping away on my portable Underwood typewriter that I, as a cricket fan, had amusingly nicknamed Derek – a note to the young: there were no computers or word processor programs in those long gone, simpler, cyber-free days – when there was a knock on my door. Someone (I forget who now) had left the university's regular Saturday night disco to come to tell me in a drunken, excited slur that Maggie had accidently stepped on some broken glass while dancing and had called out for me to go and help her. When I got to the disco, which was only a short walk from my halls of residence, I found her sitting in an inebriated heap on the floor in the corner of the room looking rather woebegone and holding a handkerchief to her bleeding foot. What she said to me at that point and why she had called for me in the first place I could not now recall. Perhaps we were much closer than I remember? In any case I helped her back to my room, her hopping on one leg and me supporting her while carrying her shoes (why I should remember that tiny detail I do not know). Back in my room I made her a sobering-up mug of coffee, cleaned up her cut foot, applied a bit of Germolene and bandaged it (I had a first-aid kit. I was such an organised young man back then!). After a while, and somewhat inevitably I suppose, we had ended up in bed.

We slept together a few more times after that but then some months later we just drifted apart (I can't remember the exact turn of events). While we must have stayed in the same friendship group, I think we stopped being quite so close. I don't recall she or I being particularly upset, we just moved on in the way things used to happen in those days (and still do as far as I know). After university I think we exchanged Christmas cards for a couple of years but I never saw her again. For some reason she didn't attend any post-university get-togethers at weddings, anniversaries and the like.

And then it suddenly struck me that someone I had been quite close to, albeit a long time ago, was actually dead, and an overwhelming feeling of regret, loss and general dread washed over me. I am at the age now where whenever I hear news of a contemporary I know, or once knew, who has died it invariably induces a momentary feeling of panic in me as I realise (as if for the very first time) that at some point in the not too distant future I will be following them in that final and irrevocable journey into nothingness.

I shook myself back to the existential present. What was the item that Maggie's daughter wanted to give to me? It was a mystery I could not even begin to guess at. Why did she want to give me it personally? Why had she not sent it through the post? Did she just want to meet someone who was marginally famous, or was there more to it than that? After a few more of these brooding thoughts I decided there was only one way to answer those questions and that was to meet up with her at the time and place she had specified in her letter.

*

I put the meeting with the mysterious Sarah Webb (Mrs) to the back of my mind while I carried on with my writing. It was four weeks until 22nd October and I had realised there were no more memories I could dredge up about her mother so it was pointless trying to speculate further about what it was she planned to pass onto me.

The days went by and I had almost forgotten about the upcoming meeting, engrossed as I was in my new novel. I had (after a while of trying and generally floundering) worked out not only the overall shape of the story but also how and why the murder would be committed, who the culprit was, and the various red herrings and MacGuffins I was going to include in order to send my future readers off on the wrong track. As usual, there would be several possible suspects for my singular, enigmatic and extremely clever police detective – DCI Sheldon Heath – to eventually gather together before dramatically revealing which one of them had perpetrated the heinous crime and what their motive for murder had been. As is always the case, once I had got the basic parameters of the plot sorted out in my mind the ideas started to flow nicely, and I was able to write my requisite two thousand words each day. I felt quite pleased, as I always do when I get to that stage with one of my novels. Another best-selling (hopefully) Sheldon Heath novel was well on the way!

By the time the 22nd October arrived I had completed almost half of the first draft and felt fairly satisfied with it. I was actively looking forward to writing the second half, along with the dramatic and clever denouement of the story. I thought a little more about that ending as I travelled on the tube into central London, jotting down a few ideas in my ever-present notebook. So engrossed was I with my plot and character ideas that I forgot to give much thought to my imminent meeting with Sarah Webb. In fact it wasn't until I was standing in the crowded, creaking and antiquated lift that took passengers up to the surface at Russell Street underground station that I started to consider what this meeting would be like. As I walked the short distance from the station to the Russell Hotel I was surprised at how nervous I felt. It was like nothing I had experienced for many years: that stomach-churning feeling that affects you when you are unsure about what's going to happen. A long time ago I used to get that sort of sensation when waiting for a job interview to begin: the extreme dryness of the inside of my mouth when my tongue seemed to stick to its roof, the nervous tic just below my left eye and the jelly-like feeling in my knees. Now I felt like that all over again. By the time I reached the entrance to the hotel I was feeling worse than I had done for a long time and was definitely looking forward to a stiff drink that I hoped would settle my nerves.

I entered the lounge bar at ten minutes to noon (turning up early for appointments is a habit I have had all my life). There were only a few people in the room, all of whom looked lost among its dark oak panelling and Chesterfield sofas. I headed for the bar and ordered a double whisky and a small bottle of dry ginger ale. After I had poured a little of the dry ginger into my whisky I took a gulp of it. The drink warmed its way down my throat in an extremely pleasant and comforting fashion. I looked around but there was no woman in a yellow mac. In fact there were no women at all in the room. I selected a table in the corner where I could clearly see anyone who entered. I did not have to wait long, for as soon as the hands on the large clock on the wall behind the bar reached twelve o'clock in through the door came a woman wearing a bright yellow plastic mac. Petite with short dark hair, she looked to be in her mid-to-late forties, and there was definitely a hint of her mother about her. I stood up so that she could see me. As she walked over to the table where I had ensconced myself, I smiled my most friendly smile, just like the one I use to greet the punters when I'm conducting a book-signing event. She didn't respond. In fact, she looked to be scowling somewhat as she made her way across the room. I held out my hand and, with a marked reluctance, she reached out and shook it in a limp, perfunctory manner.

'Hello, Mrs Webb, nice to meet you. Would you like a drink?' I asked.

'Yes, a slim-line tonic water... please,' she replied.

I went to the bar to get it while she took off her mac, put it on the back of her chair and sat down.

I ordered her drink along with another double whisky for myself. Taking the glasses back to the table I realised that my unaccountable nervousness had now lifted and had been replaced by a feeling of expectation and, yes, a certain amount of excitement too.

'I was so very sorry to hear about your mother,' I said in my sincerest voice, as I sat down and poured some ginger ale into my whisky.

She looked at me and just nodded, her lips clenched tightly together.

'Was it a long illness?' I asked.

After a pause, during which she seemed to gather herself, she answered, 'Yes, it was really. She had lung cancer and slowly wasted away. It was hard to watch.'

'I can imagine,' I said, with as much feeling as I could muster. To be perfectly honest I found it difficult to feel anything very much. After all, it had been almost fifty years since I had last seen Maggie. If we had kept in touch with each other I'm sure I would have been much more affected by her death, but under the circumstances I wasn't, although I did try extremely hard to look as sad and as solemn as possible. I sipped my whisky and waited for her to speak again.

She coughed to clear her throat, took a sip of her tonic water, picked up her brown leather shoulder bag, unbuckled it and reached inside. She took out a long white envelope and a small red box, both of which she passed to me. I took them and looked at her inquiringly.

'As I indicated in my letter, my mother instructed me, on her death bed, to give these to you.'

I peered down at the envelope. It had my name on it. I flipped open the box. Inside was a ring that I vaguely recognised: silver with a largish stone in the middle, which I presumed was a diamond. I put it down on the table after giving Sarah Webb a quizzical look that I hoped conveyed to her that I was as confused as I felt. I opened the envelope and took out a sheet of paper. I was about to read from it when I decided not to and slipped it back inside the envelope.

'Erm, I think I'll read this at home. If that's all right

with you, Mrs Webb?'

'It's fine with me,' she said sharply. 'But could you answer me one question please?'

'Erm, yes, of course… well, I'll try. I only knew your mother for a relatively short period of time and then only as part of a wide group of friends. After university I never saw her again so I can't really recall a great deal about her to tell you the truth.'

'In that case, I would like to know why, according to the diary she kept in 1973, my mother wrote that you and she had got engaged to be married at a party in the June of that year?'

Now I really felt confused. 'Erm, we didn't,' I said in a suitably baffled voice. 'I'm sure that I would have remembered something like that happening.'

Sarah Webb didn't look convinced. I thought, somewhat incongruously considering our current conversation, that if it were not for the perpetual scowl she wore on her face she would have been quite attractive.

I picked up my whisky and drained the glass before scratching my head. '1973 was our last year at university. After we had finished our finals in the summer we would have gone to several parties where everyone would have got extremely drunk I imagine, and then we all went our separate ways soon after the results came out. I never saw your mother again, sadly. We just sent each other letters and cards a few times I think. We certainly didn't get engaged; ours wasn't that sort of relationship. I have no idea why she would have wanted me to have this ring.'

She looked at me with disdain. I could see in her eyes that she didn't believe a word I had just said.

'You did sleep with her though. That's in her diary too. In it she wrote that you had told her you loved her and had given her a ring. You were supposed to meet her during the summer but failed to turn up. When you eventually rang her you told her that the engagement was off. According to her diary she was so upset that she actually contemplated suicide.'

To say I was shocked would be an understatement. I shook my head. 'It didn't happen that way,' I said. 'I can't remember the exact details of those final parties but I'm pretty sure I didn't propose to her. Yes, we did sleep together on a few occasions but that sort of thing was the norm. We were young, we were at university, people slept around but our relationship was never very serious though.'

'Well it obviously was to her. According to her diaries she never really got over the feeling of rejection. She actually died thinking of you.' Sarah Webb stifled a sob, took out a handkerchief to dry her eyes, and looked at me again, blinking rapidly. 'I'm sure she'll make it clear in the letter. It was the last thing she ever wrote.' With that she stood and reached for her coat from the back of the chair. I stood up too, out of politeness.

'I'm so sorry that all of this has upset you,' I said.

'But you must understand that there was nothing really between the two of us. If there had been I would have definitely kept in touch. Please believe me.'

She looked at me again. For a moment I thought she was going to shout or scream at me but she obviously thought better of it and just shrugged and put her mac on.

'Here's my phone number if you want to ask me any questions after you've read Mum's letter.'

She handed me a scrunched-up piece of paper she had taken from her coat pocket. I nodded. Without saying goodbye, farewell or cheerio she turned and walked out of the door, leaving me to sit down in a state of utter bewilderment wondering what the hell all that had been about.

*

Back home that evening I pondered what Mrs Webb had said. I was so wrapped up in my thoughts that when Jenny, my wife, asked me what the matter was I didn't take in what she had said and she had to tap me on the arm before I responded. The meeting with Sarah Webb and the letter she had given me had thrown my mind into total confusion. I went to the study where I had locked the letter and ring in the top drawer of my desk. I read it again – for the fifth time. I had originally looked at it as soon as Mrs Webb had left the lounge of the Russell Hotel. The contents had brought me up short and made me doubt what I thought I had known. This is what it said:

Dear Rob,

It has been a long, long time. I missed you at first but I gradually got over not seeing you, although I have to say I have probably thought about you every single day of my life since I last saw you. When you read this I will already be dead, but before I die I'm going to ask Sarah, my daughter, to give you this letter and the ring personally. Incidentally she's not yours if that's what you were thinking. I got involved with a man fairly soon after I had heard from you for the last time and she was the result. I'm quite glad it turned out that way to be truthful – it saved me the bother of getting married and doing all that domestic stuff that, I think in retrospect, would have bored me rigid.

I hope the writing is going well. I've read all of your books of course, although I have always thought that you should have turned your mind to something a bit more literary rather than keep going with all that sub-Christie genre stuff. Who knows, you might have won a Booker Prize or two! I was thinking the other day of those late nights we used to work on the university newspaper all those years ago. It was so obvious that you were the one with most of the talent. Ironically perhaps, I went on to be a reporter on a few local newspapers – even had an interview at the *Guardian* once but nothing came of it. Ended up as editor of the *Plumstead Gazette*. Oh, such towering heights! Inexplicably you became a schoolteacher I believe. I have to say I was taken aback by that news as you never seemed to me to have any obvious interest in, or empathy with, children at all. But I suppose people are always capable of doing surprising things that can appear wildly out of character!

I wish I could have seen you again and spoken to you. It has always mystified and annoyed me that you were able to let me go with such alacrity. One minute you were putting the ring on my finger and asking me to marry you and seemingly the next you were discarding me like an old, worn-out overcoat. I suppose I have always resented you for treating me in that way, but then again life is always full of such disappointments. Besides, as I have already said, I was never a great fan of marriage. I just thought it would have made you happy.

I hope you like Sarah. She's the only part of me that will be left on the earth after I have gone. She's all right generally although I think it takes people a long time to get to know her. Her marriage didn't last too long; her husband ditched her after three years. That sort of thing seems to run in the family – ha-ha!

As I approach my death my mind keeps going back to our university days and all the people we knew: Jack, Michael, Nick, Tina, Liz, Angela, Posh Rufus, Toby, Fiona and Jane. Was there an Althea? It's difficult for me to remember all the names these days. I often wonder how many of them you kept in touch with. I only ever saw Michael. We used to meet up occasionally in some pub or other. And then of course there was Stella. Beautiful, sexy, tragic Stella! I suppose she never really deserved what happened to her despite the sort of person she was. I have never forgotten that day when she died. What a shock it was! I don't expect anyone will ever know what caused her to do it, or even if it actually was suicide. Perhaps you should set your detective on to it – Sherlock Heath or whatever he's called. Who knows what he might discover?

Well, that's all I've got to say. I don't quite know how much time I've got left but not very long, I think. Maybe we'll meet each other again in heaven – or possibly hell! Who knows? In some ways either place would be just as appropriate. Be good!

Maggie x (a little kiss for old time's sake!)

I put the letter down. The handwriting was quite clear, if a little shaky, but I didn't know what to make of it. Had her mind started to go when she wrote it? It seemed unlikely; there didn't seem to be anything too amiss with her memory apart from the bit about me giving her a ring. I couldn't understand it, although I did now remember where I had seen the ring before: it had been on Maggie's finger, on one of the fingers of her right hand to be exact. Why would she invent a story about me giving it to her and saying that we were engaged when she had obtained it from somewhere else? If only I could have spoken to her about it but of course, barring a séance, it was too late now. I had another look at the ring and shook my head. I put it and the letter back in my desk drawer and locked it. How strange it all was and how much the incident had made me think back to my university days of long ago. I certainly hadn't thought about Stella for ages. The whole business surrounding her death had been so important at the time but now, like so many other things from those years, it seemed far too distant and cold to still be in any way relevant to the person I now was and the life that, until very recently anyway, I'd been happily leading.

And then I remembered where I had first met Maggie. The memory seemed to come to me from out of the blue. It was in one of the campus bars. It was a weekday evening early on in the autumn term of 1972 and I was sitting there with Toby Barker having a pint or two. Toby could always be guaranteed to lead me astray. No doubt he had turned up at my door and asked if I wanted to go for a swift half, a phrase that usually meant that I would be returning to my room many hours later after having had a skin-full of beer! Anyway, while we were sitting chatting in the corner of the bar I remember Maggie came over to us with a cigarette held between her lips, and asked for a light.

Chapter 2: *Maggie May*

Wednesday, October 1972

'Excuse me, can I have a light please?'

'Sure,' Rob said, and passed her the box of matches that sat, along with his cigarettes, on the low table in front of him. He looked at the girl as she concentrated on lighting her cigarette and smiled. She smiled back. She was smallish, very pretty, with big brown eyes, long dark hair and was wearing a black and purple jumper and smart flared jeans with embroidered flowers on the back pockets. 'Hi, I'm Robert – Rob,' Rob said, as she passed him back his matches.

'Hi, Robert Rob,' she replied, smiling. 'I'm Maggie. And who's this?' she continued, studying Toby with a twinkle in her eye.

'Oh, I'm Toby. Pleased to meet you, Maggie. Erm, can I get you a drink?'

She looked at her watch. 'Oh, okay, yes please. Er, I'll have a dry martini and lemonade if that's all right?'

It was the first week proper back at the start of the

21

new university year. Lectures and seminars had begun, and Rob and Toby were only too aware that this was the beginning of their final year. Rob had been spending a lot of time over the summer holidays thinking hard about his future. This evening he had been intent on doing some in-depth and important reading before his history tutorial tomorrow, up until the point when Toby had knocked on his door and lured him out for a drink in one of the college bars by saying, 'Fancy a swift half?' There was a great deal of work ahead for Rob if he wanted to get any sort of decent degree so these midweek visits to the bar would definitely have to stop. He had thought this all too briefly as he grabbed his jacket and wallet and enthusiastically followed Toby to Hawkshead Bar.

'Are you a first-year?' Rob asked.

Maggie laughed and touched Rob's knee. 'No, I'm in my fourth year of French and European studies. I spent last year in France working in a secondary school, so this is my final year. Sorry, do you want a ciggy?' she said, offering her packet of Embassy to Rob. 'What about you?'

'Oh – yeah, thanks,' Rob said, as he took a cigarette. 'I'm in my third year, doing history,' said Rob, as he lit the cigarette and then took a deep drag of it, grimacing a little. 'Toby doesn't smoke, by the way,' he said, noticing that Maggie had taken another cigarette from the packet and put it on the table in front of where Toby had been sitting. She picked up the unwanted cigarette and put it back in the packet, dropping the box into her large, purple shoulder bag.

Toby returned carrying all the drinks at once, holding them in his hands somewhat precariously with a packet of crisps clenched between his teeth. Rob and Maggie smiled at each other.

'Hope you both like cheese and onion,' he said, having put the drinks down, torn open the crisp packet and put it in the middle of the table.

'Thanks,' said Maggie, taking a sip of her martini and lemonade and delving into the bag to pick up a crisp.

'Cheers,' the two friends said, both taking large glugs of their beer.

Maggie looked at her watch again. 'I'm supposed to be meeting my friend Jane here at eight o'clock and going into town, but she's late.' She looked at Rob and smiled. It was a nice smile, thought Rob, friendly but alluring. Full of Eastern promise, he thought, as the tune to the *Fry's Turkish Delight* television commercial played unbidden in his head. He would like to get to know this Maggie a bit better so it was a pity she would be leaving the bar so soon tonight.

And then, as if on cue, a tall blonde-haired girl wearing John Lennon-style glasses came through the door scanning those present in the bar.

Maggie quickly finished her drink. 'There she is. I'm off. Ta for the drink, I'll return the favour next time.' She winked at Toby, looked at Rob, and was gone.

'Good-looking girl. Nice tits too,' said Toby.

'Not bad,' said Rob.

'I think she fancied you, Rob.'

'Nah, I don't think so. I thought it was you she had her eye on,' Rob replied. 'There was a definite sparkle in them when she looked at you.'

Toby smiled. 'Well, can't blame the poor girl I suppose. Putty in my hands. So which bar shall we go to next then?' he said.

*

There were six bars on the sprawling campus that was the University of the North. Opened in the mid-sixties as part of the government's expansion of higher education, the university was built out in the wilds of Cumberland and was by far the biggest single employer of the immediate area. The nearest town, Flitborough, was three miles away, but such were the services and facilities available on campus that a student could literally spend all their time there and never leave the site. As well as a large book and stationary store called Murdoch's there were two banks, a newsagent, a launderette, a bread, sandwich and cake shop, a chemist and several grocery outlets all mainly located outside of the large open area that was officially known as Queen's Plaza, but which everyone called The Square. The large building that held the university library and an attached and well-frequented coffee bar stood in one corner of The Square. A many-storied tower block containing student bedrooms was situated in another corner. A university-run travel agency took care of all the train and coach bookings that students needed for journeying to and from their homes at holiday times, and a frequent local bus service could take anyone wanting a change from campus life into town in order to visit its many student-friendly eateries and pubs. Several refectories or cafeterias could be found throughout the university campus, each one serving different styles of food all produced and served (usually with great efficiency and friendliness) by local women of varying ages. Female cleaners took care of the study bedrooms, even making the beds of those (invariably male) occupants who couldn't quite manage to do the task themselves, and a small army of repairmen clad in green overalls were always on hand to change light bulbs, fix leaky taps and perform a myriad of other maintenance tasks throughout the campus. All in all those students who occasionally reflected on the situation they found themselves in considered themselves fortunate in the extreme to have landed in such a cosseted and well-provisioned learning environment.

Rob was one of those who certainly appreciated his privileged life at the university to the full. Raised in a council house in a working-class area of an East Midlands city, he had attended a large comprehensive school and could not believe his luck when he first saw the university campus. He knew that there would be plenty of challenging studying for him to do, of course, but the facilities available on site had genuinely amazed him in those early days. On a full local authority grant he had found that generally he had enough money to pay rent, buy books and food. His intake of beer increased exponentially during his first year, however, and at times he found it difficult to keep up with the greater spending power of those students he met who came from more privileged backgrounds; the sort of people he had never had any contact with before.

During his first year, having latched on to Toby Barker who was gregarious to a fault, Rob became acquainted with a large group of fellow students from various backgrounds. Among many others there was Tina from the Surrey stockbroker-belt, Liz from the well-to-do bit of Manchester, Posh Rufus from some unspecified spot in darkest Kent, Nick – a somewhat taciturn Geordie who was very driven as well as extremely clever, Fiona – a tall, robust and sturdy-looking girl from a rural background in the South-West who was into horses in a big way, and Althea from the USA, one of the few black students at the University of the North at that time. And then there was Stella George: petite, beautiful, willowy, ethereal and notoriously distant and unobtainable. Adorned with long blonde hair, beautifully clear skin and pale blue eyes, she was the one all the males (and some of the females) would frequently fantasise about. No one could ever place her by her accent that seemed to lie somewhere between Received Pronunciation and middle Europe, with a hint of American around the edges, brought about, she would tell people, because she was the daughter of a high-ranking army officer who had been stationed in various locations around the world, forcing her to attend a large number of disparate foreign schools. Of all the people Rob got to know at the University of the North, Stella was the one he never really understood. He always maintained that he was very good at 'reading' people and seeing what made them tick, but with Stella he was never sure what she was thinking at any given time or indeed what it was that motivated her. She was a good student – there was no doubt about that – and on one level always seemed to exude poise and confidence. At other times, however, she seemed unsure and hesitant; "a bundle of nerves" as Rob's mum might have described her. On one occasion, in his second year, Rob had asked her out to the pictures and she had gripped his hand tightly throughout the tense thriller. Occasionally she looked fondly into his eyes but on the way back to the campus, when he had suggested coffee in his bedroom, she had smiled, shook her head and (annoyingly for Rob) said, "No," very firmly. As far as Rob could see no one ever had more than one date with the beautiful and desirable Stella and he could never work out why. She had plenty of friends of both sexes but nobody, with the exception of one person in particular, ever really got close to her. She rarely said much about her home life or mentioned her family, and remained an enigma, at least as far as Rob was concerned, right up until her untimely and tragic death when late one night, at the end of her final term, she had seemingly leapt from the balcony on the tenth floor of the tower block to The Square below.

From the very beginning of his first year Rob had worked on the university newspaper, which came out weekly. For a long time he had imagined a future for himself as an intrepid, investigative journalist or foreign correspondent who would, after serving a short but distinguished apprenticeship on some local rag, graduate to one of the Fleet Street national dailies or maybe even to the BBC, despite the corporation's habit of only hiring Oxbridge graduates. Getting experience working to a deadline on the student-produced newspaper, which for some reason was called *Ariel*, was one of the things that Rob hoped would stand him in good stead as far as getting started on a glittering future career in journalism.

It was a few days after he had first met her that Rob next saw Maggie. He was sitting in the *Ariel* office reading through an article that one of the reporters had left on his desk, trying to decide if it was interesting enough to include in that week's edition. After two years of working on the paper, Rob had graduated to the role of editor. He didn't find it as mentally stimulating as going out in the field and finding stories for himself but it did mean that he had a good amount of control over what was published. That sort of responsibility, he rationalised, would be invaluable when he started to look for newspaper jobs in the real world.

Maggie breezed in through the open door of the office and smiled at Rob who hadn't looked up immediately, engaged as he was with the piece of writing in front of him.

'Hello you,' she said. 'Any chance of a job?'

'Hi,' replied Rob, looking up and momentarily wearing a puzzled expression on his face. 'A job on *Ariel*? Yep, we can manage that. Always looking for new writing talent.'

'How do you know if I have any?'

'Oh I'm sure you do,' said Rob, grinning. 'How was the film the other night?'

'Good, but it made me cry.'

'What was it called?'

'*Sounder*. It was about a black boy and his dog in the Depression years in America.'

'Interesting. Well, your first job can be to write a two-hundred-and-fifty-word review of it. I need something else for the entertainments page,' said Rob, enjoying sounding like a hard-bitten editor in some Hollywood movie set in a vibrant New York newspaper office.

'Okay, will do. I'll write it now,' said Maggie, grabbing a pen and notebook from her voluminous shoulder bag, sitting down at the table and setting about her task.

Rob watched her as she wrote: her long, dark brown hair; her scrunched up eyes as she thought about her vocabulary choices; her slightly turned up nose and her frankly adorable full lips that broke into a smile when she looked up and saw him staring at her.

This was the beginning of a relationship between the two that would last for the rest of the academic year, ending with a whimper in late June 1973 as all the final-year students left the University of the North for the last time after receiving the results of their examinations.

Chapter 3: *Two of Us*

November, the present day

Up until my recent unfortunate travails, Toby Barker and I used to meet up a couple of times each year and had done so ever since leaving university. A football or cricket match was usually the focus of our get-togethers, after which we would visit a few pubs and then stagger back to whichever cheap hotel we happened to be staying in. Toby has a house in Skipton, North Yorkshire, and so our sporting pilgrimages would take place anywhere between there and South London, where I had a home. During the winter months we visited a football ground neither of us had been to before, usually a team that played in the lower leagues; the likes of Doncaster, Port Vale or Peterborough for example – teams we generally knew virtually nothing about. To be honest, our knowledge or interest in all things football did not run very deep. In the summer though we would meet up at one of the big cricket grounds – Old Trafford, Trent Bridge, Edgbaston, the

Oval or Lords – to watch an international match, if we could manage it, a county game if we couldn't. We then spent the day chatting amiably, occasionally watching the play and pontificating on batting technique, drinking far too much expensive and poorly kept beer before ending up at some local hostelry and drinking even more. I'm going to miss those times a lot.

Anyway, our next meeting took place in November a couple of weeks after I had met with Sarah Webb. We had been to see Walsall FC play Mansfield Town FC, which turned out to be a fairly uneventful nil-nil draw, and we had ended up in a pub in the middle of Walsall, a town that had obviously seen better times and was a rather sad, grimy and run-down sort of place. The pub, however, wasn't too bad and thankfully had not gone out of its way to attract a younger clientele so it was quiet enough for the two of us "old fogies" to sit and have a relaxed chat over some pleasant ale without having to shout above a cacophony of loud music or fruit machines.

We eventually got around to my strange meeting with Maggie's daughter. Toby seemed as mystified as I was about the whole affair.

'I don't remember you two getting engaged,' he had said, just before he had taken a large gulp of his Marston's Pedigree bitter.

'That's because we didn't. I have no idea why Maggie wrote in her letter saying we had.'

'Perhaps she had dementia or something?' said Toby,

looking thoughtful and taking another swig from his glass. Toby's beer intake had not lessened over the years, a fact to which his substantial girth bore testament.

'Seemingly not. The rest of the letter was completely lucid, and according to her daughter, Sarah Webb, she'd remained compos mentis right up to the end.'

'That's all very strange then. I knew you two were a bit of an item in those days but didn't realise it was quite so serious. Another pint?'

I looked at my still almost full pint and shook my head. I watched Toby as he walked to the bar. Actually these days he tended to waddle rather than walk. Carrying all that extra weight couldn't be very good for him at his age – at *our* age! Almost certainly he was a huge heart attack waiting to happen, not that it seemed to bother him much. From being an athletic young man with more than his fair share of rugged good looks, Toby had gone to seed in a big way with his once quite handsome features now puffy, florid and jowly; his face these days looking increasingly like a comical sock puppet.

When he came back with his pint, having sat down with a slight groan, he asked, 'So what is she like then, this Sarah Webb?'

'A bit sour-faced actually,' I replied. 'Obviously she was sad that her mother had just died, but I got the distinct impression that she somehow blamed me for it.'

'Seems rather unfair,' he said, taking a large gulp of

his beer.

I lifted up my glass and drank some too, realising I was being somewhat left behind in the quaffing stakes.

'I know,' I agreed. 'I can't understand it at all. Even if I *had* been engaged to Maggie, which of course I wasn't, you would think that after some forty-odd, almost fifty years she would have pretty much forgotten me. I'd more or less forgotten her. It's been quite an effort of will to piece together the few memories I have of her from that time.'

'Well, a lot of things did happen back then. Some of them are harder to forget than others,' said Toby.

'Yeah I know, but it was still a hell of a long time ago,' I replied.

'Well, some people seem to live in the past to a much greater extent than others. Perhaps that applied to Maggie? By the way, did you know that the ancient Greeks thought that nostalgia for past times was a mental illness?'

'I didn't know that, Toby.' I smiled in a perfunctory way and took a drink of my beer. Toby had a penchant for non-sequiturs and "interesting" facts. He had always taken every opportunity to drop one or two into our conversations, a habit that I usually found quite amusing. Yet on this occasion, wrapped up as I was with the letter from Maggie and wanting to talk about it, I found it rather irksome. It must have shown on my face because Toby quickly steered the conversation back to Maggie's message.

34

'So are you going to get back to this Mrs Webb?'

'I'm not sure. Don't know what else I can say to her apart from telling her again that I wasn't engaged to her mother. It's difficult to prove a negative isn't it? According to Maggie's letter, one day near the end of our final term, at a party, I asked her to marry me and gave her an expensive diamond ring. I mean, for God's sake, where would I have got the money to buy something like that back then? I was broke most of the time at university!'

'Hmm, good point. If it was at a party though you would have been pissed. Maybe you just forgot that you'd asked her? We all say stupid things when we've had a few.'

'That's true I suppose, but asking someone to marry you! Would I really have forgotten I'd done that even if I had been completely rat-arsed? And that still doesn't explain the ring. I definitely remember Maggie wearing it on her right hand but I don't recall her telling me where she'd got it from.'

'Have you had it valued? It might just be a bit of tat.'

'I have actually. Took it to a jewellers I know in Soho. It's worth a fair bit in fact. There's no way I would have been able to afford it in 1973.'

'Okay. Perhaps you just found it. Or stole it?'

'Toby! What do you take me for?'

'Well, there was that time…'

'No! I've told you that was definitely a one-off aberration. I should never have done it, I know that.

35

When I told you, it was only to get it off my chest and come clean – an act of contrition, if you like. And I did return the money soon afterwards!' I felt a little angry that Toby had brought the matter up. He did have a tendency to do that sort of thing from time to time. It made him feel a bit superior I think. There was a momentary silence and we both picked up our pint glasses and drank deeply from them.

'In any case,' I said, having finished my beer, 'the fact that I stole some money when I was nineteen years old – money that I gave back almost straightaway – can't in any way be related to the matter of Maggie's ring. Two completely different things.' I picked up my pint and drained the glass, more out of a feeling of indignation than of thirst. I stood up, somewhat shakily, and marched off to the bar to get more beer for Toby and myself. I felt embarrassed then, just as I always did whenever I thought about the incident that had, annoyingly, stayed soundly in my memory over the years. Being short of money towards the end of the Christmas term in my second year, I had taken the petty cash from the *Ariel* office. It was only a few pounds. A short-term loan was how I had justified it to myself. I lied to *Ariel's* then editor, Lorraine, the next day when I swore blind that I knew nothing about the missing money, only suggesting that I might have forgotten to lock the filing cabinet where the cashbox was kept. After the Christmas holidays, when I'd earned good money delivering seasonal mail, I returned the stolen money anonymously, via an envelope placed in Lorraine's pigeonhole. I don't think anyone ever suspected me but I felt guilty as hell for a long time and never told anyone about it until, at one of our get-togethers, when as usual I'd had far too much beer, I admitted the incident to Toby. 'We all make mistakes when we're young,' I'd said to him, half expecting some reciprocal story of a similar youthful indiscretion from Toby, but one never materialised. I doubt if the revelation made much of a difference to our relationship apart from my realisation that Toby was far more discrete and tight-lipped when it came to self-criticism and admitting past errors of judgement than I was.

The embarrassed silence between us only lasted for a very short time and soon we were back to pointless banter about football and cricket. After a few more pints and a whisky or two, both of us had put the whole matter behind us and were both intent on arguing about who should be selected for the England cricket squad for its upcoming winter tour. However, deep down, I have to say the fact that Toby had brought up the matter of the stolen money at all rankled a bit for the rest of our evening together.

*

The next morning, as we stood outside the Travel Inn ready to say our goodbyes, Toby mentioned that he was thinking of contacting old friends from university with a view to organising a reunion weekend to mark fifty years since we had graduated.

'If you could ring round a few people and test the water I'd be grateful,' he said.

I'd nodded and said that I would. Only afterwards did I ask myself why Toby couldn't contact people himself and why he had suggested I should do it. And then I decided that I quite liked the idea of getting in touch with friends from times past, some of whom I'd seen only occasionally over the years and others I'd had very little contact with at all. It would be a way of letting everyone know about Maggie's death and at the same time perhaps asking people to throw some light on her seemingly spurious claim that the two of us had been engaged. My only dispute with Toby's suggestion that I should "ring round" was the impersonal nature of it, and I decided that I would endeavour to actually visit as many people as possible and have face-to-face conversations with them.

As I drove home from the West Midlands I started to plan the order in which I would attempt to see at least a few of my old university friends. The journeys would provide a welcome break from home and from Jenny too, for that matter, as it was extremely unlikely that she would want to accompany me on any of the trips. It would be up to her, I decided. Anyway, she'd be working and would probably be pleased to see the back of me for a while too.

Later on, when I mentioned my proposed trips to her,

she seemed okay with the idea to the point of disinterest, which to be honest was the way she reacted to most of the things I told her these days.

In my study, notebook in hand, I began to do some serious planning.

Chapter 4: *Sunday Morning*

Sunday, November 1972

Rob and Maggie lay in bed smoking grass. They were in Rob's single bed in his study bedroom and were wedged tightly against each other as both lay on their backs, Rob's left arm under Maggie's neck. They had just had sex for the second time since they had fallen into bed the night before and felt warm, satisfied and quietly happy. Both stared at the ceiling, slight smiles on their faces as the drug took its pleasant hold.

'Are you working on *Ariel* today?' asked Maggie.

'Yeah, probably am,' replied Rob, carefully flicking some ash into an ashtray that was perched on the edge of his bedside cabinet. 'Oh no, hang on, I'm not actually – just remembered I've got an essay to finish first. Need to hand it in tomorrow,' he added, languidly blowing smoke out of his mouth and passing the joint to Maggie.

'Can we lie here for a bit longer though?' said Maggie, before taking a deep drag of the grass and holding the smoke in her lungs before passing it back to

Rob.

'Yeah, sure. Don't you want any breakfast?'

Maggie released the marijuana smoke in a long, thin, white stream. 'In a bit, not yet,' she said, closing her eyes, her smile growing wider.

She snuggled her head into Rob's armpit. Rob noticed how her long dark hair seemed to crackle as she did so. He turned his head to the left and kissed her forehead. Maggie sighed with pleasure.

'What were you like when you were little?' said Maggie, dreamily.

'What do you mean?

'I don't know. What sort of things did you do when you were a child at home?'

Rob sighed and thought. 'Erm, well I used to read a lot. We didn't have many books at home so I used to go to the library every Saturday morning and come back with a pile of books to read during the week. I liked American comics too – *Superman*, *Batman*, *Green Lantern*, the *Flash* and all that. I collected stamps. Built Airfix models. Erm, I used to play board games with my younger brother Paul. Didn't have that many friends actually. My mum didn't really encourage anyone to come round to our house. I think she was a bit ashamed of it – we didn't have much money – she was on her own. My dad had left her and didn't have anything to do with us. Complete bastard of course!' Rob had stopped smiling. He had a final toke on the spliff and stubbed it out in the ashtray. 'Why do you ask?' His voice was mushy and muffled by smoke.

Maggie opened her eyes and turned her head slightly. 'I just want to get to know you a bit better, that's all.'

Rob smiled as he remembered something. 'Do you know what we used to call sandwiches when I was a child?'

Maggie thought and smiled. 'No, what did you call sandwiches when you were a child?'

Rob chuckled at the distant memory. 'We called them pieces. Pieces! I suppose we got it from my mum and her parents – my grandparents. What did you call sandwiches in your family?'

'Strangely enough we called them sandwiches.'

Rob smiled. 'Very posh! So what strange little foibles did your family have then?'

'Foibles? I don't know. We're a pretty normal Sheffield family. Middle-class I suppose. My dad's a policeman. He likes Gilbert and Sullivan music a lot. When I was younger we would sometimes sing along with the records. I used to find the policeman's chorus from *Pirates of Penzance* very funny. Still do actually.' Maggie flung her left arm over Rob's body, rolled onto her side, made a sort of purring noise and squeezed further into him. Rob felt her hard nipples press into his left side. He turned his head again and kissed her.

'How's the foot?'

'Throbbing a bit.'

'It was quite a deep cut. Perhaps you ought to call in at the Medical Centre today?'

'Maybe.'

'How did you manage to do it anyway?'

'I was drunk and dancing – you know that. Some irresponsible twat had dropped a glass and didn't bother picking the bits up.'

Rob yawned and stretched. 'You should be more careful.'

'Hmm. Thanks for looking after me, by the way – in lots of ways.' Rob felt her smile against his chest.

'Why did you call out for me?'

Maggie paused. 'I was… I wanted to see you.'

'You could have asked me to go to the disco with you in the first place.'

'I did!'

'I don't remember.'

'Well I did. We were in the *Ariel* office, yesterday morning. Michael and Toby were there too.'

'No, all you said was, "are you coming to the disco tonight?".'

'That meant: shall we go together?'

'Did it? I don't think so. Not the way I heard it.'

'Well, Michael and Toby went. Toby got drunk of course.'

'As did you! Why didn't you ask Michael to help you when you injured your foot?'

'Oh, he'd gone by that stage. He doesn't really like loud music and doesn't react well to booze. He gets all teary and sentimental.'

'Yeah, but he follows you around like a lost lamb

usually.'

'He doesn't!'

'Yes he does. Everyone has noticed.'

'I suppose he does. I think it's because he likes me. Who in their right mind wouldn't?'

Rob looked at Maggie's smiling face and chuckled. Some dribble had run from her mouth and made a little pool of liquid on his chest. 'Have you been to bed with him?'

'Michael? No, of course not… well, actually we did once but nothing happened. We just lay there cuddling. I think he might be gay.'

'Hmm, I've always assumed he was.'

'Why do you ask?'

'Why do I ask what?'

'If I'd been to bed with him?'

'Just wondered.'

'You're not jealous, are you?'

Rob quickly twirled his body around in the bed, moved on top of Maggie, pushing her onto her back again and looked down at her face. 'Of course not,' he said.

'Oh!' said Maggie, her eyes opening wide after feeling Rob's obvious arousal against her thigh. 'Again?'

'Why not? Since we're here!'

'No objections from me, your honour.'

They kissed long and hard and then made love for the third time.

Chapter 5: *Meet on the Ledge*

November, the present day

Over the next few days, I ruminated on the subject of Toby's proposed university reunion. I had a number of thoughts, mainly along the lines of how such an occasion could easily fall flat and turn out to be a dismal failure. The chances were that after the initial excitement had died down everyone would proceed to get very drunk, and old resentments that had lain dormant for so long could resurface and the whole thing would end up in piecemeal and petty disagreements, or worse. Still, helping to arrange it, even if it was destined never to take place, would give me an opportunity to speak to some old friends and maybe ask a few pertinent questions regarding Maggie and our relationship in those long-gone university times.

Tina and Nick had been a couple all throughout our time at the University of the North and quite soon after graduating they had married. They'd had three kids and were still together after forty or so years; a major achievement and well-nigh unique among my contemporaries from those days. I'd decided that they were going to be my first port of call as they lived relatively close to me.

In many ways they were totally unlike each other. At university Nick did a chemistry degree and Tina studied sociology. He went on to get a Masters degree and eventually got a very well paid job with a major pharmaceutical company while she became a social worker in a deprived area of North London. Now retired, they lived in a large house in Wimbledon, and I had met up with them sporadically over the years, mainly for birthdays, weddings, anniversaries and retirement bashes. Tina was a petite woman and whilst her once lovely long chestnut-coloured hair had since turned grey with age, she was still extremely attractive in her sixties. Partial to an amusing turn of phrase when the fancy took her, she had been an absolute stunner at university and everyone had been very envious of Nick, who despite being tall, dark and handsome was a far more serious individual who could seem a bit of a cold fish until you got to know him. Oddly perhaps, he emerged as our main supplier of cannabis and other narcotic substances whilst we were at the University of the North. Whether that was something to do with his chemistry background, I was never too sure (you didn't ask too many questions about the drugs traffic in those days and I'm sure the same is true today). It certainly demonstrated that he was a natural entrepreneur and was someone who was interested in maximising his earnings from a very early stage. Strangely, Nick himself never appeared very interested in using the products he seemed to have an unending supply of; I don't think I ever saw him smoking a joint or popping any of the pills he was more than happy to sell to others.

I also remembered that he and Toby, for some reason, tended to rub each other up the wrong way. In one particular instance, when we were all sitting chatting outside a pub on a warm summer's evening, our pints of beer in hand, the two actually came to blows over something one of them had said or done and had to be separated. What it was that had angered one or both of them I have now forgotten, if in fact I ever actually knew. After that they tended to keep away from each other, being coldly polite whenever they were forced to be in the same room together. If we did have a reunion it was obvious that we would need to keep a close watch on them, particularly Toby who could be massively undiplomatic when he was drunk (which was most of the time to be honest).

I gave Tina a phone call and she and Nick seemed delighted to be asked to meet up for a chat. She suggested that Jenny and I should go round to theirs for dinner on the following Saturday and then stay over. I agreed but later had to ring her back and explain that Jenny was unwell and so I would be visiting on my own. Tina said she and Nick were sorry to hear that and wished Jenny a speedy recovery. In fact Jenny was perfectly well but the truth was she had never liked meeting up with my university friends. 'I have no shared history with them,' she announced on one occasion. Actually she was perfectly correct in that assertion as she's my second wife and is also some twenty years younger than me. My first marriage to Sylvia didn't work out very well. After five years and one daughter she had decided we were not suited, packed her bags and left me. She moved in with someone she had known at her own university and made it as difficult as possible for me to see Jessica, our daughter. However, things gradually improved over the years and eventually I was able to meet up with Jessica on a more regular basis, having her over at weekends and occasionally taking her away on holiday. These days – well, up until very recently anyway – I have had an extremely good relationship with Jess. She's now in her early thirties, has a house near to mine and has two children of her own who I used to enjoy seeing every other weekend.

I met Jenny when I was Head of History at a large and successful comprehensive school in London. She was a newly qualified teacher who had just got a job there. We married a year later and a few years after I was able to quit teaching to become a full-time writer. Up until then I had been writing in my spare time, such as it was, and had gained quite a decent following with my first three crime novels. Being able to write on a full-time basis meant I could knock out my books with much greater regularity and my earnings skyrocketed, just as

Jean, my agent, predicted they would.

Jenny and I were very happy at first but (and perhaps this happens in all marriages) we eventually grew to have less and less in common with each other. I suppose the rot began to set in when she had to go out to work each day and I would stay at home, even though I handled most of the shopping, cooking and housework duties. And then there was the lack of children. Jenny was very keen – I wasn't that bothered to be honest – but we tried and tried and nothing happened. Gradually it dawned on her that for some reason she wasn't going to become pregnant. She inquired about IVF treatment and was quite keen on the idea for a time, before dismissing the whole thing and seemingly becoming resigned to the situation and prepared to move on with her life. However, as she became older, a growing resentment seemed to develop in her and for some reason she began to blame me for her failure to get pregnant. I did point out to her, on more than several occasions, that I had actually fathered a child, a fact that made her all the more morose. In the end we both tacitly agreed never to mention the subject again, which worked to some degree, although things were never quite the same as they had been before. Our relationship seemed to exist in a state of veiled and unspoken disappointment and despair, and we both started to live increasingly separate lives while maintaining, as far as the outside world was concerned, a close and loving marriage.

Anyway, Saturday soon rolled around and I found myself sitting in Tina and Nick's extremely smart dining room, with its dark wood furniture, oak wainscoting and William Morris wallpaper, enjoying a very good meal. Tina is an excellent cook and the food she'd put in front of us all evening was uniformly delicious. After they had both asked me to pass on their love to Jenny and again hoped that she would soon be feeling better, they diplomatically didn't mention her absence again and my suspicion was they had guessed the real reason for her non-appearance.

We spent the first part of the evening chatting about the foreign holidays we'd been on recently and giving status reports on our grandchildren (they had several). I then got around to broaching Toby's idea about a university reunion. As I had predicted Nick didn't seem too keen on the idea but Tina's enthusiasm soon seemed to win him round. Again I made another mental note to myself to do my best to keep Nick and Toby apart as much as possible.

Both were saddened by my news about Maggie, as well as intrigued by my meeting with her daughter and the revelation about the letter and the mysterious ring. I wasn't that sure how much they would remember about Maggie but Tina quite surprised me with the details she could recall about her.

'So you don't remember asking her to marry you then?' she said, as we started to munch on some cheese and biscuits.

'No, and I'm absolutely convinced I didn't,' I replied, just before putting a large chunk of Stilton in my mouth.

'Did her daughter say which party the deed was supposed to have taken place at?' chipped in Nick.

'No. If you remember there were quite a lot of them in that final couple of weeks of term while we were all waiting for the results of our finals.' As I spoke, Tina filled up my glass with red wine from a newly opened bottle. We'd already imbibed a fair bit during the previous three courses and I imagine that all three of us were slurring our words somewhat.

'There were a lot of parties,' agreed Nick, somewhat redundantly.

'Hmm. Do you remember the one in that house in the middle of nowhere? They had rigged out the cellar with disco lights. For some reason I specifically remember dancing to *'All Right Now'* and feeling really happy,' said Tina.

'That's because you were probably pissed as a newt,' laughed Nick.

Tina turned to him with a look of exaggerated forbearance on her face and smiled in the slightly mock-haughty way I was familiar with; it was a signature expression of hers.

'That's undoubtedly true. And wasn't there also a lot of pot being smoked by everyone?' she said.

'I guess so,' I replied. 'That was usually the case at the time. Do you remember if Maggie was there? My mind's an absolute blank about it. I do remember the house and the cellar. Did it belong to one of the lecturers?'

'Not too sure. It may have done,' said Tina, shaking her head.

Nick, who had been deep in thought suddenly piped up. 'I remember now: I couldn't go to that particular party because I had to go to my Auntie Nora's funeral.'

'That's right!' Tina and I said at the same time.

'I certainly recall Maggie being there. She was dressed in black I think,' said Tina.

'She was always dressed in black – or purple. It was her usual look,' I replied, emptying my wine glass and grabbing the bottle to fill it up again.

'I've also got a vague memory of her being in tears at one point,' said Tina.

'Really?' I said. 'I've absolutely no recollection of that.'

Adorably, Tina had screwed up her large eyes, trying to draw down more details from her memory. 'Yes!' she said triumphantly. 'She was standing on her own, crying. Liz and I went and spoke to her.' Tina screwed up her deep blue eyes even tighter.

'What did she say?' I asked.

Tina opened her eyes. 'I can't remember,' she said, deflated. 'We were all pissed or high or most probably both. I just remember the loud music and Maggie standing there looking sad.'

'Yeah,' I said. 'My memories of that night are very

cloudy.' I rubbed my eyes. I felt tired and more than a little drunk, which considering the amount of wine I'd put away wasn't at all surprising.

Shocked enlightenment suddenly lit up Tina's face. 'God! It wasn't long after that party that Stella... you know...'

'It was the day after in fact,' I said. 'At least, I think it was,' I quickly added.

'Was Stella at the party?' asked Nick.

'Yeah, I believe she was,' I said. 'She left early for some reason – I think. If you remember, she was one of the few people at the time who actually owned a car. Other than that I can't recall very much about the party.'

We sat in silence for a few seconds and then Tina topped up our glasses and we all gratefully changed the subject. We spoke about other things for a bit: family matters, various acquaintances we had in common and minor medical issues that were just starting to raise their ugly heads due largely to our advancing age. Eventually, Nick brought us back to the proposed reunion and when it was likely to take place.

'I don't know really. I imagine it would be summer of next year. That'd be more or less fifty years after we left university, for most of us anyway. Early stages yet, of course. Apart from Toby, you're the first people I've spoken to about it.' I hoped I hadn't sounded too downbeat about it all. I had the distinct impression that Nick was looking for reasons not to turn up whatever time of year it took place.

After a bit more drinking and a little more chatting – most of it relaxed and convivial – we left the dining room, drank some coffee and ate a few After Eight mints. Soon afterwards I found myself in Tina and Nick's spare room lying in bed. It took me a long time to get off to sleep. My mind was racing away, replaying the things that had been said during the evening, and a vague feeling of unease had begun to brew in my mind. When I finally drifted off, I proceeded to have a vivid and nonsensical dream where I was being chased by an immense white horse that had a madly grinning and jodhpur-wearing Fiona (another of my university friends) mounted on its back. In her hand she carried a horsewhip, which I knew if she ever caught me she would certainly use with great ferocity on my back and rear end.

Chapter 6: *Will You Love Me Tomorrow?*

Friday, June 1973

It was Friday night. Grasmere Bar on the campus of the University of the North was crowded and noisy. Plumes of blue-grey smoke rose up to the pine-covered ceiling. Some students, along with a few of the younger lecturers, stood together having animated conversations while others sat at low tables drinking, smoking and talking. Some had serious expressions on their faces; others were looking happy and relaxed. All were pleased that the term's work was almost over and that chatting, smoking and drinking were the only activities required so close to the end of the academic year. Some of those present would proceed to have one or two sociable drinks before returning to their rooms where they might read a couple of chapters of their current book before falling asleep. Others would carry on drinking throughout the night as well as smoking some pot and then end up with a head-splitting hangover when they finally emerged from their own bed, or that of someone else, round about lunchtime on Saturday. A few would swear that they would not touch a drop of alcohol ever again, before, later in the day, ending up in another one of the six bars on the campus happily drinking once more.

In one of the relatively quiet corners of the bar, Rob was sitting next to Tina McCloud. They had been talking together for two hours or so and both were now on their sixth drink. Rob was drinking pints of bitter; Tina was drinking rum and blackcurrant. Rob looked longingly at Tina whose long brown hair had tousled and curled down onto her white blouse in what he thought was a thoroughly gorgeous and alluring way. Their conversation that evening had ranged far and wide. They had talked about music, which groups they liked and disliked, their chances of doing well in the recently completed exams (the results of which would shortly be announced) and what they planned to do in the future. Rob had been carefully leading up to asking Tina a particular question.

'Erm, by the way, are you going to Tim's party tomorrow night?' he asked her, sitting as close to Tina as he could and noting that she had not attempted to inch away from him.

'Hmm, not sure,' Tina replied.

'What would stop you?'

'I don't know if I can be bothered, what with Nick being away this weekend.'

'Oh, come on, Tina, it'll be fun. Tim's got a big cellar

in his house apparently and he's providing loads of free drinks. It doesn't get much better than that.'

Tim was one of the young lecturers in the history department who Rob got on with particularly well, often sharing a surreptitious joint with him in his office at the end of the day.

'I might. I'll see how I feel.' Tina slurred her words somewhat and was looking tired. 'I'll probably go if Liz does.'

'Liz is bound to be there,' Rob said. 'She said she'd get her new boyfriend to give people a lift in his car – Tim's house is out in the wilds. Er, anyway, how long is Nick away for?'

'He's back on Monday. He thought it would be best if he spent Sunday with his mum and dad after the funeral.'

'Right, of course. Good for him. Always very important to spend some time with your folks after such an occasion. Do you want a last drink?' Rob said, quickly finishing off his pint and standing up.

'Better not. Feel a bit pissed already to be honest.'

'Oh, go on. It won't hurt. I'm having another.'

Tina smiled. 'Okay then, if you're twisting my arm. But don't blame me if I throw up all over you.'

Rob smiled in return. 'Same again?'

Tina nodded.

When he returned with the drinks Tina was lighting a cigarette. She offered one to Rob who took it and then held Tina's hand steady as he lit his cigarette from hers.

He remained holding her hand for a second or two longer than was absolutely necessary. As he did so he looked into Tina's eyes. They were slightly glazed and sleepy-looking but still, in his opinion, quite the most fetchingly beautiful eyes he had ever seen. She smiled back and blushed slightly.

'What's Liz's new boyfriend like then?' said Rob after a pregnant pause.

'He's all right. Quite nice in fact. He's called Donald. Works in the labs in the chemistry department. He comes from Scotland – friend of Nick's.'

'And he's got a car. Always useful!'

'Do you know what I think?' slurred Tina, suddenly deciding to tap Rob on his knee with her index finger in a drunkenly familiar way that Rob saw as very promising. 'I think that you and Liz would have made a very good couple, and to tell you the truth, I'm quite surprised you didn't go out with her on a regular basis after you and she had that short fling, or whatever you called it. I know that she wanted to at any rate.'

'Really? I didn't know that. I thought it was just a two-ships-passing-in-the-night situation. Actually, I'm not sure it would have worked in the long run. After that time we slept together things were never quite the same between us,' Rob replied.

'Hmm,' said Tina. 'Why was that do you think?'

'I honestly don't know. Bit of a mystery I suppose. We're still friends though.'

'So what about you and Maggie? You've been

together for quite a long time now.'

'Oh, that's never been much of a thing to be honest. We just get together when we're feeling a bit lonely – or bored.'

'One day they'll probably have a name for that sort of relationship,' said Tina, taking a sip of her drink.

Rob could have sworn that there was a hint of disdain in her voice, but decided to ignore the slight, if that was the case. 'So how are you and Nick getting on these days?'

'Fine. Good. We're fine… all fine, I think. Actually, sometimes I can't really tell though. He can blow a bit hot and cold. And of course he works very hard; he often gives it all of his attention. He wants… he *needs* a First and sometimes that outweighs everything else in the world.'

Rob noticed that as well as slurring her words a little Tina looked quite sad as she revealed rather more about her relationship with Nick than she ever would have if she had been sober. Rob took it as another good sign that tonight could be his night as far as he and Tina were concerned.

'Er… I suppose it's time to go. They've already called last orders,' Rob said, as he finished off his beer. He looked into Tina's eyes. 'I'll walk you back to your room if you like.'

Tina smiled. 'I don't think that will be necessary,' she said, then stood up unsteadily and would have fallen over if Rob hadn't grabbed her around her waist. 'Oops!

59

I'm obviously not used to drinking quite so much. Perhaps I will need you to accompany me home after all.' She gave a discrete little belch, putting her hand up to her mouth, before smiling again in a sexily drunk sort of way, Rob thought.

As they walked hand-in-hand down University Boulevard (the rather grand name given to the main thoroughfare that ran right through the middle of the campus) Rob found himself having to slow his walking pace to compensate for Tina's erratic side-to-side movements. He let go of her hand and instead put his arm around her waist so as to guide her in a more efficient way. It had been a warm summer's day but now an unseasonably cold wind was blustering its way around the university buildings; buildings that always looked so stark and rather ugly late at night when there were not many people about. Rob pulled Tina closer to him, feeling the comforting warmth and shape of her body. She didn't object.

With some difficulty Rob guided her up a flight of stairs, and when she stopped at the top to lean against a wall Rob smiled and moved his face closer to hers. She smiled back at him and did a little chuckling sound in her throat but didn't move her head away as he took his chance – the chance he had waited for so long – and kissed her. He felt her lean into him, her petite body lithe, supple and compliant. Her quick tongue darted into his mouth. Rob sighed as they slowly withdrew from each other's lips and then the pair, smiling and continuing to hold on to each other, moved down the corridor until they were outside Tina's room where she fumbled for her door keys in her shoulder bag.

Inside, Tina gratefully slumped down onto the bed and Rob sat next to her. He smiled at her and kissed her again. Her lips were warm and moist. Her breath smelled headily of alcohol and tobacco and their tongues joined with each other again like long-lost friends. His right hand moved to her left breast and he squeezed gently thinking that at last, after so long, he would soon be lying naked next to her and would be able to explore every aspect of her body during what he assumed would be a long night of discovery. He would take it very steadily, he thought. He would savour watching Tina take off her clothes at the same time he took off his and then they would make love slowly and languorously.

Rob had just slipped his hand between Tina's legs and had begun to search for the zip on her jeans when the door to the room burst open.

'Hi, wondered if you were… oh no! Sorry!'

Rob pulled himself away from Tina's mouth and looked up at the horrified face of Liz as she stood in the doorway. In his time Rob had seen beetroots that were not quite as red as Liz's face was at that moment. Frozen in time for a few seconds, Liz then repeated her puzzled and garbled apology and quickly left the room, closing the door behind her.

Rob turned his head back toward Tina's, ready to

carry on where they had left off. However, the incident seemed to have quickly sobered Tina up because she now had a serious look on her face as she gently pushed Rob away and stood up.

She smiled an embarrassed-looking smile. 'I'm so sorry, Rob. I'd really like to, but I can't. It wouldn't be fair on Nick. So sorry.'

'Nick's miles away, he wouldn't know,' said Rob in a tone of voice that even to him sounded pleadingly needy and pathetic.

Tina looked genuinely shocked. 'Yes he would. I'd have to tell him.'

'Oh right, of course. Sorry. My fault. I got carried away.' Rob felt worried and a little surprised that Tina would have been quite so truthful to her boyfriend. 'Er, this isn't going to spoil things, is it? We can still be friends?'

Tina looked down at Rob who was still sitting on the bed hoping that his very hard erection would soon release him from its remorseless grip and he would be able to walk out of Tina's room with some of his dignity left intact.

'Of course! Nothing important has happened. Just two friends sharing a little time together and then having a bit of a drunken snog. No damage done.'

'You won't tell Nick then?'

'No, of course not. No need to worry.' Tina smiled reassuringly.

'What about Liz?'

'Oh I'll explain things to Liz. She won't say anything. She's very loyal to me.'

'Okay then.' Rob now felt able to stand and moved towards the door. Smiling, he said, 'Will you still be going to the party tomorrow night?'

'Yes, of course,' said Tina, smiling back.

Rob smiled again, looked at Tina longingly and then left the room.

Tina leant against the closed door and let out a sigh that was part relief and part regret. If pressed, she would not have known which of those two feelings was currently the greater.

*

At first Rob meant to go straight back to his room and, following his frustrating encounter with Tina, do what was necessary before falling soundly asleep, but in the middle of The Square he stopped and looked up at The Tower, wondering if Maggie was in her room. He worked out where her room was: tenth floor, one above his, three doors down the corridor from the lift-shaft. Yes, her light was on. Rob smiled. Earlier in the day, while they were having a coffee together in the *Ariel* office, she had asked him what he was planning to do that evening. He'd lied, telling her that he was going for a few drinks with Toby.

'I did mention it before. It could be one of the last times we can do that,' he had said.

Maggie had agreed that it was important that he should meet up with Toby.

'Oh well, I suppose I could have a night in and do a bit of reading or I could go and see Jane – and we'll be at the party tomorrow night won't we?' she had said, more brightly than Rob had expected.

'Of course,' Rob had replied. 'Looking forward to it. Bit of drinking, bit of bopping. It'll be great.'

Maggie looked happier. 'Well, have a good night then. Make sure Toby doesn't drink too much!' She had laughed out loud and given Rob a peck on the cheek.

After his failed attempt to sleep with Tina, Rob now decided he didn't want to go back to his room where he would lie in bed feeling frustrated, lonely and sorry for himself, so he headed into the lobby area at the foot of The Tower and pressed the button to call the lift. As was always the case, loud and disturbing clanking and grinding noises came from the lift shaft until, after an interminable wait, the doors shuddered open to an empty lift compartment that unusually smelled strongly of urine.

On the tenth floor Rob stood outside Maggie's door, listening out for any noises coming from within. He could hear a Carole King song (one of Maggie's favourite singers) playing softly on her record player. Rob smiled and, remembering Liz's thoughtless throwing open of Tina's door earlier in the evening, decided to go for a much subtler approach to entering this room. After all, he thought, Maggie probably had fallen asleep while listening to her *Tapestry* LP and he certainly didn't want to frighten her. Gently opening the door, he peered into the room. The light on Maggie's bedside lamp shone dimly through the red cloth she had draped over it and the room was fuggy and pungent with the aroma of cannabis and joss sticks.

'Hi, how are you doing? Thought I'd just drop in and see you,' Rob whispered softly, taking off his t-shirt and shoes. His thinking at this stage was if Maggie were asleep, as seemed likely, he would just get quietly undressed before slipping into bed with her. She would doubtless wake up, be really happy that he had called in to see her and then be only too pleased to indulge in some gentle love making before they both fell into a deeply satisfied sleep.

Rob noticed some movement in Maggie's bed as she evidently began to stir, disturbed by his arrival. *Just right*, thought Rob, as he took off his remaining clothes, leaving his jeans, socks and underpants on the floor where they fell. Gently holding up the sheet and blanket of Maggie's bed he was suddenly startled at the sight of two bodies entwined there together, both of which were making little groaning and sighing noises as they were locked in a passionate embrace. Noises of lovemaking were soon replaced by surprised yelps and gasps as both participants in the bed sat up, looking shocked as they desperately tried to conceal their nakedness. Rob stepped backwards, almost falling over his discarded clothes, and tried to work out the reason why Maggie would be lying naked in bed with an equally naked Stella George.

The recriminations were not as drawn out and as vociferous as Rob thought they might be. Stella had demanded that he turn around while she got out of bed, found her clothes, got dressed and then left the room rather sheepishly. Maggie was more annoyed and more vocal as she lay in the bed and demanded by what right he had to come barging into her room and invading her private space. After a while, however, Maggie had calmed down enough to tell Rob (who by now had got into the warm bed next to her) how the incident with Stella had come about.

'She knocked on my door to see if I wanted a coffee. I said I had a bottle of wine and some grass and did she fancy sharing them with me. She said, "yes". We got talking and, you know, one thing led to another. We started kissing and then ended up in bed – as you saw.'

'Do you often sleep with women?' Rob asked, smiling, obviously interested in the possibilities this revelation now offered.

'No!' replied Maggie, delivering a punch to Rob's upper arm. 'Oh, and don't think it's something that you would be invited to take part in, in any case.'

'Didn't you think I might be a bit jealous?' said Rob, as he began to stroke the inside of Maggie's thigh.

'Would you be really?' Maggie smiled and ran her fingers through Rob's long curly hair.

'Of course I would. Not as much as if you were

sleeping with another bloke though!' Rob gave a gentle slap to Maggie's bottom.

'You know I wouldn't do that,' Maggie said, offering her mouth to Rob.

Rob smiled and they kissed.

Outside the window the unseasonably cold wind whistled persistently and noisily around the tower block.

*

They awoke early next morning; the single bed made it difficult for them to go back to sleep once the June sunlight had flooded into the room. Rob's inevitable early morning erection made Maggie smile and she kissed him with passion. After they had made love again Maggie got up, slipped on Rob's t-shirt that still lay on the floor and, bare-footed, she padded out to the communal kitchen where she made them mugs of tea.

As they sat up in the single bed drinking their tea, Maggie, still wearing the t-shirt and still smiling, asked Rob about the party that was due to take place that evening.

'How are we going to get there?'

'I'm not totally sure. Thought I might ask Liz. Her new boyfriend has a car.'

'Won't Nick and Tina be going with them?'

'Nick's not here. He's gone home for a funeral apparently.' Rob thought about the previous night. He remembered the taste of Tina's lips and the feel of her body. He had been so very close to ending up in bed with her. If only...

'What time are we going?' asked Maggie.

'I don't know! Why can't you work out some of these things for yourself?' Rob snapped back.

Maggie flinched. 'Why are you suddenly being annoyed with me?' she asked.

'What? No reason. No, actually, there is a reason: last night when you were in bed with Stella, did you consider my feelings at all when you were going at it with her?'

'We weren't "going at it"! It was just two people being friendly with each other. It didn't mean anything.'

'It didn't mean anything? You had sex with another person! The fact that it was a woman doesn't really alter that fact you know. *I* should be enough for you. You should only want and need to go to bed with me. No one else!'

'But we had great sex last night and this morning. That should prove that it's you I want to be with. Stella's just a friend. We just got into bed with each other for a bit of fun.'

'When I wasn't around?'

'Yes! And by the way, I saw your eyes light up when you thought there might be a chance for you to join in,' Maggie said angrily.

'I've had enough of this,' said Rob, as he struggled out of the narrow bed and searched for his clothes on the floor before pulling on his pants, jeans and socks. 'I'll have my t-shirt back please,' he said, sounding annoyed as he bent down to tie his shoelaces.

Maggie smiled and took off the t-shirt slowly and sexily hoping that her provocative mock-striptease might persuade Rob to come back to bed. It didn't. He snatched his shirt from her and quickly put it on while marching to the door, which he flung open.

'I'll let you know about tonight,' said Rob. '*If* I decide to go!'

Maggie sat looking at the open door to her room, half expecting Rob to slink back and blow her a kiss. He didn't. She felt miserable and misused. She had become used to Rob's occasional mood swings and had been quite adept at calming him back to normal. Now, however, they were running out of time. Soon she and Rob would be heading off into the big wide world and she still didn't know if he would definitely be joining her in Cardiff in September at the start of her postgraduate journalism course. She sighed and patted dry the tears that had begun to run down her face with the edge of her bed sheet.

Chapter 7: *Who Knows Where the Time Goes?*

December, the present day

I sat at my desk in the study going through my address book, trying to decide which of my old university friends I should contact next about the reunion. I was suddenly taken aback by the realisation that it would be a fifty years' reunion. It didn't sound right. How could fifty years have gone by so fucking fast? The thought made me smile. That expletive was one I had employed only very occasionally over the years. So much had changed; indeed, in many ways the 1970s decade was like a foreign country where they really did things very differently.

Some of those many differences I looked back on fondly: beer had been ten pence a pint in the university bars; most lads, myself included, wore their hair long, and the clothes were pretty good. Afghan coats, the ubiquitous army surplus greatcoats, mini-skirts, bell-bottoms and loon pants. But a few of the differences, now seemed absolutely crass and outlandish. For example, a popular television programme at the time was called *The Black and White Minstrel Show* and was watched by millions each weekend. In it, white male singers would 'black up' in what was presumably seen by its fans as a piece of charming nostalgia that brought back memories of the happy-go-lucky American slave-owning southern states of the nineteenth century! There were a number of other TV programmes that were equally awful and insensitive. Google them – you'll be surprised!

Another difference between then and now (in my view at least) was the frequency of swearing and in particular the number of times people used the f-word I had just used under my breath. As far as I can recall, it just wasn't used nearly as often back then as it is today, when many seem to utilise it as a sort of punctuation mark merely to separate one group of words from another. That definitely wasn't the case in the past, at least not in the circles in which I moved. After all, it was only in 1965 that Kenneth Tynan first used the word on live British television, causing such an uproar and shock that questions were asked in parliament, and some Tory backwoodsmen members of parliament even called for the famous theatre critic and writer to be horsewhipped, gaoled – or worse. Today, quite normal everyday conversations in all sorts of TV programmes seem to be so peppered with "fucks" that the old Anglo-Saxon swearword has lost much of its impact and potency. I've always thought that we need to jealously preserve such

71

strong words for those times when we're in extremis and we desire to express the most powerful oath we can muster; those occasions when you stub your toe or accidently hit your thumb with a hammer.

Those thoughts about the distant past were just some of the things that rushed unbidden through my mind as I sat trying to decide who I should next get in touch with from those far off university days. Many of those individuals I had once mixed with I had not seen or spoken to for a very long time, although over the years I had kept in contact with most of them by letter or via the occasional interaction on Facebook (which represented the outer limits of my cyber expertise). After a bit of hesitation and general dithering I decided to ring Michael on my mobile phone, something we didn't have back in the 1970s of course. How on earth did we manage? Michael was someone I had known reasonably well at university. He had been very close to Maggie and certainly needed to be informed about her death, if he hadn't already heard. He seemed very interested to hear from me but, unsurprisingly I suppose, he became extremely quiet when I told him about Maggie having died; so much so that I had to ask him if he was still on the line.

'Yes, I am,' he said.

'Are you okay?' I asked.

'Yes – your news came as a big shock, that's all.'

'Yeah. It was terrible news for me too,' I said, hoping that I sounded sincere. 'I half thought that you might have known already and even gone to the funeral.'

Michael went very quiet again. When he finally spoke there was a catch in his throat. 'No, I hadn't heard. I would definitely have gone if I'd known about it.'

'They should have let you know.'

'Yes,' he said.

'I remember that you and Maggie were close at university,' I said.

'Yes. I suppose we were quite close,' he replied, sounding very tearful.

'How's Paul?' I said, thinking that a slight change of subject was needed.

'He's very well thanks,' he said.

I congratulated myself on remembering the name of the chap that Michael was currently living with (I probably only did so because he had the same name as my brother). Since coming out about twenty years ago Michael had lived with a number of partners (none of whom had stayed with him for very long) but he and Paul had been together for about three years now and hopefully he had, albeit late in life, found some sort of long-term stability with another person. At university, when the gay liberation movement seemed to make being homosexual much more socially acceptable and indeed almost trendy – at least among students – Michael Key (always Michael and never Mike, Mick or Mickey) refused to say whether he was gay even though everyone assumed he was. He went out with women from time to time, I suppose in an attempt to show people, and perhaps convince himself, that he was straight. He genuinely didn't seem to realise that all the people he knew and who liked him weren't bothered one way or the other about his sexual orientation (not that we would have used that particular phrase back then). At university he had been a good-looking guy, tall with long dark, almost black, curly hair and certainly never had too much trouble attracting members of the opposite sex, but I think he just wasn't very interested in them, apart from Maggie that is. I had always quite liked Michael, and he could be surprisingly good fun in the university bars when despite his apparent shyness he would be only too happy (after a few drinks that is) to lead us somewhat incongruously in the singing of an array of filthy rugby songs and, even more incongruously, in a number of Irish rebel songs (I think one or both of his parents had originally come from Ireland). Of course, the person he spent most time with was Maggie. He had first met her one afternoon in the *Ariel* office early on during our final year at the University of the North after which he would follow her around, seemingly doting on her every word and endeavouring to be in her company as much as possible. Invariably they would be observed sitting together in the library, or having a quiet coffee in The Square's café. I vaguely recalled that sometimes when I went to her room Michael would be there, seemingly having deep and profound conversations with her. To tell you the truth, on occasion, I had been a little jealous of the time he spent with her. I managed to dredge up a memory of one occasion where I had to have a friendly but firm word with him about getting in the way, particularly when I felt the need to spend a bit of private quality time with her. Memories such as that had gradually started to filter back into my mind.

Anyway, back to our phone conversation. I eventually got around to asking if he'd be interested in the reunion.

'No, I don't think I would,' he said.

'Why not?' I replied.

'I don't think I fitted in very well at the time and I'm pretty sure I wouldn't feel part of the group now. Besides, it was such a long time ago. Would anyone really be very interested in meeting me, or even remember me?'

'I think people would be extremely interested in seeing you actually. I remember back in the 1990s when your documentary series was on telly how people were really grabbed by it.' (Michael had gone into television production and had overseen a series of films about archaeological digs throughout the world, which had briefly caught the public's imagination).

'Yes, perhaps they might. Actually if Maggie had been there...' Michael didn't need to finish the sentence.

'Well, think about it anyway. Toby Barker is very enthusiastic about a big get-together as are Tina and Nick,' I said, lying slightly.

'Okay,' said Michael. 'Will partners be invited?'

'We hadn't thought that far ahead but I don't think anyone would object if you bought Paul along.' Actually I wasn't sure about that but we would cross that particular bridge a little nearer to the time. 'In her last letter to me, Maggie said that you and she used to meet up regularly,' I said.

'Yes, we did. We'd meet for lunch or dinner at some nice little bistro or gastro pub, and then about a year ago I stopped hearing from her. I just thought she'd got bored with my company.' He gave a sad little laugh that was full of regret. 'I sort of suspected at the time that she may have disapproved of me living with Paul after all the failures I'd had with other men. I guessed she thought it would all end in tears, like the other times. Ironic really. Anyway she didn't get in touch again. But now I know it was probably around that time that she was being diagnosed and treated for cancer, so it was understandable I suppose. I guess all that chemotherapy and whatnot would have made her illness all too obvious. Shame really. I could have helped her and...'

At that point he dissolved into tears over the phone, which to tell the truth was more than a little embarrassing. All I could do was tell him that there was little he could have done and that Maggie always was a fairly private person. Over the years she would certainly have cherished her relationship with him.

When Michael had regained control of his emotions I suggested to him that we should get together and have a good chat about old times. Michael agreed and suggested one of his 'nice little bistros' for us to meet up at on the following evening, which being a weekday would enable him to book a table easily. Jenny wasn't too pleased when I said I would be staying at Michael's overnight so I had to come up with a stratagem that would win her over to this trip as well as all the others I intended to make. I eventually did this by promising that the two of us would go on a luxury river cruise down the Rhine in the following spring, something she'd always wanted to do and, as it turned out, a holiday we were destined never to go on. Such is life!

*

The next evening I found the bistro easily. It was actually very nice and was also tastefully decorated for the Christmas season. Over an excellent three-course meal and a good bottle of red (Michael, I discovered, was very knowledgeable about his wines) we continued our conversation. This was one of the few times I had seen Michael since university and the march of time had taken its toll on him, as it had done on us all. Gone were the long dark locks. Instead, Michael had chosen the all-over-shaven-head look that so many balding men had decided to adopt in recent years. In contrast to the lack of hair on his head, he now sported a small, neatly trimmed and almost totally white beard. However, he had managed (unlike some of us) to avoid piling on the pounds and had kept himself surprisingly fit and trim-looking in his old age. I tried to avoid thinking that this was a gay thing and congratulated him on his slim profile while patting my somewhat protuberant stomach at the same time.

Michael was as polite, pleasant and attentive as I remembered and still had that rather sad look in his eyes and hangdog expression that, I recalled, had also been a feature of his general demeanour back in our university days. When he spoke about Maggie he looked even sadder and I noticed little tears welling up in his eyes that he quickly wiped away with his table napkin.

'I really wish I could have seen her one more time,' he said.

'Yeah, that would have been nice for both of you,' I replied.

There was a short period of silence while we ate our excellent desserts (both of us had chosen crème brûlée) and Michael, with his giveaway watery eyes, was so obviously thinking about Maggie and times past.

'Michael, can I ask you something about you and Maggie back in our time at university?'

Michael looked up; his small dessertspoon paused in mid-delivery to his mouth. 'Yes of course. What do you want to know?'

'Why did you like her so much? She was a nice enough girl back then of course, attractive and everything, but what made her so special in your eyes?'

Michael looked thoughtful for a moment and I had

the impression that he was endeavouring to choose his words carefully. 'That's a difficult question,' he said, looking directly into my eyes. 'I think that it was mainly because she liked me. She understood me, she listened well and was always kind to me. She was one of the few people in my life I could say that about. It certainly wasn't the case where most people have been concerned. And that includes my own parents by the way.'

I nodded in what I hoped demonstrated my sage-like understanding. 'I never knew you felt that way. You had a lot of friends,' I added.

'No, not really,' he replied. 'I knew a lot of people but I don't think they really wanted to get to know me all that much. I was just part of the furniture as far as most of them were concerned. Maggie was the only one who really understood what made me tick. We used to have some really deep conversations about families and relationships. Up until I met her I felt more or less alone at university. I wasn't sure I actually belonged there; I was never close to anyone. I was just the friend-of-a-friend type of person. And then I met Maggie in the *Ariel* office one day and we just clicked right away. I knew she liked me from the start. Everything just felt so right about us.' Michael dabbed his eyes with his napkin again, drank some of his wine and then smiled at me in a sad sort of way.

'Can I ask you… were you in love with her?'

'I think I was, in a way. With her as a person, I mean.

I regretted not being able to fancy her sexually – but I didn't. I knew right from the start that I would never... er, be able to satisfy her in that regard. I suppose I saw her as the big sister I never had.'

I nodded again. Although I couldn't really understand the concept of being in love with a woman without wanting to have sex with her, Michael's point about a big sister figure sort of made sense.

Once the meal was over Michael paid the bill (I let him as he insisted) and we walked the short distance back to his house. Over coffee we chatted some more and I tried hard to convince him that he would enjoy the reunion and that everyone would be pleased to see him. Paul was there and he joined in our conversation for a bit. I'd never met him before and he seemed genuine enough, although I had a quiet smile to myself when Michael introduced us as he and Michael looked so very similar to each other. He was a few years younger than Michael but sported the same lean figure, goatee beard and shaven head. It would have been difficult to come up with a more archetypal-looking gay suburban couple to be honest. I was pleased when Paul said that Michael ought to go to the reunion. Paul then went to bed and left the two of us drinking brandy and talking into the early hours. That was when I finally got around to my second reason for seeing him.

'Michael,' I said. 'Do you remember anything about Maggie and me getting engaged?'

'Engaged? Erm... no, I don't think so. *Did* you get

engaged?'

I explained and told him about my meeting with Sarah Webb and the ring. He seemed as dumbfounded as I was about it all.

'Because you and Maggie were so close, she would have definitely told you if something like that had happened, wouldn't she?' I asked.

'Yes, of course she would have done. Well, I think so. She often spoke about you but never anything about the two of you being engaged.'

'Do you remember her wearing the ring?'

'No, sorry. I was probably too self-obsessed to notice anything like that, but I do remember her telling me that she and Stella George had slept together on a few occasions. Did you know that?'

I vaguely remembered Maggie's brief fling with Stella but amid all the tragedy that had taken place concerning her death I had definitely pushed that knowledge to the back of my mind. 'Yes, sort of,' I said, not committing myself fully. 'She confided in you about it?'

Michael nodded. And then, no doubt fortified by the very good brandy he had provided that we had been drinking far too much of, he suddenly decided to remind me that I had also once criticised him for seeing too much of Maggie. 'I was really hurt by that,' he said.

'I don't remember that.' (I was lying but only because I wanted to hear what he had to say about it).

'Really?' he said, looking a bit disbelieving.

'Yes,' I said.

'Well, it did have a big effect on Maggie and me. Our meetings went underground; we had to get together in secret.' He looked triumphant.

I nodded in what I hoped was an understanding and apologetic way. At which point, after those minor revelations, I managed to change the subject and we had an extended conversation about various other people we had known at university, including one or two of the lecturers we had in common (Michael also did a history degree).

After several more brandies I was eventually shown to the spare room where I slumped onto the bed in a drunken haze and quickly drifted off to sleep. However, my night-time repose was again disturbed by another strange and vivid dream. This time I seemed to be dressed in a fox costume and Fiona, resplendent in a bright red jacket and again sitting astride a large white horse, led a pack of ferocious, slavering, half starved-looking dogs that were seemingly intent on hunting me down as I ran around looking for a suitable fox hole to dive into and hide.

Chapter 8: *Paranoid*

Tuesday, March 1973

'Why don't you just tell Michael to get lost?'

'Why should I? I like his company. He's a nice person.'

Rob was sitting on the steps of The Square when Maggie had walked past on her way to her room. Although it was only mid-March it was a warm day; by far the warmest of the year so far and the first really spring-like day of Rob's penultimate term at the University of the North. He had been sitting in the sun reading a chapter of a required text for his next essay when he noticed Maggie emerge from the library, holding hands with Michael and then smiling at him as he headed off into Murdoch's. Rob had called to Maggie and, continuing to smile broadly, she gave him a little wave and walked to where he was, sitting down on the step beside him. Despite the balmy weather she was still dressed (as she usually was) in black. When she had tried to kiss Rob's cheek he had pulled away.

'But why the hell are you being so pally with him? Holding his hand and everything!' Rob continued.

'Why shouldn't I be pally with him?'

'Because you shouldn't. It looks strange. Why were you holding his hand for everyone to see?'

'Because he's my friend, and he's nice and kind!'

'He may be "nice and kind" but he's also weird, creepy and is probably queer,' said Rob in too loud a voice. One or two people, sitting on the steps nearby, looked over to him.

'That's not fair! He always says how much he likes and admires you,' Maggie replied.

'I'm not sure I particularly want him to like and admire me,' Rob said with a sneer. 'And I don't think you should go around holding his hand. It looks a bit pathetic – like something out of *Winnie the Pooh*!'

'We're friends. That's what friends do! Besides, I like *Winnie the Pooh*. And why are you being so possessive?' Maggie tried to stand but Rob grabbed her arm and pulled her back down again. 'Ow! That hurt!' she said, rubbing her arm and flashing her large eyes in rebuke at Rob.

'I'm sorry,' said Rob, suddenly feeling guilty and stroking her arm where he had grabbed it. 'I didn't mean to be rough but you know… it just annoys me a bit the way he… you know… clings to you all the time. It is weird, you must admit.'

Maggie smiled, although she was still rubbing her upper arm before rolling up the sleeve of her jumper and examining her arm for a bruise. 'Okay it is a bit, but he is very nice to me all the time. He likes me; he is lovely to me in fact. He bought me a jam doughnut in the café today.'

Rob smiled back although his eyes still looked annoyed. 'Well, that's all right then. One jam doughnut and he's your friend for life.'

'Yes, I think he will be. And by the way you've never bought me a cake of any description and we've known each other now for six months.'

'I'll make a note. What are you doing tonight?'

'Not much. I've done all the work I needed to do just now in the library. Shall we go for a drink?'

'Okay but don't tell Michael otherwise he'll turn up too.'

'I won't.' Maggie smiled and gave Rob a lingering kiss on the lips before standing and picking up her voluminous and heavy shoulder-bag that was stuffed full with books and a thick A4 writing pad. 'See you at about eight then?'

'Yeah. Come down to my room – the music's better.'

Maggie stuck out her tongue and then trotted down the steps toward the entrance to The Tower. Stopping halfway she turned around and shouted back to Rob. 'A jam doughnut!'

Rob smiled and watched her as she disappeared through the door of The Tower's lobby before getting back to his book. He suddenly stopped reading, looked up, slammed the book shut and stood. He had decided in that moment that he wasn't just going to ignore the matter with Michael. He was going to have a word with him, and now was as good a time as any.

*

Michael was in Murdoch's browsing books in the history section when Rob walked up to him and tapped him on the shoulder.

'Got a minute, Michael?'

'Hi. Yes of course, Rob,' said Michael, smiling.

'Not here. Let's go to the office.'

Michael knew "the office" meant the two rooms just off the University Boulevard where the *Ariel* newspaper was produced each week.

'Anything wrong with the article I gave you yesterday?' said Michael, as the two of them made the short walk to the office.

'No, it was fine. Really well written as usual.'

'What's the problem then?' Michael could see that Rob was annoyed about something but he couldn't think what it could be. His relationship with Rob, as both the editor and as a friendly acquaintance, had always been good and Rob had often praised him on his writing for *Ariel*.

'I don't think you should be seeing quite so much of Maggie,' Rob said, after they had entered the office and he had closed the door behind them.

'What do you mean?'

'What I mean is I think you're spending too much time with Maggie and you ought to give her a bit more breathing space.'

'I don't understand. Has she complained to you about me? Has she asked you to speak to me?'

Rob briefly thought about saying yes but then realised that Maggie would certainly object to being lied about. 'No, she hasn't. This is me asking you as a favour.'

'Rob, I still don't understand. I'm just friends with Maggie. We don't do anything but talk, if that's what you're worried about? It's totally platonic between us.'

'You have been to bed with her though.'

'No... er, well yes, once, but we didn't do anything. I don't fancy her in that way. We really are just good friends.'

'So how can you end up in bed with someone you don't fancy? That just doesn't make any sense!' Rob could see that Michael was on the verge of tears. This was a really good time, Rob thought, to force home his point.

'It was during a period of time last term when I felt really lonely. I ended up pouring my heart out to her and... well, I suppose I needed to be cuddled. So we just... ended up in bed together.'

'With your clothes on?'

'Yes... no... just our underwear.'

Rob noticed that Michael's eyes were watery and that little tears had begun to form in the corner of his eyes.

He shrugged. 'Well look, you've heard what I've said. If you want to keep on the right side of me just don't bother Maggie so much in the future. I don't think that's too much to ask really, is it?'

'No I suppose not,' answered Michael weakly.

'Okay. We'll leave it there then. Just think a bit more in future before you go about with her holding hands and… the other stuff.'

'Can I go now?' said Michael.

'Yeah. Okay. I'll see you for the editorial meeting on Thursday.'

'Yes. I'll be there.' Michael quickly rubbed the tears from his eyes and left the room, being careful to close the door quietly. He didn't want Rob to think he was in any way annoyed with what had been said to him, fearful that he might lose his writing privileges for the newspaper in the future. Michael knew that Rob was a stern taskmaster; somewhat of a perfectionist who did not suffer fools in any way gladly.

Rob smiled to himself as soon as Michael had left the room. To be honest he had always liked Michael as a person as well as appreciating his work ethic and his writing. However, he was absolutely sure that if he continued to see Maggie as often as he had up to now he would make sure that Michael would never again write another article for *Ariel*.

Rob left the office after locking up, heading over to see if Toby was in his room. He needed to tell him that he wouldn't be meeting him in the bar that evening as he was going to spend some time buttering Maggie up. Toby would wink suggestively in his usual fashion before making an even more suggestive action with his clenched fist and forearm. All in all Rob felt that the last hour or so had gone quite well and that Maggie and Michael had both got the message. He hoped so anyway.

Chapter 9. *Changes*

January, the present day

Age is such a strangely subjective thing. Most of the time I don't actually feel any different to how I felt when I was twenty-one or even younger. Occasionally however (usually in the morning when I've just got out of bed and before I've done a spot of exercise), aches and pains and stiffness in my various joints quickly remind me that I'm now closer to seventy than I am to sixty. Lately, due to my radically altered circumstances when any sort of exercise is at a premium, I have started to feel my age on a more regular basis. In my darkest moments I fear that I will simply fade away to nothing in this awful place in which I have recently found myself and never again set eyes on the outside world. At such times, when it feels that my mind is "full of scorpions" (to quote the Bard) I have to shake myself out of such depressive thoughts and spend a bit of time counting what blessings still remain. I have my health; I think I still have most of my marbles intact; I'm still able to write my stories and, of course, I am able to continue with this short memoir that I hope will eventually help to put the record straight about everything that has happened. We shall see; only the slow and remorseless passage of time will tell I suppose.

So, back to when I was dealing with the reunion plans. Having already met with Tina, Nick and Michael, and in light of the dreams/nightmares I had recently been experiencing, I decided to get in touch with Fiona in order (hopefully) to stop my sleeping mind conjuring up the night-time horrors in which she appeared to be taking a starring role, as well as asking her about the reunion and what she remembered about Maggie and me.

Fiona Oakman (née Wells) lived in a small, picturesque village in Dorset not far from where she had been born and raised. Always very well to do, being the only daughter of a very privileged mother and father, she had gone on to marry a wealthy widower who was considerably older than her. He had died a few years ago (I, along with some of her other ex-university friends, had dutifully attended the funeral) and had left her with a large bank balance and an even larger eighteenth century pile in a beautiful area of the rural southwest. I hadn't actually contacted her since her husband's funeral so she was surprised when I rang her up one day and suggested we could meet early in the new year to discuss Toby's idea for a reunion.

And so, after a quiet Christmas Day spent at home

with Jenny and a much busier Boxing Day entertaining my daughter, her husband and my two grandchildren, I found myself in the first week of January driving to Dorset and the chocolate-box village of Piddleton Magna, the home of Fiona. For a while I sat outside what could only be described as the manor house she had inherited, marvelling at both its size and location at the end of a long, wooded drive. I even saw a deer trotting across the driveway as I approached the house.

Before I went to university, the council estate I was raised on was, to me, the extent of the known world; a world I seldom left. The houses, the streets, the doctor's surgery, the rows of shops and the schools were all that I knew. Naively, I had no real idea that some people lived in houses they actually owned rather than ones they rented from the local housing authority. (Mrs Thatcher's 'Right to Buy' plan had not yet happened – a policy that would eventually help to destroy the community nature of the sort of area where I was born and raised.) The thought that one day I would have a friend, or at least an old acquaintance, who lived in an actual honest-to-God mansion would have been completely outside the extremely limited parameters of my imagination at that time.

Eventually, after sitting in my car for several minutes musing about such things, I got out and walked up to the porticoed front of the house where I rang the bell, half expecting an agéd family retainer (perhaps called Dithers) to open the door and ask me to wait while he informed madam of my arrival. Somewhat disappointingly that wasn't the case, as the door was actually opened by Fiona herself, accompanied by five small dogs that sniffed enthusiastically round my ankles. Fiona, now even more domineering in her manner than she had been at university (and that was saying something), brusquely shooed the dog-pack out of my way, gave me a quick hug and peck on the cheek before ushering me inside. I remembered now, from my only previous visit at the time of her husband's funeral, the vastness of the hallway (which probably took up the equivalent floor space of most people's entire houses) and the great wooden staircase that Fred Astaire, dressed in top hat, white tie and tails, would no doubt have enjoyed dancing down on his twinkling feet.

Fiona looked extremely well and seemed as robustly healthy as she always had done in the past, despite now sporting steel grey curls and a pair of reading glasses that dangled from her neck. Dressed in a shapeless woolly jumper, riding trousers (inevitably) and smoking a cigarette (she had never kicked the habit, unlike most of us) she led me into her kitchen where she filled the kettle.

'Tea?' she asked in her usual stentorian tone.

'Yeah, that'd be great.'

'I've made some rock cakes. Want one? If we don't eat them the dogs will end up scoffing the lot!'

'I'd love one,' I answered – actually the drive had made me pretty hungry.

I moved one of the dogs out of the way with my foot as I sat down at the large farmhouse-style kitchen table that, despite its size, seemed rather lost in Fiona's massive stone-flagged kitchen that was equipped with the inevitable cream-coloured Aga.

'Still managing the house on your own?' I enquired, as I was bothered by one of the dogs that had suddenly decided to nibble my ankle.

'Just give him a kick; he'll soon get the message,' said Fiona, noticing the errant hound. 'Yes, I manage very well thank you. Not quite decrepit yet, although I do get a cleaning woman in twice a week and there are a few local girls that pop in occasionally to help with the horses. Oh, and the gardeners of course,' she added, stubbing out her cigarette and straightaway lighting another she took from the packet on the table. 'And how are you and that very young and extremely beautiful wife of yours?'

Fiona had always had a direct approach to most things in life and never beat around the bush; she preferred to tear up any bothersome bushes by their roots and feed them to the nearest available four-legged animal.

'We're fine thanks, Fi. Jenny's still working for a living of course, unlike us lazy sods who do nothing all day!'

'Speak for yourself! I'll have you know that I work like a Trojan looking after the horses and dogs and giving riding lessons to assorted local youngsters. I'm practically a social worker. I wouldn't be able to fit any sort of real job into my busy schedule!' Fiona poured tea from the sturdy brown teapot she'd plonked down on the table. 'Milk? Sugar?'

'Just milk please,' I answered, picking up the rock cake she had placed in front of me and taking a bite from it. 'Very good,' I said, probably spraying cake crumbs all over the place.

'Glad you like them. They usually turn out a bit dry. I only really make them for the dogs to be honest.'

'Hmm,' I said. 'I hope I'm not depriving one of them of their treat!' The ankle-nibbling dog was staring at me with undisguised hatred as I finished off the cake and picked the remaining crumbs and currants from the plate.

Fiona sat down opposite me at the table and sipped her tea. She hadn't eaten one of the rock cakes, which I thought was not a good sign. She looked as impressive as ever. Almost as tall as me, "broad in the beam" (as she would have doubtless described herself) and with large but attractive facial features, she was still recognisable as the posh eighteen-year-old student I first spoke to at university fifty years ago (at the end of a history tutorial, if I remembered correctly). Back then she seemed to represent an alien species as far as I was concerned, like no one I had ever met before in my sheltered and totally uneventful working-class life. She was supremely confident, outspoken (albeit in the poshest accent I had ever heard in real life), very attractive in a robust "jolly hockey sticks" sort of way and with long, ash-blonde hair that she often wore tied in a ponytail. She also had the most magnificent rear I had ever seen. From the moment I had first set eyes on her backside (shaped, I would later work out, by daily horse rides through the Dorset countryside) I fancied her like mad. It took me a long while before I did anything about it though. I don't remember the exact circumstances but it happened sometime in my second year and followed events at a disco when both of us were almost certainly drunk as skunks! I had a vague recollection of going to her room where we ended up in bed together. Goodness knows what the sexual encounter was like (highly robust and athletic I presume) but I'm pretty sure it was a one-night stand and nothing of a similar ilk ever took place again, although we maintained friendly relations throughout our time at university and, indeed, up to this particular meeting around her substantial kitchen table.

'So what's all this about a reunion then?' she asked.

'Well, just what I outlined on the phone really; trying to get as many people from those times back together again.'

'And what would we do once we're back together again?'

'Toby and I haven't worked out things that far ahead yet but I would guess there would be something like a nice meal and civilised drinks on one evening – say on the Friday we arrive – and then a disco, or whatever they call them these days, on the Saturday with lots of 60s and 70s music.'

'Sounds like it could be fun. Would people bring their partners?'

'Erm, not sure about that,' I replied, thinking back to my conversation with Michael when I'd implied it wouldn't be a problem. 'I don't think you'd be able to bring all your dogs though.'

'Oh no, the mutts would have to fend for themselves for the weekend. I'm sure one of the girls would throw them some food occasionally. But I wouldn't want to be a goosegog or left sitting all on my lonesome in the corner looking completely sad, pathetic and bereft all evening!'

'I very much doubt that would happen, Fiona.'

She looked sceptical.

'I will personally make sure you have someone to talk to all night,' I said, smiling.

'All night? Well, that's the best offer I've had for some time!' she said, grinning in a definitely predatory way.

I wondered then how much she remembered about our little intimate encounter all those years ago.

'By the way, you know I have certain reservations about Toby. Would I have to speak to him at all? I certainly wouldn't want to sleep with him again!' she said, in a matter-of-fact way.

'Not if you didn't want to,' I replied. I'd forgotten that she and Toby had a bit of a thing as well. I found it hard to imagine that particular scenario taking place these days. 'I think the whole thing ought to be as laid back as possible and no one should feel any pressure to do anything – except take part in karaoke of course!'

'Oh well, that is something I would be happy to have a go at.'

'Well it's definitely a possibility,' I said, finding it difficult to imagine Fiona holding a microphone and belting out *Born To Be Wild* or something similar (it was an even more outrageous concept than her and Toby getting it together in bed again).

There was a pause in our conversation and then Fiona suddenly looked at me with a serious expression on her face. 'Will anyone have a go at me about Stella George?' she said, blowing out a plume of smoke and looking uncharacteristically worried.

'What do you mean?'

'Well, you know about the disagreement I had with her not long before she topped herself?'

'I only remember that vaguely,' I replied.

'Well I certainly wouldn't want to go through all that again.' She looked only partly mollified by my answer. 'I remember being questioned by an extremely rude policeman about it at the time.'

I tried to recall the events that led up to Stella apparently leaping to her death from The Tower, our nickname for the university accommodation block where she was living at the time. I vaguely remembered hearing that Fiona had got into an actual fight with Stella at the party that had taken place the evening before Stella died, but I couldn't remember any details other than that.

'I'm pretty sure that the subject of Stella won't be brought up,' I said, attempting to sound reassuring. 'No one would want to discuss that particular event when we all have so much else to talk about.'

'Not sure I'd be as positive about it as you are. I think there will still be a few grudges from that time waiting to be aired again,' replied Fiona, shrugging as though to indicate that the subject was not worth spending any more time on. 'More tea?'

'No thanks, Fi, I already find myself increasingly having to pee every ten minutes these days as it is!'

'Yes, this getting old business isn't much fun, is it? My knees aren't anywhere near as good as they once were,' she said, as she poured herself another cup of tea and lit another cigarette. 'By the way, I was so sorry to hear about Maggie.'

I had let her know in my initial phone call and was quite surprised that she had sounded quite so affected by the news.

'I didn't know her as well as some of the others did but she always seemed to me to be a thoroughly kind and pleasant girl.' She pronounced it "gal" of course.

I nodded my agreement, noting that Fiona looked surprisingly close to shedding a small tear or two.

'Right then,' she said, visibly shaking herself and reverting to her usual commanding tones as she finished her tea and stubbed out her cigarette. 'Time to walk the dratted hounds I think! Did you remember to bring some suitable footwear? It's going to be very muddy out there with all the blasted rain we've had lately.'

'Wellies all right?'

'Absolutely hunky-dory!'

The five dogs, energised by the word walk, had suddenly congregated in the kitchen, excitedly running around in circles and yapping enthusiastically; their paws and claws tapping out a staccato rhythm on the stone floor. After popping out to the car and pulling on my wellingtons, we set off across a large open field that for all I knew was part of Fiona's back garden.

*

That night, full of excellent roast beef, Yorkshire pudding and home-made apple pie, as well as a great deal of wine and most of the contents of a very nice bottle of single malt whisky that Fiona and I had worked our way through, I lay on the bed in one of Fiona's many spare rooms staring at the ancient exposed beams of the ceiling. We had whiled away the rest of the evening relating memories of our time at university (rather worryingly, her memory seemed much better than mine). Once asleep I had a peaceful and dreamless night, and in the morning, having awoken feeling fresh and rested, I was able to reflect on the fact that my recent recurring nightmare of being set upon by Fiona and her pack of ravenous, salivating hounds had mercifully seemed to have gone away.

Chapter 10: *In a Broken Dream*

Saturday, June 1973

The Rolling Stones' *Brown Sugar* was booming out at full volume as Rob walked down the steps into the surprisingly large cellar with its several arched alcoves. The atmosphere in the underground room was warm and fuggy with smoke, and smelled of pot, beer and sweat in equal parts. Rob noticed the unmistakable figure of Fiona Wells as the multi-coloured psychedelic lights played across the room's dancing bodies. As always he glanced at Fiona's bottom, encased as it was on this occasion in a pair of tight pink loon pants. He smiled and waved to her, noticing that she was dancing with a tall bloke with short dark hair who he had never seen before. Fiona waved back and grinned broadly. Momentarily, Rob wondered why he and Fiona had only slept together the one time but then he remembered how exacting and downright exhausting that single encounter had been. To say that Fiona liked to organise and dominate proceedings would be an understatement.

He recalled that the next day he had felt bruised and sore in one or two of his more intimate places.

Keeping in time with the music, Rob (still smiling at the memory of Fiona bouncing on top of him for most of the night they were in bed together) walked over to where Maggie stood on her own aggressively smoking a cigarette and holding a bottle of Newcastle Brown ale. When she saw Rob her lips pursed in annoyance.

'Where have you been?' she said, angrily. She had to shout into Rob's ear to make herself heard above the music.

'Sorry I'm late. I went to the pub in the village with Toby and Rufus – you know what they're like,' Rob replied.

'I've been here on my own for ages!' Maggie shouted. 'You said you were looking forward to being with me tonight!'

'I'm here now. Do you want to dance?'

'No. I've gone past that now.' She brushed Rob's hand away as he squeezed her shoulder.

'Maggie, don't be miserable. Come on, let's have a bit of a bop. You like this one.'

Free's *All Right Now* had just begun, put on the turntable by a guy Rob vaguely knew who was acting as DJ for the night. Maggie shrugged belligerently, put her beer bottle on the floor and, looking extremely miserable, stepped towards the crowded area that had been designated as the cellar's dance floor.

As they began to move to the music Rob waved a

hand at Tina who was dancing with Liz in the corner below one of the cellar's arches. She looked as beautiful and desirable as she always did and Rob again felt regretful about the previous night and considered how differently it might have turned out if Liz had not stormed into Tina's room at a crucial moment.

Maggie noticed Rob's wave and his admiring and thoughtful glances in Tina's direction. 'Would you prefer to dance with her?' she said, poking Rob in the chest to get his attention.

Rob looked confused at first, not quite fully hearing what Maggie had said. Then, having realised, he grew angry. 'Oh for God's sake, Maggie! I'm sick of this! Why don't you grow up?' he shouted, and then turned and stormed off, pushing his way through people in the crowded cellar and stomping his way up the stone steps.

Maggie slowly dragged herself back to where she had left her beer. She stood facing the whitewashed cellar wall, tracing the pointing between the bricks with her fingers before lighting another cigarette and picking up her bottle of Newcastle Brown. Tears began to stream down her face as *All Right Now* finished playing and the DJ followed it with Elton John's *Crocodile Rock*.

Still facing the wall and with her eyes full of tears, Maggie felt a tap on her shoulder. She turned around, wiping her eyes, half-hoping a chastened Rob had returned to apologise. Instead, Tina and Liz stood in front of her looking concerned. Tina placed a hand on

Maggie's shoulder, squeezing gently.

'Are you all right?'

'I'm fine,' Maggie said, putting her beer down again. She took a handkerchief out of her jeans' pocket and gave her nose a good blow.

'Do you want to go outside and get some fresh air?' said Tina.

Alongside her Liz nodded her support.

'Er, yeah, okay,' she answered miserably.

Tina put her arm around Maggie, with Liz looking concerned on the other side, and the three young women left the cellar and headed upstairs where they went through a door that led to the back garden of the house.

*

Outside the early June air was still warm and sultry, although a stiff breeze had just begun to rustle the trees. Maggie took a big swig of her beer and then a long drag of her cigarette. Tears still ran down her face and she allowed Tina to wipe them away with a handkerchief.

'It is clean,' Tina said.

Maggie smiled and gave a little phlegmy laugh. 'It's Rob,' she said, in answer to a question she had not been asked.

'What's he done?' asked Tina.

'Oh you know: one minute he's all nice and kind, and the next he's having a go at me for something or other. Last night for example he came round to my room really late and was lovely and understanding about a little mistake I'd made when I thought I wouldn't be seeing him, but then this morning he went all funny and strange and stormed out. And then he said he'd meet me here and then goes out drinking with Toby and Rufus instead and has only just turned up and… and…' at which point she dissolved into sobs again and was comforted by Tina and Liz, who stood on each side of her gently patting and rubbing her back.

After Maggie had calmed down a little Tina said, 'Did you say Rob went round to your room late last night?'

'Yeah he did. He'd been out drinking with Toby and must have felt a bit on the… y'know, horny side, so he came to my room. I was sort of… asleep actually – a bit annoyed with him to be honest. But he was so nice and… well, he knows very well I can't resist him.'

Tina looked at Liz and shook her head. She would have liked to tell Maggie about the previous night but had sworn Liz to secrecy and didn't see how she could justify blurting out the truth in this situation. However, she patted Maggie's back slightly more aggressively than before.

*

After Rob had left the cellar he headed out to the front garden of the house and stopped to light a cigarette. There were a few people in small groups drinking from

106

bottles or paper cups, talking and smoking as the summer sun finally set behind some distant trees. He had earlier left Toby and Rufus drinking in the village pub and his first thought was to re-join them there, but he paused when he noticed Stella George standing on her own, leaning against a large horse chestnut tree. She was smoking and looking lost in thought as Rob wandered over to her.

'Hi,' said Rob, lighting a cigarette of his own. 'You okay?'

'Yes, I'm fine,' she said in her strange polyglot accent. 'I just needed a bit of a breather.'

'Did you come here on your own?' asked Rob.

'Yes I did. I fancied a drive and then remembered about the party so came here.'

'Look,' said Rob. 'I'm sorry about interrupting you and Maggie last night. If I'd known…'

Stella looked embarrassed and smiled. 'I'm sorry too. We just got carried away a bit. I was feeling lonely and… you know, things just happened.'

Rob looked at Stella: her perfect features, large eyes, and beautiful golden hair. She was certainly one of the loveliest-looking girls he could ever imagine seeing.

'Actually… the thing is, Stella, it wasn't a one off, was it? It's been happening fairly regularly.'

Stella looked even more embarrassed. 'Who told you that?'

'Toby told me tonight actually. There isn't much he doesn't know,' smiled Rob.

'You shouldn't believe everything Toby tells you – he often doesn't have other people's best interests at heart – but yes, I do like Maggie and I don't mind admitting it. We're good together. We respect each other. We satisfy each other.' Stella looked at Rob as if to challenge him to disagree.

'I'm sure you do, Stella, but it's a bit unfair isn't it?'

'Why? What do you mean?'

'Because Maggie and I are going out with each other – we're a couple – and... she shouldn't want someone else as well as me.'

'But you and she are not exclusive, are you?'

'What?'

'Well, you sleep around with other women, don't you?' Stella looked triumphant, the hint of a sneer curling around her beautiful mouth.

'What? No! Who told you that?'

'Oh plenty of people – Fiona for one. You and she have ended up in bed together. And don't deny it! Maggie would be so upset if she knew.'

Rob looked at Stella. Her eyes glinted in the light from the fading sun. 'You wouldn't tell Maggie though would you? Please don't – it would probably wreck us.'

'Save her from your deceitful behaviour you mean. Maggie deserves someone better than you, Rob. She should have someone who respects her not someone who can't keep his jeans zipped up for more than a few minutes.'

Rob looked angrily at the beautiful but suddenly

cruel-looking features of Stella. 'If you break me and Maggie up I'll—'

'You'll what? You know, Rob, you really are quite a nasty piece of work aren't you? Maggie thinks you're a thoughtful and caring person but some of us know differently!'

'You… you bitch! Someone ought to shut you up and…' Suddenly worried that he felt like striking out at her, Rob did not finish his sentence but turned and walked out of the garden. He wasn't going to hang around here any longer. He would go back to the pub in order to calm down and get his thoughts straight.

Stella watched Rob as he left the garden and walked on up the lane that led to the village pub. She smiled and lit another cigarette.

*

In the back garden, Tina and Liz were still consoling Maggie.

'I'm all right now. Thanks you two for looking after me.'

'Are you sure?' said Liz.

'Yeah I'm fine. I just let things… you know… get on top of me a bit.'

'Well I'm sure things with Rob will be all right. We all know what men can be like sometimes,' said Tina.

'Yeah, I'm sure you're right.' Maggie smiled at them in a reassuring way. 'I think I'll go inside and get another drink now.'

'Good idea,' said Tina. 'Let's go and get really pissed and dance the night away!'

'Sounds good to me,' laughed Maggie.

The three girls locked their arms together and walked off in that special and exclusive form of sisterly solidarity that women can do so naturally and easily, and which has always been hard for males to emulate – or even begin to understand.

Chapter 11: *Gotta See Jane*

January, the present day

You may be wondering at this point why I decided to become a teacher rather than the journalist I had always planned to be. I could of course explain my fundamental change of mind by employing some devastating points of argument and profound reasoning. For example, I could say that I decided I needed to give something back to the society that had given me the chance to get on in life, or that I suddenly realised that education is the one silver bullet that can totally transform an individual's life for the better. But to be absolutely honest, that wouldn't be true – at least not for me. No, when it came to the put-to I simply chickened out; I didn't trust myself to be able to cut the mustard in the journalistic world. I saw myself languishing in the stagnant shallow waters of some dead-end local newspaper just covering weddings, funerals and local football matches, never being quite good enough to work in Fleet Street – as it then was – or at Broadcasting House. And so I took the easy way out. Not that teaching itself is easy of course, it's certainly not, but the actual transition from university to teacher training college and then to school was simple and straightforward enough and it seemed to lack any serious degree of jeopardy. After all, I knew a lot about schools, I knew about learning and I knew my subject. Career structures in secondary schools seemed to be well defined and far less fraught than the prospects of a reporter beginning work on the *Slough Bugle* or the *Islington Herald* or wherever. In the end, you see, I opted for the familiar, the commonplace and the routine and, as I said before, I chickened out. Did I ever regret my decision? No, not really. I did well in the teaching profession; I was pretty good at the actual teaching. I had lots of good ideas and I was efficient and well organised. Most of the kids liked me, even though I was quite strict and demanding, but they always knew where they stood with me. And I rose up the career ladder smoothly and rapidly. Within five years I was running my own department at a big and well-respected comprehensive school. Did I want to go further? Become a head teacher and go into school management? I thought about it at times but no, I never really fancied that at all. Managing a department seemed satisfying enough most of the time, and I enjoyed the cut and thrust of dealing with young people every day in the classroom, something I didn't want to lose. Sitting in a headmaster's office pretending to be busy never really appealed to me. In any case, as you already know, after a few years I was able to ditch teaching completely and turn to full-time writing, though that only led to me doing exactly what I had always despised about the headmaster job... yes, you guessed it, sitting in an office all day (albeit my own office at home) pretending to be busy!

Anyway, back to my journeying around the country.

I left Fiona's stately home after breakfasting on a huge plate of bacon, egg, sausage and black pudding (all produced on local farms she told me), only slightly put off by several hungry-looking dogs salivating and staring reproachfully at me for daring to eat when they were not. I had put Fiona's name in the 'Definitely Yes' column of my imaginary reunion scorecard; she'd given me a hefty hug (she still felt strong enough to arm-wrestle a lumberjack) and a kiss on the cheek before I got into my car and drove off deeper into the South-West, heading for Cornwall. As it was the middle of winter the roads were comparatively clear – or as clear as they are ever likely to get these days – and the weather was surprisingly clement for January. I made good progress and soon found myself in the town of Penzance, standing on its wide promenade looking out on a stormy sea, a blustery wind blowing away the mental cobwebs left by my drive. I was thinking how nice it must be to live by the coast and be able to look out at the ocean every day – a recurring thought I have every time I visit the seaside.

I had arrived in Penzance to see Jane, who I had

known only vaguely at university. She had been one of Maggie's close friends and had remained a bit of a mystery to me during that time. Jane had been one of those people who was always there, or thereabouts, during my final year, but I had never really got to know her. I think she had followed the same languages course as Maggie and they had met up occasionally to exchange notes during their year abroad in France. I remember seeing her from time to time with Maggie and I thought that she might be able to shed some light on the ring and engagement issue. So I had rung her, told her about Maggie (she cried down the phone) and asked if I could visit her for a chat about old times. She agreed and so I booked myself into a Penzance guesthouse for a couple of days, thinking that I might do a spot of coastal walking as well as meeting up with her. I had visited the town a few times over the years and had thought that if ever I left London it was the sort of place I'd like to end up at. I also remembered a pub that I'd found that was particularly nice – the Admiral Benbow on Chapel Street – and thought that it would be relaxing to spend some time there. I'd mentioned this to Jane who said that she knew the pub and agreed to meet me there in the evening for a meal (they did extremely good pub food, if my memory was correct).

We met at seven o'clock that evening. I had been a little worried that I wouldn't recognise her (I hadn't actually seen her for forty-eight years after all) but as it turned out I did, and she also recognised me. She was still tall and slim and wore glasses, although her previously longish fair hair was now short and quite grey and, like all of us, she had acquired a few lines on her face. We both agreed that the passage of time had inevitably left its mark but under the circumstances we weren't doing too badly, all things considered.

Over a hearty meal (I had an excellent steak and kidney pie and mash, washed down with a few pints of a very nice local ale – how I miss those simple pleasures) we talked at length about Maggie. Jane was soon close to tears again as she spoke about her relationship with her former friend, particularly about the time when they were both based in Parisian schools during their year abroad.

'Maggie and I were close for a long time,' she said. 'After university we used to go on holiday together each year. Sarah, her daughter, was very young and Maggie was on her own so it gave her a chance to get away for a change of scene. We went all over Europe but never back to France, which was a bit odd I suppose as we were both pretty fluent French speakers.' She looked into the far distance with watery eyes when she spoke about Maggie. 'And then we just lost touch. I got married and soon after had my children. We stopped seeing each other – just drifted apart – although we still sent Christmas cards to each other. The very last time I saw her must have been about fifteen years ago when I was in London for a meeting and rang her to see if she wanted to meet up. We did meet briefly for a coffee and then she had to dash off to interview someone, or do something else connected with the newspaper she was working for. I can't remember now. I never saw her again.' At this point Jane shed some more tears.

'Hmm, that's such a shame,' I said. 'And no one let you know about her death and the funeral? I would have thought Maggie's daughter might have contacted you?'

Too emotional to speak, she just shook her head. All I could think of doing was placing my hand over hers on the table top in what I hoped was a warm and sympathetic gesture.

After allowing her a bit of time to recover, I decided to ask her whether she remembered Maggie mentioning anything about the two of us getting engaged or about a ring.

'Oh yes,' she said, sniffing and drying her eyes for the umpteenth time. 'I remember her telling me about that, and how tearful she was when you called it all off and didn't get back in touch with her again. She was so upset about it – inconsolable for ages. We went on holiday together in August just before she started her journalism course at Cardiff University and it was all she could talk about.'

I must have looked quite shocked. For a moment I was struck dumb by this revelation. Jane had provided the first concrete evidence that Maggie had actually mentioned this story to someone at the time and had not made it up later on.

After quickly gathering my thoughts together I

questioned Jane further. 'Do you remember her saying when and where we had decided to get engaged?'

'Yes. It was definitely at a party because I remember her telling me the next day. She was so excited.'

'Which party? Do you remember?'

'I think it was at a lecturer's house somewhere. I know that I was really fed up because I couldn't actually go as I was languishing in the university medical centre with glandular fever. I remember I was lying in bed on the Monday morning when one of the nurses told me that Stella George had committed suicide by jumping from The Tower.'

'Oh right. Wow – I'd forgotten that you were ill at that particular time. There was so much going on. Do you remember exactly what Maggie said to you?'

'Now you're asking! It was an awfully long time ago!'

'I know,' I said. 'But please try – it's quite important to me.'

Jane gave me a funny look but then shut her eyes in an attempt to think back to that time. 'Hmm, it's so hard to remember things exactly but I do remember Maggie coming to visit me in the medical centre and bringing me some grapes. We laughed about that – it seemed so grown up. As I said, she was excited and obviously couldn't wait to tell me something. I can't recall exactly what she said but I definitely remember her telling me that you had asked her to marry you the night before.'

'Okay,' I said, feeling quite shocked at this

confirmation. 'Did she say anything about a ring?'

Jane screwed up her eyes in thought and then opened them and shook her head. 'I can't remember if she said anything about it then but I do recall that she wore an engagement ring for a long time afterwards, despite you having called it all off,' she said, looking somewhat reproachfully at me.

I looked into Jane's eyes to try to ascertain if she was telling the truth. I couldn't think of a valid reason why she would lie to me. She obviously felt that I had hurt Maggie all those years ago but was that enough for her to concoct a story just to support her now deceased friend? I thought it was pretty unlikely she would do that. So if she *was* correct, why was it I had forgotten the events of that night, to the extent that I couldn't remember asking someone to marry me? It just seemed totally insane.

The rest of the evening went by and we had a polite conversation about our other university memories, our working lives (Jane, now retired of course, had worked for a publishing company) and our families, especially grandchildren (she seemed to have dozens of them). However, throughout the rest of the evening it was a struggle to stop my mind from going back to the revelation that (according to Jane anyway) I had indeed asked Maggie to marry me all those years ago. I did eventually get around to asking Jane about the reunion and although she didn't dismiss the idea completely, I did get the impression that without Maggie she thought there would be little point in her going to such a gathering. I put her down as a probable "no" on my mental list of likely reunion attendees.

We left the pub and I walked Jane back to her house, which was only five minutes away. Then I strolled back down to the promenade and spent some time looking out to sea again, ruminating on what I'd been told that evening. I watched the occasional distant, moving lights far out on the ocean and wondered what sorts of ships they belonged to as I huddled into my fleece to try to keep out what was by now a bitterly cold wind. When I was a kid we rarely went on holiday because my mum always found it difficult to make ends meet, and so I'd never really got used to being at the seaside. Even at my advanced age I found it exciting and strangely unnerving to look out at the vastness of the sea, particularly on a cold winter's night. The sight had always provoked in me a state of deep contemplation, and as there were no other people about on the promenade that particular evening, the feeling was even more pronounced than usual.

I eventually stirred myself and found some steps that led down to the beach. I walked along the sand for a while, taking in that special coastal aroma of fish, salt and rotting seaweed. A few hundred yards along the beach I found some more steps, climbed back up to the promenade, tried to knock the sand from my shoes and wended my way back to the guesthouse where I was thankfully able to get warm again in my small but homely room. There I lay in bed, too full of thoughts to immediately fall asleep. My chat with Jane had answered some questions but raised many more. Why had I, at that party in 1973, asked Maggie to marry me when I had never considered our relationship a particularly important one? And why on earth had I forgotten all about it? As I was in the process of drifting off to sleep, I presumed I would have a troubled night with a plethora of nightmarish dreams, probably populated by various people from my past including a posthumously irate Maggie. However, as it turned out, for the second night running, I had a surprisingly undisturbed and welcome night's sleep.

Chapter 12: *Without You*

Saturday, June 1973

Stella George threw her cigarette onto the ground and stubbed it out with the heel of her white sandal. She watched Rob make his way back towards the village pub before she turned and went back inside the house.

She looked in the lounge, scanning the people there. Two were sat slumped on a Habitat sofa that had seen much better days while others lay around the room on large red and blue floor cushions, all languidly smoking pot while listening to an Incredible String Band album. She smiled her sweetest smile as she looked around the room to ascertain whether Maggie was there. After deciding she wasn't, Stella went into the kitchen, where just a few people were standing around chatting, and poured some white wine from an almost full bottle into a paper cup. Carrying the bottle and another cup, she took small sips of the wine as she walked into the hallway that smelled strongly of jasmine joss sticks and where several people sat on the floor talking, smoking and listening to the music that wafted out from the lounge. Squeezing past a male and a female who were ensconced on the stairs kissing, oblivious to everyone else, Stella climbed the staircase.

Upstairs she looked in the bathroom, which was empty, and then peered in at the open door of a bedroom that was also empty apart from a pile of coats lying in the middle of the double bed. Two more bedroom doors were closed and Stella put her ear to the doors but couldn't hear any noises coming from either. She thought about quietly opening the doors and taking a look inside but decided against it. No point making life even more dramatic by opening the door to discover a couple having sex in there, she thought.

She finished her wine before making her way back down the stairs, still clutching the wine bottle and the extra paper cup and ignoring the couple who were continuing to kiss. In the hallway she found the steps to the cellar and made her way down them. Loud rock music was playing as she stood at the bottom of the steps, letting her eyes adjust to the low-level lighting. Disco and strobe lights pulsed around the room, highlighting its occupants and the cigarette smoke that hung in a blue-grey pall above the dancing bodies.

Stella noticed that a beaming Fiona was dancing with a tall, good-looking guy she'd never seen before and nearby, also dancing, was Althea with another man she didn't know. Then she spotted Maggie at the far end of the cellar standing with Liz and Tina. Stella made her way over to them. She caught Maggie's eye and smiled. Maggie smiled back, although Stella noticed there was a slight hesitancy about the way she did so.

'Hi,' Stella said, and gave Maggie a hug, the wine bottle still held tightly in her hand. She poured some wine into the spare cup and gave it to Maggie. 'Sorry, you two, I've only brought two cups,' she shouted above the music to Tina and Liz, as she refilled her paper cup and proceeded to drink from it.

'That's okay. We were just going for a dance anyway,' replied Tina diplomatically, as she put her hand on Liz's shoulder, squeezed gently and directed her to the dance area.

'I can see your eyes are red. What has he done now?' asked Stella, looking at Maggie, concern on her face.

'Rob? Oh, we just had a bit of a row and I took it too much to heart, that's all. Nothing to worry about.'

'I do worry about you though.' Stella reached out and stroked Maggie's long dark hair. 'I've just seen him heading for the pub.'

'Thought he probably would. I imagine that Toby and Rufus will be there till closing time.' Maggie put her wine down and reached for the cigarette packet she had tucked into the back pocket of her jeans. She took one out and lit it before offering the packet to Stella who shook her head.

'You ought to ditch him you know. He's really not anywhere near good enough for you.'

Maggie took a deep drag of her cigarette and smiled.

123

'Sometimes I think that, but then when I'm with him – when we're together – I can't imagine ever being with anyone else.' As she spoke wisps and curls of smoke issued from her mouth and nose.

'Does that include me?'

'No, of course not, but with you... it's different. We both know that our thing isn't meant to be permanent. It's just a temporary fling... friends just having a bit of fun. Isn't it?'

Stella's face suddenly looked crestfallen. She looked at Maggie and then down to the floor, her disappointment all too evident. When she looked up again her eyes were ablaze with indignation, bordering on hatred. Maggie had never seen such a stark look on Stella's beautiful face before. She took a step backwards.

'Stella, I'm sorry. I didn't realise you were so serious. I honestly thought we were just having a bit of fun. I'm not... you know... that way inclined really. I prefer men. I didn't...'

'How can you say that?' Stella spoke slowly and deliberately. 'You've been as keen as I have to jump into bed together. We are good for each other, Maggie. We know how to please each other. And now you say you prefer Rob – who's a cheating rat by the way. I always thought you were much better than him but now... I don't think so!' Stella spat out her last few words.

Maggie took another step back, colliding with the

cellar's brick wall. She looked puzzled. 'What do you mean, cheating?'

'Do you know, Maggie, sometimes you are an absolute fool. You must be the only one who doesn't know the type of person Rob really is. He'll sleep with anyone with tits. He's in and out of bed with loads of girls and you... you think he's exclusively yours? You're just a complete idiot, aren't you?'

Maggie stared at Stella. In that brief moment she hated Stella more than she had ever hated anyone or anything in her entire life. 'Get away from me you... you bitch! I love Rob and I'm sure he loves me. And...' Maggie broke down in tears, dropping her half-filled paper cup, the spilled wine forming a quickly expanding puddle on the stone floor.

Stella shook her head and smiled. 'Well if you want to know how faithful Rob is, ask Fiona or Althea or Tina or Liz and probably quite a few others too. I feel so sorry for you.' She shrugged, took a swig from the wine bottle and turned, leaving Maggie standing with tears running down her face for the second time that evening.

Stella stopped at where Fiona was dancing with the tall man and, smiling at both, began to dance with them. She passed the wine bottle to Fiona who smiled back at her before drinking from it and then passing it to the man.

*

Once again, Liz and Tina noticed Maggie's distress. They went up to her and comforted her, putting their arms around her and again softly patting her back.

'Is it true?' Maggie managed to gurgle through her tears.

'Is what true?' said Tina and Liz in unison.

'That Rob… cheats on me? That he sleeps around all the time?'

Tina gently but firmly took Maggie by the arm and led her upstairs out of the cellar. She was concerned that the loudness of the music would make their conversation even harder than it was obviously going to be already.

Stella watched them leave as she danced and smiled again.

*

In the garden, Tina looked at Liz and then at Maggie. 'Now, Maggie, what are you so upset about?'

'Stella told me… that Rob hasn't been faithful to me after he told me he was! I don't know… whether I should believe her… or not,' Maggie sobbed.

Tina raised her eyebrows and pursed her lips in the closest she would ever get to a sneer. 'You shouldn't believe everything Stella tells you. She can be very bitchy at times.'

'But she said that he had slept with you, Tina… and you, Liz. Is that true?'

If Maggie's eyes had not been so full of tears she might have seen Liz's face, for the second time in twenty-four hours, turn a very deep shade of red.

'Erm… well, yes I did sleep with him,' said Liz. 'But it was ages ago – a year ago – I think before you two even got together. And it didn't really mean very much.'

Maggie's face flared red with anger. 'Why do people always say that?' she shouted. 'They always say that it didn't mean anything but of course it meant something, otherwise it wouldn't have happened!'

Liz looked shocked at Maggie's outburst and took a step backwards. A couple of people standing nearby in the back garden looked over at the three women.

'And what about you, Tina? You always look so bloody well innocent! When did you go to bed with Rob?'

'I didn't… we haven't. Look, Maggie, I was with him in the bar last night but nothing happened afterwards. He just walked me back to my room. Really – nothing happened at all.'

'Last night? You were with him last night? He told me he was with Toby last night.' Maggie's wet cheeks were glowing in the dying sun's crepuscular light. Soon it would be dark and the cold, stiff breeze that had been so apparent over the last few nights would again begin to blow and quickly bring the evening temperature plummeting downwards.

'I don't know what he said to you, Maggie. All I know is that nothing happened between us. I'm faithful to Nick. You know that.' Tina looked at Liz for confirmation and she nodded a shade too enthusiastically.

Maggie shook her head. She lowered it and looked at the ground. One or two teardrops fell by her feet. 'I'm sorry... I'm so confused. I don't know what to think anymore,' she said. 'I thought we were okay together and now...'

'Do you know,' said Tina, 'I don't think Stella will always have your best interests at heart. She can be very scheming, and if she takes against someone...'

'I don't know,' Maggie said wearily. 'I need to speak with Rob. I think I'm going to walk to the pub and talk to him... see what he says.'

'Okay,' said Tina. 'Do you want us to come with you?'

'No, it's all right,' Maggie said, smiling in a bit of a lopsided way. 'I'll be all right now. I've pulled myself together. The fresh air will do me good. I'm sorry for getting annoyed with you both, you didn't deserve it.' She smiled at the two women as warmly as she was able to and then left the garden, heading for the pub. Tina and Liz watched her as she walked away, her head bowed.

Chapter 13: *American Pie*

January, the present day

The day after my meeting with Jane I wrapped up warmly in my fleece, scarf, gloves and woolly hat and had an extremely enjoyable (albeit very blustery) few hours walking along part of the Cornish coastal path; a little solitary journey that gave me plenty of time to ponder and brood about what Jane had told me the night before. In the evening I went to two more extremely nice Penzance pubs before ending up back at the cosy and inviting Admiral Benbow with its log fire. Over a few pints of local cider, I had an interesting chat with a chap who was a self-proclaimed expert on the Cornish language and who put forward a case as to why Cornwall should be independent from the rest of the UK. Surprisingly, considering the amount of alcohol I'd put away during the evening, I had a relatively clear head when I woke up the following morning. Maybe it was due to the coastal air – or the local apples!

After a very nice full English breakfast and good

coffee at the guesthouse, I set out for South Wales. The drive was uneventful as I headed for Caerphilly where Althea lived with her husband James. Althea originally came from South Carolina in the USA and had spent a year at the University of the North as part of the "Study Abroad Year" scheme run by the university. After a year or two back in the States, she came to the conclusion that she actually preferred living in Britain and so decided to settle here permanently. Apparently she considered that as a person of mixed race (my mum would have referred to her by that awful phrase "half-caste") she felt that she had less chance of being discriminated against in the UK than she did in the US. I was never quite sure about that but she seemed convinced, so who was I to argue? After a couple of years she met James Jones in Cardiff while she was working there (she taught English literature at a secondary school and he was a civil servant) and they married soon afterwards. She was so in love with him and the area that Althea even learnt the Welsh language, and in doing so I suppose she became an honorary Welsh woman. They now lived in Caerphilly, having had a couple of kids who now had their own families and lived nearby.

We had met up on various occasions in the past and I had always got on well with both Althea and Jim. I particularly enjoyed telling people the story of how I made her fall on the floor with laughter. It was during my third year at university and I was doing some cooking in the communal kitchen that was down the corridor from my study/bedroom (as the small rooms were so grandly called). At the time I had a fairly limited culinary repertoire: eggs on toast, beans on toast, cheese on toast, tinned spaghetti on toast – you get the picture. On this occasion, however, I'd decided to splash out on a meal that my mum had occasionally served up for us at home: frozen faggots. These were basically meatballs made from liver and other bits of offal, the recipe originating in the Black Country apparently. Well, you can probably guess the rest. As I was standing at the cooker heating up and stirring the faggots and gravy in a small saucepan, Althea, who lived on the floor above and looking bored and in need of a sociable conversation with someone, appeared in the kitchen. She quickly took an interest in what I was doing, attracted no doubt by the pungent aroma the food was giving off.

'What are you cooking up there, Rob?' she said.

'Faggots,' I replied.

'What?'

'Faggots,' I repeated.

When I looked at her again she was doubled up in what could only be described as paroxysms of laughter. She then graduated (if that's the right word) to sitting on the kitchen floor with her face screwed up in total and utter amusement and disbelief. When she was able to speak coherently again she explained to me (at the time I was so obviously very naïve and unworldly) just what the word faggot meant in the United States.

Althea was always very easy to talk to and rarely took a judgmental stance on what today would be referred to as "political correctness" or "wokeness". I remembered telling her the story of how I was once with my mum in a Woolworth's store in Leicester when she proclaimed, in a loud voice, that she needed some "nigger-brown cotton". I did my panicky best to shut her up but she never really understood why she couldn't say that particular word without causing offence. As far as she was concerned, she was simply describing a product in a traditional hue that people had referred to quite naturally in the past. Surprisingly, perhaps, Althea laughed along with the story and told me how her mum (she said "mom" of course), who was African American, had also made faux pas of various sorts. All in all Althea Stokes (as she then was) and I got along pretty well and at some point during that first term of my third year we had slept together a couple of times. She was, after all, very attractive: tall and slim, often wearing an embroidered Afghan coat and with her hair done in the archetypal "Angela Davis" Afro style that was very 1970s. I can't remember if I ever admitted my unfaithfulness to Maggie who it now seemed, from what I had gleaned from the memories of others, was far more attached to me than I had originally thought.

Part of Althea's attraction, on top of her undoubted physical attributes, was that she was another of those females who would have seemed so amazingly exotic to me with my very limited life experience prior to going to university. Named, at her mother's insistence, after the black American tennis player Althea Gibson, who had broken through many racial barriers in the years after the Second World War, she was someone I was extremely glad to have known. If somebody had told me back in the days when I lived on a Leicester council estate that one day I would have a relationship with a beautiful black girl from America I would not, of course, have believed them in the slightest.

There was another reason for me being very keen on the idea of having a romantic liaison with Althea and that harked back to an experience I'd had at the end of a long-standing relationship with a girl called Christine when I was in the sixth form at school. She was studying A-Level French and I had been attracted to her right from the time one lunch break when she had translated into English for me the incredibly sexy sounding words of the hit song *Je t'aime... moi non plus* by Serge Gainsbourg and Jane Birkin (banned by the BBC of course despite it getting to number one in the charts). The conversation that ensued was, up until then, by far the most erotic incident of my life, which wasn't really saying very much, it being a fairly low bar. Christine and I carried on going out right up to the time I went to university, when one of the last things she said to me on the night before I left was that if ever I broke up with her I should definitely not then go out with a black girl. It was the first occasion I realised that she had such

133

racist tendencies; I had been blinded I suppose by her physical charms up to that point. I never contacted her again apart from sending her a letter, written on my first day at the University of the North, in which told her I didn't want to see her again when I was back home during the university holidays.

Anyway, back to Caerphilly. Althea and Jim seemed really pleased to see me and were happy to put me up for the night (I'd already phoned them before setting out from London a few days before). Of course, Althea now looked somewhat altered from our halcyon days at university, as we all did. Her wonderful Afro cut was sadly reduced to a short, cropped grey hairstyle and she was now rather stooped over by the effects of age along with some particularly bad attacks of osteoarthritis she'd suffered from over the years. However, I tried not to dwell on the inevitable changes that the passage of time had wrought on us both, but instead concentrated on the things that were bothering me in the present. After a brief look around the town of Caerphilly along with its impressive castle – a place I'd never been to before – we went back to their home for a very nice meal along with (again) lots of wine. Althea had made American meat loaf and key lime pie, both of which were totally delicious. I was pleased that she still kept in touch with her original country's culinary style at least.

Over dinner I broached the idea of the reunion, which both Althea and James thought was a good idea and said they would be happy to attend as long as people's partners were allowed. Althea and I then talked about the friends and acquaintances we remembered from those times (she was someone else who seemed to have a much better memory than I did) and we briefly dwelt on the death of Stella. It appeared that she and Althea had fallen out not long before Stella's apparent suicide, prompting the police to interview her, just as they had done with Fiona. I didn't recall that event but concluded that I probably never knew about it in the first place, having been totally obsessed about my own future at that stage; it would have been around then that I made the decision to train to be a teacher rather than a journalist. We also spoke about Maggie's death. Althea expressed her sympathy but did go on to say that she hadn't really known Maggie very well, although she had been aware that she and I had been in a fairly long-term relationship. I was glad that Althea did not allude to our brief fling in front of her husband.

After skirting around the subject (while again consuming a great deal of wine) I then asked Althea whether she recalled anything about Maggie and me possibly getting engaged.

'Do you remember me or Maggie, or anyone else for that matter, actually talking about it?'

'Well, like I said, I didn't know Maggie very well so I don't believe I had too many conversations with her, but I seem to remember that someone did mention to me that you and she had spoken about getting engaged,' said Althea.

'Really?' I said. 'Do you remember who that was?'

'Actually I think it might have been Toby Barker.'

'Are you sure about that, Al?' I was quite taken aback by this revelation.

'No, not totally sure at all but I have a vague recollection that it was him.'

'Do you remember when it was he might have told you?'

Althea looked into the far distance as she tried to recall what for her must have been a very insignificant conversation from so long ago. 'No sorry, I don't. It would probably have been when I was really busy organising going back to the States.'

'Of course,' I said, as I helped myself to more wine. 'Might it have been at a party at a house in the countryside that was owned by a lecturer called Tim? It would have been right before the exam results came out.'

Althea thought hard again. 'No, sorry, although I did go to that party – I remember the place pretty well. I remember dancing in the cellar and arguing with Stella in the garden – she said some really horrible things – but I've got no detailed recollection of the conversation with Toby. It may have taken place outside the house but that's all I can say. Sorry to let you down, Rob.'

And that was the total extent of the conversation that pertained to the thing that was at the very top of my list of concerns. The rest of a very pleasant evening was spent talking about the usual topics: families, holidays we had been on, the current dismal state of politics in the UK, the USA and the world in general, and so on – all helped by a great deal of wine. (I had set out from home on this 'road trip' with twelve bottles of wine in the boot of my car to share with those friends I visited – just in case you thought I was doing a great deal of sponging off people without offering anything in return!)

That night I lay in Althea and Jim's spare room feeling more confused than ever. For the second time I'd had a confirmation (if only a vague one) that Maggie and I had openly spoken about marriage, and that Toby (of all people) could be one of those who knew more about it than he now admitted.

When I eventually slid into sleep I was again transported to a strangely half-familiar but desperate nightmarish landscape where I was running away from a pack of madly snarling and fearsome-looking dogs. This time there were two figures mounted on huge white horses. One of those leading the baying hounds was Fiona, now seemingly dressed in biker leathers, and atop the other horse, and looking mightily uncomfortable, was the rotund figure of Toby who was waving around a large sword that was dripping with blood. It took me a moment or so to realise that the blood was mine.

Chapter 14: *Days*

Saturday, May 1973

It's a Saturday lunchtime. The location is The Slipway Inn in Flitborough. Rob and Maggie are huddled in the corner of the crowded pub munching their way through some large steak baps. Glasses of beer sit on the table in front of them – a pint of bitter for him, a half for her. The beer isn't that good but Rob and Maggie are not yet very discriminating where drink is concerned. It is, after all, the year 1973 when ubiquitous real ale is still some way off in the future, perhaps just a tiny and hopeful glint in the eye of the editor of *The Campaign for Real Ale's Good Beer Guide*, published for the first time the previous year.

Rob and Maggie's conversation is about the future and what it may hold for them.

'Do you know that in the year 2000 I'll be forty-eight years old?' said Maggie.

'Yeah, same here,' mumbled Rob, his mouth full of meat and bread and his attention fixed mostly on the sports pages of a *Daily Mirror* he'd found discarded on the table.

'You've got some mustard on your cheek,' Maggie said, wiping it from Rob's face using a paper serviette. 'Forty-eight! It doesn't seem possible!'

'It's a long way off.'

'Yeah, but we'll get there one day. Isn't that worrying to you?'

'Well, not as worrying as not getting there I suppose,' said Rob, briefly looking up from his newspaper.

'That's true. Do you think we'll still be together then?'

'What?'

'Do you think we'll still be together in the year 2000?'

'In the year 2000?' Rob said.

Maggie noticed a sheepish look on his face.

'That's twenty-seven years away. Best just to concentrate on the present I always think.' Rob took another bite of his steak sandwich and looked again at the county cricket scores in the *Daily Mirror*.

'Hmm,' replied Maggie. She had come to the definite conclusion that every time she suggested anything about how their relationship might develop in the future Rob would always brush it away as unimportant or he would quickly change the subject. She watched him as he slowly chewed his steak, studied the paper a bit more and took a big swig of his beer.

'Well this is nice, isn't it?' Rob said, looking up,

realising that Maggie had gone quiet. 'I think it's good to get away from the campus occasionally. How about we go and see a film this afternoon?'

'Okay,' Maggie replied.

Rob looked at his wristwatch to check the time and then looked thoughtful. 'Do you know that back home at my mum's the clocks are always half an hour fast?'

'What? Really! Why?'

'My mum has always had them that way. Her parents did too apparently. Says it's to make sure she's got more time than she thinks she has. My brother and I just thought it was normal behaviour. I was quite surprised when I discovered that not everyone does it and most people have the correct time showing on their clocks and watches.'

Maggie grinned. 'Do you get on well with your mum?'

'Yeah. Okay. Better now that I don't live at home for most of the year.'

'I'd like to meet her at some point.'

'Hmm, yeah... great, of course. We'll have to arrange that some time.'

There was that sheepish look again as Rob went back to his food and newspaper. Maggie watched Rob eat some of his steak bap.

'Is she nice, your mum?'

Rob looked up again and drank some beer. 'Er, yeah, she's okay I suppose. She's had a rough time in the past. I remember my dad always arguing and hitting her pretty frequently before he left. She has a much better life now.'

'How old is she?'

Rob scratched his chin as he thought. 'She's quite old – forty-six later this year.'

'Same as my mum.'

'Really?'

'Yeah, just a bit younger than we'll be in the year 2000.'

'That's interesting,' Rob said without any real interest, as he looked down at his newspaper again.

'Hmm,' said Maggie, as she picked up her beer, drank some and took another bite of her roll. She found it difficult to eat as the steak was really tough. She pushed the plate away and took out a cigarette, lighting it with the lighter Rob had given her for her birthday. She blew a line of smoke from her mouth. 'What film shall we see then?'

'Eh?' Rob said without looking up.

'What film shall we see at the pictures?'

Rob looked at her. 'I don't know. What's on?'

'I'm not sure,' she replied. 'I can go and find out if you like.'

'Actually, I think I'm quite happy to stay here for a bit.'

'It was your idea,' said Maggie, suddenly sounding disconsolate.

'Yeah, I know,' Rob replied, still reading.

Maggie glanced at the front page of the *Daily Mirror*

Rob was studying. *Nixon Did Know!* shouted the banner headline. She looked around the pub at the people drinking, smoking and chatting. There were a few obvious student-types scattered about but most of those present were not from the university. She had heard that there were occasional contretemps between students and local youths from the town but she had never experienced any problems herself. She guessed that most of the locals were used to the university being on their doorstep as it had been in existence for about eight or so years now, and people must certainly appreciate the employment opportunities that it had brought to the area.

Soon she and the majority of her friends would leave the university and start to experience life in the "real world". Mostly she was looking forward to the future and in the past few days had been trying to decide what she should do for a living once her cosseted life as a student was over. She would have liked to have made some sort of career decision already, but Rob had not told her anything about what *his* intentions were for next year and where he was going to be living. Rob had many times told her that he wanted to train as a journalist after he had got his degree. The University of the North didn't do a postgraduate journalism course but a few places around the country did. Recently he had mentioned that he might apply to one at Cardiff University but he'd not told her of any firm plans. The last few months working on the university newspaper had convinced her that she would also like to try journalism as a career and she had been hoping that she and Rob might end up on the same course together, but he had been very tight-lipped about his plans in recent weeks. Maggie had originally considered teaching as a career option and had gone so far as to look at a number of teacher training college prospectuses, but until she knew what Rob planned to do she was loathe to set any of her ideas in concrete.

Biting the bullet, Maggie tapped Rob on the knee. 'Have you decided yet where you'll be next year?'

'What?' said Rob, looking up from his newspaper.

'Have you decided what you're going to do next year?'

Rob looked suddenly quite flustered. It was obvious to Maggie that his mind was working quickly in order to give her a non-committal answer. His face coloured slightly. When he spoke he did so slowly, carefully choosing his words.

'Hmm, still not sure where I want to do the journalism course. There are a number of options that I'm still considering: Cardiff, Coventry, Preston Poly, one or two others. Too much choice really. Why do you ask?'

'What do you mean, why do I ask? I'd like to know what's going to happen next year between us and whether we'll be together somewhere.' Maggie had raised her voice and one or two people in the pub were looking her way.

Rob's face had coloured again. 'Maggie, for God's

sake there's no need to shout.'

'I wasn't shouting! All I want to know is where I stand as far as next year is concerned. I'd like us to be together then but time's running out. We need to make some quick decisions.'

'Yes I know. There's still time. Don't worry. I'll let you know as soon as I can. I'm about ninety-five per cent certain I'm going to apply to Cardiff. Their journalism course seems pretty good, but I just need to give it a week or so to tie up a few loose ends.'

Maggie considered asking Rob what exactly those few loose ends actually were but decided that there was little point in pressing him further. Despite his seeming procrastination, which was quite out of character, it sounded like Rob was almost certain about Cardiff next year so it made sense for her to get her application for the journalism course in as soon as possible too. As she finished her beer and watched a still slightly red-faced Rob continue to read his paper, she decided that as soon as she got back to her room on campus she would fill in the application form, post it off and then hope like mad that Rob would soon do the same.

Rob carried on looking at the sports pages. He was aware that Maggie was staring at him. He knew why she was concerned and why she had sounded so angry a few moments ago, but he found it impossible to tell her the truth. For three years and more his intention had been to go into journalism after leaving university. Applying for a journalism course was obviously the first step in that plan but last night, as he was attempting to fill in the application form for the year-long postgraduate course at Cardiff University, he had experienced a massive crisis of confidence. Would he be able to achieve anything in that profession? Was he good enough to be anything more than a second-rate hack on a local newspaper? Would he actually enjoy working on a newspaper or for a broadcaster anyway? He was, in fact, close to dropping the whole idea and considering something else. Already he had visited the university library and had taken a look at a number of prospectuses for postgrad teacher training courses at colleges of education. Wouldn't becoming a teacher be a much more sensible option for him? Wasn't it a profession he would be more suited to? He would have to decide soon, he knew that, but he couldn't talk to Maggie about it – not yet anyway.

Rob looked at Maggie's slightly annoyed face. A bit of distraction was needed at the moment, he decided. He put the *Daily Mirror* down on the seat beside him and finished off his beer. He smiled at Maggie. 'Shall we go to the pictures now then?' he said cheerfully.

Chapter 15: *You're So Vain*

January, the present day

After an extremely filling breakfast of American pancakes and maple syrup, which Althea had made especially for me, I drove away from her house still feeling a little unsettled by my dream of the night before. As I tried hard to forget the details of the nightmare, I eschewed the habitual '60s and '70s music contained on my iPod (now an out-dated piece of technology someone was telling me recently) and listened instead to an interesting programme about general elections since the Second World War on *Radio 4*.

I've never been much of a political person apart from a generalised feeling that those on the left of politics seem to have beliefs and policies that tend to benefit the vast majority of people. Of course I did the usual sort of studenty stuff back in the '70s: I put my student grant in the National Westminster Bank rather than Barclays because of the latter's involvement in apartheid South

Africa; I marched on an anti-Vietnam War demo in London in 1971, and I chanted "Maggie Thatcher – milk snatcher!" along with the best of them, but I never really got too involved with politics, leaving it to others to sort out – rightly or wrongly. Because of that I never got to mix with those inveterate politico types at university, apart from knowing Posh Rufus that is.

Rufus St John Munro was, along with Fiona, one of the poshest people I met at the University of the North. He came from a wealthy family who appeared to own large swathes of Kent, but by the time I first met him in 1970 he had revolted against everything his family stood for and had joined a Trotskyist splinter group whose name I have now forgotten (there were so many). For the next three years he seemed to spend much of his time writing political tracts and standing for election to various student offices, and in spite of this he (annoyingly) still came away with a decent degree. In most of these electoral endeavours he was successful, mainly due to the fact that he possessed a fine rhetorical style when delivering speeches to large groups of his fellow students. He also had a range of well-honed invective that mainly consisted of swearwords and interesting (if biologically impossible) imagery – aimed at his political opponents – that could be very funny. To be fair he also had a great deal of organisational skill that seemed to come very naturally to him. For these reasons he was not really the sort of person I would normally have got to know, but early on in my first term

I ended up in the same history tutorial group as him and shortly after that he became friendly with Toby, who brought him into our circle of friends. Rufus was soon given the sobriquet Posh Rufus (which of course he never really liked), due to his hard-to-conceal refined accent. To be fair, despite his political leanings and his somewhat patrician air, Rufus was always very likeable and amusing. He was a natural raconteur who seemed to have an endless supply of stories and jokes and, in those early days, wasn't above occasionally poking fun at himself. He also had a great liking for beer and would often join Toby and me for an extended evening in one or more of the campus bars.

Anyway, after leaving university he moved to London, did a Master's degree, began a PhD (that he eventually dropped out of), and for a time ran a left-wing bookshop called The Ragged-Trousered Philanthropist. Occasionally, when I found time outside of my teaching job, I would meet up with him in Camden Town where he lived, and we'd have a few pints together. Eventually, in the late 1970s, and having mellowed somewhat (he'd decided that he would like to pursue a serious political career), he got into Labour Party politics. After proving himself a decent candidate in an unwinnable constituency in his native county, he got selected for a safe seat in central London and was elected to parliament for the first time in the 1987 general election. During this period, as you can imagine, his politics went from far left to firmly in the "acceptable" centre of the Labour Party, and by the time Tony Blair and New Labour heaved into view in the mid-1990s, Rufus was well placed and well respected enough to take up an important post in Blair's government following the Labour landslide of 1997.

During the time he was a government minister I rarely saw him, although we did keep in touch, and on one occasion Jenny and I were invited to meet him at the House of Commons, which was quite a thrill for the two of us. He often appeared on television news programmes as one of the important kingpins of New Labour and had an obvious skill for deflecting awkward questions by answering completely different ones and sounding totally sincere as he did so. For a brief time he was even spoken about as a possible future prime minister but, as they say, all political careers eventually end in failure, after a scandal involving a number of investment deals he had made with some dodgy foreign companies he was shuffled off to the House of Lords where the pomposity that he was always rather prone to was allowed to flourish unremittingly.

I had decided early on that after my trips to Devon, Cornwall and South Wales it was probably a good idea (if I wanted to keep on the right side of Jenny that is) to head back home. Before I did so, however, I had decided to make a bit of a detour from the M4 motorway and visit Rufus who had a home in Long Barton, a small village somewhere between Oxford and Aylesbury.

I made good time and got to Rufus's extremely

impressive-looking thatched cottage at around lunchtime. He and his long-suffering wife, Sarah, were expecting me as I had phoned them on the previous evening. As usual Rufus was very welcoming and gave me a big hug, although I was quite taken aback by the strong smell of alcohol on his breath so early in the day. We had a very convivial lunch, provided by a local and highly thought of chef, who apparently was often called upon by the Munros to provide delicious food for special occasions. I felt honoured!

After we'd eaten, Sarah left us saying, 'You two men have a bit of a natter,' and disappeared somewhere into the depths of their large, old and rambling house while Rufus and I retired to his snooker room.

As you might imagine, the room had a well-stocked bar, and we sat drinking after-lunch coffee and cognac. Rufus regaled me with an assortment of highly entertaining and amusing Westminster tales including a number of scurrilous stories about members of the present Conservative government who apparently had trouble keeping their trousers zipped up in the presence of their female staff.

As I listened to him I realised that, perhaps more than anyone else I had known in my student days, Rufus had changed the most. In the place of the young student activist with his drab green ex-army jacket, long black curly hair and Zapata moustache, in front of me now sat a self-satisfied, florid-faced, wispy-haired individual who looked somewhat older than his sixty-nine years.

In many ways he reminded me of those James Gillray political cartoons that depicted red-nosed, overstuffed, eighteenth century country squires and I found myself trying to imagine what Rufus would look like in a powdered periwig. It was evident that he had almost completely reverted to the type of person his rich over-privileged family had always expected him to turn out like. If he hadn't deserved the nickname Posh Rufus back in the '70s he certainly did now. He had indeed come full political circle from student revolutionary to his current position of well-heeled New Labour Party grandee without ever closing his mouth on the way.

In saying all of that, Rufus was still very good company, and asked all the right questions about my family, my writing and myself. I think that deep down he always had a grudging respect for me at university and that had carried on up to the present.

Eventually, with some effort and perseverance, I was able to turn the conversation around to the reunion idea to which Rufus gave his hearty agreement and promised to be there. That was expected of course; any opportunity to engage with an audience, especially a captive one for the weekend, was heaven-sent as far as Rufus was concerned. I then told him about Maggie dying (he had already picked the news up on the grapevine apparently) and asked him about whether he remembered anything about our apparent engagement.

'Can't say that I do, Rob. Should I?' He said this while lighting up a large Havana cigar (Rufus was another who had never abandoned the smoking habit).

'Just wondered,' I said. 'Apparently I asked Maggie to marry me but I can't actually remember doing so.'

Rufus smiled. 'I used that approach a few times when I wanted to get a woman I fancied into bed.'

I forced a smile. 'No, we'd already been to bed a few times by then. This was just before the end of our final term. I am supposed to have asked her at a party that was held at a lecturer's house just before the exam results came out. Trouble is, I can't remember.'

'Oh I remember that party. The lecturer was called Tim I think – History department. Toby and I went to the village pub and got absolutely bladdered. Weren't you there?'

'At the pub?'

'Yes.'

'I've got a vague memory I might have been, but nothing concrete.'

'Let me think.' Rufus closed his eyes (it's strange how so many people do that).

His face, once dashing and handsome and now reddened and bloated by good living and general excess, was a picture of absolute concentration. I noticed how a vein in his forehead palpitated a little as he sucked on his Churchillian cigar, his eyes still closed, his hand rather theatrically placed on his chin. When he spoke his eyes remained shut; it all seemed a bit weird and transcendental to me actually.

'The pub was called the White Swan. Toby and I

were there. You were there too. Then you went away for a while and came back later. I think Maggie also showed up at the pub at one point. Believe it or not I was very drunk and spent most of the time chatting up a rather splendid-looking barmaid with huge knockers. Toby got into an argument with one of the locals at one stage I remember.' Rufus opened his eyes.

I'd never really looked at his eyes so closely before and had certainly not noticed how blue they were. 'That's an impressive display of memory, Rufe,' I said.

'I've always had good recall. It's an important attribute to have in politics. Always useful to remember when you've lied and who you've lied to!' Rufus smiled in the familiar and reassuring way that anyone who had seen him do on television over the years would have recognised.

'You said that Maggie turned up at the pub. Do you remember the conversation we had?'

'No sorry, old sport. I must have been pissed as a fart by then. I have a vague recollection that she was upset over something that had happened earlier but I've absolutely no memory of what that was or what the two of you said to each other. I was obviously too busy trying to shag the barmaid.'

'Thanks Rufe, that's useful anyway.'

'Glad to be of help. I don't get too many people telling me I've done anything useful these days. Not like the old days when I used to get more compliments than I could handle. Fully deserved of course!' Although he smiled, he also looked rather wistful and sad and, to be honest, I almost felt sorry for him.

I left soon afterwards. I got a hug and a kiss from Sarah and a handshake and hug from Rufus and headed off back home. As I drove into London I reflected on the short "road trip" I had made and what had been said to me by the people I'd visited. I decided that in spite of knowing a little more about what happened all those years ago, I was still more or less completely in the dark about whether, or indeed why, I'd asked Maggie to marry me and if I'd actually given her an engagement ring. To be honest I was probably more confused than ever. As I arrived home I decided that there were a few more people I needed to visit if I was ever going to get to the bottom of this problem.

Chapter 16: *All the Young Dudes*

Saturday, June 1973

The White Swan public house in the Cumberland village of Burnside was surprisingly quiet for a Saturday night in June. The day had been very warm, and many of the villagers and local farmers had popped in for an early quick drink before going home for their dinners and to watch the latest episodes of *Dad's Army* and *The Dick Emery Show.*

Toby and Rufus sat at a table in the corner of the bar and were gradually becoming louder as their beer consumption levels rose, much to the annoyance of the few locals still left in the pub. Sometime before, Rufus had been standing at the bar where he had bought another two pints of bitter for the pair as well as flirting with the pub's blonde barmaid whose name, somewhat coincidentally, was June. Back in his seat, enthusiastically supping his beer, Rufus continued, every now and again, to essay his broadest and cheekiest smiles to June who, he was pleased to note, smiled back at him in a somewhat shy fashion.

'What absolutely wonderful tits she has,' exclaimed Rufus in much too loud a voice.

A young tousled-haired farmer, standing at the bar and who considered himself to be June's boyfriend, turned and looked daggers of hatred at him.

'Not bad. I've seen better though,' replied Toby, drinking from his pint pot.

'Really? Well, any port in a storm and all that. There's not much else going on here.'

'We could go to the party. They'll be lots of women there.'

'Plenty of time' it's still early. Parties never get warmed up until it's properly dark anyway.'

'True. What do you think your chances are with her?' asked Toby.

'With June? I don't know. Prepared to give it a try though. The shy ones are always the dirtiest in my experience.' Rufus finished his beer and then ran his hand down his dark moustache to get rid of any drops of liquid left on it. 'Another?'

'My round, mate.'

'No, I need to get to the bar to have another crack at the sexy June.'

Toby quickly drank what was left of his pint and gave his glass to Rufus who sauntered to the bar; his best smile beaming out at June who was in the process of having a quiet conversation with her boyfriend.

'June! Another two pints of your best bitter, my

gorgeous-looking angel. And have a drink yourself,' said Rufus loudly.

June's boyfriend looked at him with utter distain but kept silent as he leant against the bar and drank some of his beer.

'Thanks, I'll have a half,' she said, as she pulled the pints. 'So I'm an angel then, am I?' she said smiling, as she handed the two, newly filled foaming glasses back to Rufus.

Rufus leaned towards her and whispered, 'How do you fancy coming to a party when you've finished here? I can show you how to be a fallen angel.'

June smiled. 'I don't know about that. My boyfriend wouldn't like it if I went to a party with you,' she said, indicating towards the young man stood at the end of the bar.

'Well, he can come too. The more the merrier!' Rufus turned his head and grinned at the young man, who scowled back at him.

Back at the table, having returned with the two full glasses, Rufus drank some of his beer. 'I think I'm in there,' he said, as he placed his glass down. 'She was like putty in my hands! Right, must go for a quick slash. Don't drink any of my beer, Tobes,' he announced, as he stood again somewhat unsteadily.'

'I'll try not to,' Toby replied with a chuckle.

In the toilet Rufus stood at the urinal for a considerable amount of time relieving himself (he had already drunk several pints of bitter). He heard the door open and then was aware of someone standing close behind him as he shook his penis, popped it back in his jeans and zipped up his fly. As he turned around, he saw the young man from the bar standing in front of him. He looked angry.

'Hi,' said Rufus, giving the young farmer one of his most winning smiles. 'Can I help you?'

'Leave her alone.'

'What?'

'You heard. Just leave her alone.'

'And what would occur if I do not, as you put it, leave her alone?'

'You'll regret it – that's what,' said the young man uncertainly. 'I'm not given to fighting but if you don't leave June alone, you'll regret it.'

'So you've already said,' said Rufus, his smile turning into a sneer. 'I think I'll go back to the bar now if you don't mind.'

The young man stood to one side and Rufus pushed past him, ensuring that his shoulder made firm contact with the other man's.

Back in the bar Rufus sat down. He looked over to June and smiled. She looked concerned and half smiled back.

'Everything all right?' asked Toby.

'Yeah, no problem. Just a minor contretemps in the bog with the country bumpkin.'

Toby and Rufus both looked in the direction of the toilet door as it opened and the young man walked out.

He was a little red in the face.

'Did he threaten you?' said Toby.

'He tried to but he's not cut out for confrontation. I summed him up very quickly.' Rufus smiled at the man who now took up his place at the bar, lowered his head and concentrated on looking at his half-filled pint glass.

'Think we should sort him out?' said Toby.

'No. Not worth it, Toby.' Rufus, smiling broadly, raised his glass to June behind the bar who still looked worried.

'I don't think he should get away with making threats though. What gives him the right?' slurred Toby, who looked at the young man resentfully. 'Another pint?'

'Yeah of course. You can ask June if she's coming to the party too.'

'Will do,' said Toby, as he got up and marched to the bar.

'Two pints please, June.' He stared at her with interest as she filled the glasses. 'By the way, the party should be really good. You should come along with us. You'd have a great time. Plenty of booze and good music to dance to. I don't suppose you get much excitement round here.' He looked at the young man as he spoke. The man looked back at him. 'That's unless you've got any objections, mate,' Toby said.

'Leave her alone. An' I'm not your mate.'

'Shouldn't you be out muckspreading or something rather than trying to stop people having fun – *mate*?'

'We don't do muckspreading this time a-year.'

'Well, I'm sure you could find other things to do that'd be useful – planting potatoes or shagging sheep or something?' said Toby, as he took a belligerent step towards the young farmer.

The young man stood up straight and clenched his fists.

'Okay, stop it, both of you!' June said, sounding worried that a bar-fight was about to break out in the pub while she was in charge. She handed Toby two full pints. 'Here, take these and go and sit down.'

Toby smiled at her then sneered at the young man and returned to his seat. June, still looking concerned, reached over the bar and touched and stroked the young man's forearm and began another whispered conversation with him.

'Thanks, Toby. Looks like you've totally queered the pitch for me now. Don't think I'm going to get to shag the delicious June tonight after all.'

'I'm sure you could do better, but I'll go back and chat her up a bit more if you like.'

Rufus was about to reply when the door to the bar opened and Rob walked in.'

'Hi, you two. Want a pint?'

'Just got one. But you could go and convince June to come to the party with us,' said Toby.

'Who's June?'

'The beautiful barmaid of course, Rufus wants to knock her off! Watch out for the boyfriend at the bar though, he's a bit of a dick.' Toby laughed.

Rufus looked thoughtful.

'Think I'll pass on that. Got enough troubles of my own as it is,' said Rob, as he walked to the bar and asked for a pint of bitter.

'What's your problem then?' Toby asked when Rob had returned with his beer and sat down.

'Oh nothing much. Maggie was a bit pissed off that I came here first rather than meeting her at the party.'

'Totally under the thumb then,' laughed Rufus.

'No, not really. I'll put everything right later – she'll be okay. By the way, I saw Stella at the party too. She was outside having a fag. Just been talking to her.'

'Now there's someone you could shag tonight, Rufus. She really is blonde and beautiful,' said Toby.

'Don't I know it, and believe me, I've tried on several occasions. She makes an ice cube seem like it's on fire,' replied Rufus.

Rob and Toby laughed.

'Yeah well, she's also an enormous bitch. She seems to think I've been horrible to Maggie. Fancies her herself apparently,' said Rob, full of resentment.

'Really?' said Rufus. 'Didn't realise she was a lezzie. That accounts for why she didn't want to sleep with me then. All is now absolutely crystal clear!' said Rufus, as he took a long, satisfied slurp of his beer.

'I've heard that from a few people actually. Not only a lesbian but also nasty with it. Best keep well away from our Stella,' said Toby, also taking a deep drink of his pint.

'I'd never seen that side of her before tonight. Was quite surprised by her to be honest,' said Rob.

'Well what she needs is a damn good shagging. That'd put her right,' said Rufus.

'Good luck with that,' said Toby.

'It's a bit worrying though. If Stella is going to try to spoil things between Maggie and me, God knows where everything will end up,' said Rob.

'Don't worry,' said Rufus, giving a now somewhat reluctant-looking June some big ostentatious smiles, 'She'll come round. Knows where her bread's buttered that one. Think I'll have one more go at getting June to come to the party with me.'

Toby and Rob laughed as Rufus sidled up to the bar, all smiles and intent. 'Good luck!' they said together.

Chapter 17: *Maybe I'm Amazed*

January, the present day

Since beginning this little memoir, as you can doubtless appreciate, my mind has been concentrated (if not totally fixated) on the years I was a student at the University of the North. In the process of doing this, many memories – some insignificant, others of greater importance – have found their way back into the frontal lobe of my brain; often to a surprising extent. One example of this was a fairly detailed recollection of something that happened on the same evening as a very special and unusual rock concert that took place sometime in the February of 1972.

First of all, the day itself was unusual. Most of the concerts at the University of the North took place on a Friday but this particular one happened on an ordinary weekday (it may even have been a Monday). Secondly, until the afternoon no one on the campus knew about the concert because it was arranged at the very last minute when a band of musicians turned up at the door of the students' union office and asked if they could play on that particular evening. Normally I suppose, in most cases, this group would have been told in no uncertain terms to go away and come back at a more appropriate time. However, under the circumstances the chap who ran the students' entertainment committee felt it was an important enough band to cause him, very quickly, to book the university's Grand Hall and put the musicians on stage that very evening. He then proceeded to tour the campus with a megaphone advertising this very special concert, much to the utter surprise and disbelief of most students. And so that is how I (and about one-thousand other young people) got their first sight of the group known as Paul McCartney and Wings.

'Do "Beatles" have wings?' someone asked, as Toby and I queued to get into the Grand Hall. Everyone in earshot laughed excitedly.

I eventually paid my fifty pence (fifty pence!) and had my hand stamped with the student union's motto, "All Power to the People". I don't remember too much about the concert to be honest, or most of what the group actually played, although I remember them performing a song called *Give Ireland Back To The Irish*, which seemed, even then, to be an uncharacteristically political song for McCartney to sing (I'm sure it's possible to find out on the Internet what the night's full playlist actually was). In any case, the thrill of seeing the former Beatle on stage just a few yards away from where I sat was huge and obviously extremely exciting (incidentally, sitting on the floor for concerts was the very restrained, somewhat 'far out' way we did things in those days!). I later heard that the members of the band gave the £500 they had earned that night to a miners' charity, which says quite a lot about the sort of people Paul McCartney and his fellow band members were.

Anyway, it was after the concert that something else happened that was also quite unusual. I was walking along University Boulevard with Toby, heading to Grasmere Bar, when we were stopped by a woman who had a portable tape recorder slung around her shoulder and was holding a microphone stretched out like a fencer's épée toward us. She explained that she worked for BBC local radio in Manchester and wanted to interview people about the Wings' concert. We said that was fine and invited her to the bar where I bought her a drink (possibly half a lager) as well as the requisite two pints of bitter for Toby and me.

We sat in a quietish corner of the bar and, if my memory serves me correctly, she got Toby to record a few words on tape first. Now I have to be honest, after racking my brain, I can't for the life of me recall what the woman's name was so I'm going to call her Felicity for the sake of this narrative. Anyway, after Toby had finished his contribution she turned her microphone to me. Now again, I can't recall what I actually said, but I do remember what the woman looked like. She was a little older than we were – perhaps late twenties as opposed to our early twenties (that seemed quite a big gap back then). To us who were no more than callow youths only just out of our teens, Felicity seemed like the height of sophistication. After all, she was working for a living, and was a broadcast journalist at the BBC – something that, of course, I was aspiring to at the time. She also had the most magnificent shoulder-length red hair, was extremely attractive, wore a green mini-skirt that showed off her very long legs, and had a nice, if rather refined, northern accent. All in all (as you can probably tell) I was pretty well smitten with Felicity. And so was Toby; I could see the signs: he was much less interested in his beer than normal, he kept smiling at her, finding reasons to touch her arm, and he was doing his best to be charming, humble and ingratiating, which was not in any way his normal state of being. Unfortunately for Toby, however, it gradually became clear that Felicity was more attracted to me than him. As she asked me questions and pointed the microphone at me she got closer and closer until our thighs touched in a most provocative and promising way. After being so briefly interviewed by her, Toby, looking visibly disappointed, left us and went off to drink and seek solace with other people he knew who were sitting at a nearby table (he always had a much wider friendship circle than me).

After a while, and a few more drinks, I invited Felicity back to my room for coffee (one of the great euphemisms of those days!). By the time we got there I think all thoughts of coffee had quickly disappeared, and I remembered that we were barely through the door before we had feverishly thrown our clothes on the floor and began some frantic and quite memorable sex. Lying in my bed afterwards she told me that she was engaged to a fellow journalist at the BBC and was due to get married in a big wedding that summer (it seemed that I was one of her last flings as a single woman. I was quite chuffed about that!). She also told me she had an English degree from Oxford University and had been recruited by BBC radio soon after graduating, something that I, as an aspiring journo, found interesting if somewhat daunting. If the BBC were only keen to take on Oxbridge graduates what hope was there for me coming from one of the new provincial universities? She also told me that she had been hoping she would be able to crash in some student's room (she didn't specify male or female) so that she could pocket the expenses money she could claim for staying at a nice Flitborough hotel. I must say, I felt a little used at that particular news.

We eventually drifted off to sleep after the partaking of a couple of joints and woke early the next morning. We had sex again before she got dressed, gave me a surprisingly passionate goodbye kiss, picked up her tape recorder and left. I never saw her again in the flesh, although many years later (perhaps about twelve or so) I did see her on a BBC television news programme where she was reporting on the latest famine somewhere in Africa.

So why did I remember that incident in such detail when my memories of a lot of other things from that time are more than a little cloudy? Well, it all came down to what happened on the day after, when Toby and I ended up falling out for the first and (up until quite recently, of course) the only time.

I must have been busy with lectures and seminars, or *Ariel*, during the day as I didn't see Toby again until the evening. As usual he was sitting in Grasmere Bar, and was on his own reading a newspaper when I walked in. I knew something was wrong straightaway as he seemed uncharacteristically quiet and withdrawn (normally it was a struggle to shut him up). When I asked him what the matter was he was quick to air his grievances with me about the night before. The conversation went something like this:

'I was about to get off with that BBC woman last night before you spoiled things for me. You'll do that once too often one day.'

'I didn't know you were interested,' I said, lying through my teeth.

'Well I was, but you elbowed me aside... you clown!'

'I certainly didn't mean to – it just happened. She seemed interested in me.'

'Well, one day you might realise that the world doesn't revolve around you,' Toby said, somewhat nonsensically.

'Look I'm sorry, Toby. You should have said something.'

'What could I say? Piss off Rob while I try and shag this girl?' (Actually that sort of thing *was* his usual approach to such situations!)

'No. Sorry.'

'I presume that you shagged her. Was she any good?'

'Er, yeah – she wasn't bad. She's getting married in the summer.'

'Not to you I presume?'

I laughed. 'No. Some bloke at BBC Manchester.'

Toby looked at me. For a minute I thought he was going to ask if I wanted a pint and that the whole thing would be forgotten, but unusually for Toby, who was not (or so I thought at the time) one to harbour grudges, he got up and walked out of the room. He had left some beer in his glass, an event that was totally unheard of before that evening.

I didn't see him again for several days after that. It wasn't until one afternoon when I was in the *Ariel* office writing up a story that he walked in (Toby wrote an occasional music review for the paper). He said, 'Hi,' and we chatted as though nothing had happened. That evening (it was a Friday night I think) we went on our usual weekend bar crawl around the campus. Nothing was said about Felicity the BBC reporter ever again and I presumed that the matter was all over; one of those flash-in-the-pan glitches that occasionally arise in long-term friendships. However, I didn't realise until many,

many years later that Toby's resentment of me had been quietly bubbling up for a long time, and that it would eventually boil over, ending up with me languishing in a prison cell forlornly counting the passage of the long hours, days and months of tedium and regret.

Chapter 18: *A Thing Called Love*

Saturday, June 1973

When Maggie walked into the White Swan public house Rob was in the process of laughing in that rather ostentatious way drunken people tend to do. Rufus had just told a joke and he had a very skilled and well-honed way of delivering a punch line that invariably sent both Toby and Rob into fits of sustained giggles. However, on seeing Maggie standing in the doorway, Rob stopped laughing, leapt to his feet and walked over to greet her, unsure of what mood she was likely to be in. Maggie allowed him to give her a peck on her cheek, which he thought was at least a tiny bit encouraging.

'What do you want to drink, love?'

'Nothing for me ta. Just wanted a bit of a chat.'

'Okay.'

'Outside.'

Rob looked a bit unsure. 'Okay. Just let me finish my beer.

'All right. I'll be waiting.'

Maggie left the bar without acknowledging Toby and Rufus. Rob returned to the table, picked up his pint glass and drained it.

'Sorry, lads, I've got to go and have a word with Maggie. Bit of a situation apparently. See you later. Wish me luck,' said Rob, raising his eyebrows.

'Totally under the thumb just so you can get a bit of nooky tonight! By the way, you'll need to hurry if you want another pint – the lovely June's about to call time,' said Toby, as Rob serpentined his inebriated way to the door.

*

Outside, Maggie stood waiting, arms folded, almost (but not quite) tapping her foot. She held a newly lit cigarette in the fingers of her right hand.

'Are you all right, Maggie? What do you want to talk about?' said Rob, swaying slightly. The large amount of alcohol he had consumed during the evening, mixed with the fresh air, was starting to have an adverse effect on his balance.

'About us,' said Maggie.

'Okay. What about us? If it's to do with that little argument back at the party that was just you getting all upset for no real reason.'

'More than about that, although you did promise that we would be together all night tonight.'

'Yeah okay, but I did have to clear things up in the

172

Ariel office, which was why I couldn't see you earlier.'

'And yet you came to the pub before coming to see me! But it's not really just about that. I want to know where we stand with each other – I've got to know – a lot depends on it. It's almost the end of term and I've no idea whether we'll be together next year or what I'll... what *we'll* be doing.'

'Oh. Okay, okay. I was planning to talk to you about that tonight actually, just before you caused me to storm off in fact.' Rob didn't think he sounded very convincing. He was going to have to do better than that if he was to get back into Maggie's good books (and her bed) this evening.

'Good. Well go on then – talk to me about it now.'

'Well, we've been going out together for quite a while now, haven't we?'

'Yes. About nine months in fact.'

'Okay. So that's quite a long time, isn't it?' said Rob, who was aware that he was slurring his words a little.

'Yes. Now, having established that it's a long time, what have you got to say about it?'

'Well, it's like this: we both leave university soon and we need to sort out what we're going to be doing next year, right?'

'Yes – again, we both know that. What is it we're going to be doing once we've left? And are we going to be doing it together?' said Maggie, starting to sound exasperated and sucking on her cigarette.

'Well, I thought that we should... in fact... take our

173

relationship to the next stage.'

'What does that mean exactly?'

'Well, I thought that should be pretty obvious.'

'Not to me. Spell it out please.'

'Well, I've been thinking about this recently and it seems to me that... on the whole... all things being equal... it would be a good idea if we, at some point in the not too distant future, if we decided to agree on the idea – if it's all right with you of course – that we should get... er... sort of engaged? If we decide to call it that. Erm, what do you think?'

'I think you've just suggested that we should get engaged. Is that correct?' Maggie looked confused and excited in equal measure, a hesitant smile slowly beginning to form on her face, her eyes still red and puffy from her earlier tears.

'Er, yes... in a nutshell... that'd be it... I think.'

'Oh, come here!' Maggie, all smiles now, dropped her half-smoked cigarette on the ground and threw her arms around Rob, hugging him until he found it quite difficult to breathe.

'Great. I'm so glad you're happy about it,' said Rob, as with difficulty he managed to disentangle himself from Maggie's embrace. 'Er, the one fly in the ointment is that I haven't actually got any money to buy you a ring... sadly. So until I do, it's probably best if we keep the whole thing quiet and don't actually tell anyone yet... only until we can afford to do it properly and throw a party for all our friends and all that of course.'

'I know!' said Maggie, smiling triumphantly. 'We can use this!' She held up her right hand and pointed enthusiastically to the ring she was wearing on her third finger. 'It's what my gran left me in her will. It was her engagement ring. It's quite valuable I think – Edwardian. That's what she used to tell me, anyway. Here, have a look.'

Maggie slipped the ring off her finger and put it in Rob's outstretched hand. He looked at it in some disbelief. It was an expensive-looking ring – silver with a single large stone, which he assumed was a diamond.

'It's really nice,' he said, as he offered it back to Maggie.

'No, no, you've got to give it to me properly, and put it on my ring finger yourself.'

'Oh, okay,' said Rob, with about the same amount of enthusiasm as someone standing at a mysterious crossroads in the middle of the night about to sell his immortal soul to the devil. He took Maggie's left hand, kissed it (a nice romantic gesture he thought) and slipped the ring onto her finger. Maggie, beaming, held her hand up and looked at the ring admiringly. Even Rob felt quite emotional as he looked at the hand with the diamond ring resplendent in place on Maggie's finger.

'Thank you,' she said. 'I really love you.' She grabbed Rob, kissing him and hugging him again.

Rob would have found it difficult to break away from her grasp even if he thought it had been a wise thing to do at that precise moment.

'Do you love me?' she said.

'Erm… yes, of course I do,' Rob replied.

'Well say it then.'

'I love you,' Rob said, almost through gritted teeth.

'Oh, I'm so looking forward to us being together next year,' said Maggie, sounding happier than Rob had ever heard her.

'Yes… me too,' said Rob.

Maggie beamed with delight and pressed her face back into his chest. Had she looked up, she would have seen the look of realisation and abject horror on Rob's (all of a sudden) pallid face, and might have been a great deal more uncertain about his overall true intentions. Of course, she was also unable see his hands behind her back and the way his fingers were crossed as tightly as he could make them.

Chapter 19: *You Can't Always Get What You Want*

March, the present day

Memory is such a strange thing. This morning I remembered in perfect detail a joke that Rufus (I'm pretty sure it was Rufus anyway) told me back in the 1970s about a rich man, his butler and a hot water bottle. It was a silly, Pythonesque joke but it made me laugh again after all these years. And then I realised with some degree of horror that I couldn't actually remember what I'd had to eat yesterday. I suppose that's not too surprising – prison food is not exactly very memorable (although it is somewhat better than how it's often depicted on television). However, it is more than a little worrying to forget things that happened so recently while still being able to recall events (albeit selectively) that occurred in the far distant past. The dreaded pitch-black cloud of dementia is always hovering somewhere so very near to individuals of my age!

Anyway, let us put that depressing thought to one side, as much as it's possible to do so. After seeing

Rufus, I spent a few weeks at home mulling over where I now stood. It seemed highly likely that I had actually become engaged to Maggie at some point at the end of my final term at university. Confidence in my own memory had been shaken somewhat by Jane's revelation and to a lesser extent by Althea's. Could it be true? Was it possible that I had made such a life-changing proposal to Maggie and then had forgotten all about doing so? If that was indeed the way it had happened it also must mean that I had broken off the engagement unilaterally very soon afterwards. I have long realised that I may not be the nicest or the most reliable person on God's earth, but that would have been a particularly shitty thing for me to do!

I half thought about ringing Toby on the pretext of telling him about how many people had "signed-up" for the reunion and pressing him about whether he had actually known about Maggie and me becoming engaged, as Althea had intimated. In the end though I decided to keep my powder dry on that one and tried to enjoy being at home with Jenny. We cooked some very nice meals together, went out to dinner a few times and saw a couple of films at the cinema before I started to get restless again. I felt determined I was going to get to the bottom of the conundrum soon and so began to consider which of my university friends I should visit next.

The most obvious candidates were Liz who, perhaps more than most, was at the centre of the events that took place in our final term at university; Angela, who was close to Liz and Tina, and Jack, who was possibly one of the soundest and most straightforward people I had ever met and was one of those people who always seemed to have his finger on the pulse of things. Both Jack and Angela lived quite close to each other and so, after ringing them up and arranging things as best I could, I let Jenny know that I would again be taking a little trip down memory lane and visiting them. Out of courtesy I invited her to come along too (I had arranged the trips to fall on a weekend) but she refused, as I knew she would. I was pleased on the whole. It meant that I could just concentrate on talking to my friends about the things that really mattered to me and would not have to waste too much time complimenting them on their choices of clothes and hairstyles, or looking at endless photos of their holidays and "cute" grandchildren.

Jack was top of my list, and it was to be the first time in forty-nine years that I would meet up with him. I had booked in at a hotel in Oxford where he lived (when I rang him he didn't offer me a bed at his place) and we met at a pub he said he was a regular at. It was one of those crowded national chain pubs that was the home of inveterate elderly drinkers from early in the morning, due to the fact that it sold cheap (but actually surprisingly good) ale, as well as the ubiquitous lager, and also served affordable food that was just about passable if you were not too discriminating. Jack and I ate our steak and chips enthusiastically enough, alongside a few pints of decent beer (thank goodness you can get the good stuff in most places these days – although not in prison of course! I do so miss going down to my local for a quiet pint).

Jack Barber, to be honest, turned out to be a bit of a disappointment. I remembered a big, reliable, quietly ebullient young man at university with a great many interests, both academic and extra-curricular. He did a geology degree, played rugby union for the university, often went sailing and rock climbing in his spare time and was rarely sedentary. Because of this he was universally known as Jumpin' Jack Flash or simply JJ for short. He also played a mean game of chess and he and I would occasionally meet up in his room or mine to play. We were pretty well matched in this regard and perhaps oddly, given the cerebral nature of the game, he was the only person at university I ever played chess with.

However, to say that he hadn't aged well would be a bit of an understatement. He looked downright dowdy, dusty and unshaven with dishevelled grey hair. As we sat talking, he would keep popping outside for a smoke, which was strange as I didn't remember him smoking at all at university. As we chatted it soon became clear what his problem was – and it was a major one. His wife of forty-odd years had unfortunately died a few months before and her death had caused him to pretty much give up on his own life. I expressed my condolences and regret of course, and told him that if he needed any help he should just ask. Unfortunately I think he had gone past the help stage and it was obvious to me that life, for him, had become a pointless drudge and was something he no longer wanted to have anything to do with. It even seemed, from what he said, that his two daughters (one lived in Scotland and the other in Australia) had given up on him too and he had little expectation of seeing either of them again in the near future. All in all he cut a sad, morose and pathetic figure, and it was hard work trying to have any sort of meaningful conversation with him.

Endeavouring to change the subject from his manifold woes I mentioned the university reunion, thinking that it might give him something to look forward to and focus on. He didn't say no exactly but I got the distinct impression that he simply didn't expect to be around in a year or so, an assessment that his smoking and consumption of beer and whisky (he drank a great many doubles during the evening) seemed to confirm. It was all very depressing and soon my main objective was to find a way to curtail our meeting and extricate myself from his company as quickly as possible.

Towards the end of our get together I, somewhat nervously under the circumstances, told him about Maggie dying and for the first time I saw a flicker of emotion in his rheumy eyes; he even had to wipe away a tear. I think the news had obviously brought back memories of his wife who I'd eventually remembered was called Pamela. They'd met at teacher training college (he was another who had gone down the schoolteacher route) and had got married once they'd both started work. He told me, still with tears in his eyes, that she, like Maggie, had died of cancer and it became obvious that thoughts of her occupied every second of his waking (and probably sleeping) life. He had a wallet full of pictures of her and he showed me every one several times over. It was all very sad and if I were another type of person there is no doubt that I too would have ended up sharing some sympathetic tears.

Again endeavouring to change the subject, I then went on to talk about Maggie and me possibly getting engaged. Back when we were playing chess together he and I would often have long conversations about life in general and I always valued JJ's opinion, probably more so than anyone else at university. I was hoping now to get some insight into my situation from someone who at one time I used to hold in pretty high regard. To that end I was again greatly disappointed.

He told me, in a sort of distant fashion, his eyes often seeming to focus on something invisible in the far distance as he spoke, that he couldn't recall me discussing that situation with him at the time. He explained that he always liked Maggie a lot and that as a pair we seemed very well suited, but as for whether we were engaged or not he couldn't really help me.

'Are you certain that you can't remember me saying anything about it? Perhaps after one of our chess matches?'

'No. Sorry Rob. Thinking about it, I'm not sure we played many chess games at that time, it being nearly the end of our final year and all, and I think I went off to do some climbing just before the exam results came out.' He spoke in a bit of a distant way although I did notice a certain wistfulness in his voice as though he was nostalgic for happier, simpler and more straightforward times; times that for him were now sadly long gone.

*

Later on, when the pub had finally stopped serving, I walked him back to his house. I had to steady him a little on the way to stop him veering about the pavement. After shaking his hand and saying our goodbyes, I watched as he fumbled around with his keys, awkwardly trying to unlock his front door. He dropped them a couple of times and then had to scramble around on the ground, searching for them in the dark. When he had finally managed to let himself in I stood outside his house for a while, imagining him on the inside, bumping into the furniture and staggering around as he quickly grabbed a whisky bottle and poured himself another drink, before falling into an inebriated sleep on his sofa. It was quite obvious to me that he was well on the way to quickly drinking himself into a disappointed oblivion. I took one last look at his house and its completely overgrown, unkempt front garden before heading back to my hotel. All things considered I didn't think we would be seeing JJ – Jumpin' Jack Flash – at our university reunion, or anywhere else in the future for that matter.

Chapter 20: *(If Paradise Is) Half As Nice*

Thursday, June 1973

'JJ, it's your round,' shouted Rob when the tall figure of Jack Barber entered the room.

Rob was sitting at a table in Coniston Bar along with Toby, Rufus, Maggie, Liz, Michael, Tina, Angela and Nick.

'That doesn't sound very fair. I've only just walked in,' said Jack, smiling benignly.

'Climbed any good mountains lately?' said Toby.

'No. No time. We've been doing these final exam thingys if you hadn't noticed,' replied Jack.

'I didn't bother with any of those!' said Rufus untruthfully.

'Okay, so what do you all want to drink then?' said Jack.

'Rum and black please, JJ,' said Tina.

'Same for me,' said Liz.

'Lager for me,' said Maggie.

'And me,' said Angela.

185

'And pints of bitter for the rest of us!' shouted Rob and Toby, almost in unison.

'Okay. Will do,' said Jack, smiling and taking out his wallet from his jeans' pocket.

'Watch the moths fly out when he opens it!' said Rufus laughing.

Jack smiled back indulgently.

'Put something on the jukebox as well!' shouted Maggie, as Jack walked to the bar.

'Actually I'll do that,' said Rob.

'The usual?' said Maggie.

'Of course,' replied Rob.

Rob put some coins into the jukebox that he and Maggie regarded as possibly the best one in the world and chose the two songs that they always selected when visiting Coniston Bar. With the strains of Harry Nilsson singing *Without You* coming from the machine, he walked back to the others and sat down between Maggie and Toby.

'Isn't it nice not to have any more exams to do,' said Maggie in between singing snatches of the song.

'It certainly is,' answered Rob.

'How do you think you've done in them?' said Toby, looking at Maggie.

'Oh, I don't know. Okay, I think. Maybe... how about you?'

'Cocked up a couple of papers, but I'll probably scrape through,' said Toby.

'Hey, Tobes,' shouted Rufus from across the table,

'are we planning on hitting all the bars tonight?'

'Each one at least twice I would think, Rufe!' Toby replied, and everyone in the group cheered.

'Hurry up with those drinks, JJ. We're all getting very, very thirsty here,' Rufus shouted, and waved at Jack who stood at the bar.

He turned and smiled benevolently at the group who now started to chant, 'Why are we waiting?'

'Hold your horses, you rabble! I'll be there soon!' said Jack.

'Shush, our song's playing!' said Maggie, as the somewhat strangulated tones of Andy Fairweather Low's singular voice emerged from the jukebox performing the Amen Corner's (*If Paradise Is) Half As Nice*.

Those around the table gave a general groan as Maggie sang along with the record, holding an imaginary microphone in her hand before they all joined in.

'Not this old thing?' said Jack, as he started to ferry the drinks from the bar to the table.

Maggie, still singing along with the record, stuck her tongue out at Jack who smiled back at her.

'Very sad!' he said, shaking his head before fetching the rest of the drinks. 'Cheers,' said Jack as he returned from the bar, sat down at the table and held up his pint of bitter. 'Here's to the future, and God bless all who sail in her!'

Everyone cheered and took big swigs from their

respective glasses. Maggie turned to Rob, smiled at him and landed a big kiss on his cheek.

'Hold on,' said Rufus. 'Shouldn't we all get one of those?'

'Later,' replied Maggie in a mock coquettish mode.

'Oo!' said Rufus. 'Can't wait.'

'Me too!' said Toby.

'And me!' said Jack.

'Well, *you* can have one right now for always being so nice,' said Maggie, as she leaned across the table and planted a kiss on the side of Jack's face. He smiled and went a little red.

'Shall we have some more music?' said Angela, who was sitting next to Toby and looking sad and close to tears.

'It's all right, I'll go. We might get some decent music that way,' said Nick, who was sitting opposite to where Toby was sat; it being the furthest away from him he could be without actually being at another table.

'I'll go with you then,' said Angela sniffing, getting up and extricating herself from the crowded group of friends.

Maggie was just about to ask Jack about his next trip to climb a mountain when Stella walked into the bar. Maggie gave her a little wave and got up and walked over to her.

'Here, I'll get you a drink,' said Maggie.

'Just a tonic water please. I want to stay sober tonight,' said Stella.

'Any particular reason?' said Maggie.

'Oh, I just need to have a conversation with someone and it's best to have it when I'm not drunk,' replied Stella.

'Okay. Who with?

'What?'

'Who's your conversation going to be with?'

'Sooner not say. I'll tell you afterwards.'

'Oh, okay,' said Maggie, a puzzled expression on her face. 'Just a tonic water it is then.'

Back at the table Toby had noticed Stella's entrance and looked thoughtful. Rufus, seeing a frown develop on his friend's face, turned and looked over to Stella as well, and for the first time during the evening he also looked downcast. Maggie returned to where Stella was standing and gave her the tonic water.

'Erm, shall we just pop outside for a sec and sit in the sun? I could do with a breather from all this lot,' suggested a smiling Maggie.

'Okay,' said Stella, smiling back.

Outside the two young women sat down at one of the picnic benches that had been set up in the courtyard outside Coniston Bar. Maggie lit a cigarette after offering the packet to Stella, who shook her head.

From inside the bar the tones of Michael raucously singing a rugby song started up. Maggie smiled to herself. It was early in the day for people to have persuaded him to sing one of his extremely naughty songs. He must already be drunk, she thought.

'*The Mayor of Bayswater had a very fine daughter…*' sang Michael.

'So who are you planning to talk to then?' said Maggie.

'Okay I'll tell you. Thought I'd have a quick word with Rob,' replied Stella, keeping her eyes fixed on Maggie.

'Thought so. You're going to tell him that we've been sleeping together, aren't you? Please don't, Stella.'

'Yes, I was going to tell him. It's only fair.'

'Fair for who?'

'Fair for me and you, mainly.'

'But look… I like what we do occasionally – it's fun, it's different, it's exciting – but I think Rob and I are going to be together in the future.'

'Really? Don't you think you're fooling yourself about that?'

'No I don't. I think he's ready to ask me about living together next year, he just hasn't said anything yet.'

'I'd be very surprised if that happened, Maggie.'

'Why would you say that? You don't really know Rob do you? You can't base everything on having gone to the pictures with him on one occasion last year. He really wants me and him to be together. Otherwise why would we have been going out for so long?'

Stella was about to speak but hesitated. Was now the time to tell Maggie about Rob's infidelity? Did she really want to be responsible for breaking Maggie's heart? 'I guess he must like going to bed with you. But,

Maggie, just because you're good in bed doesn't mean he's in love with you.'

'Well I think he is in fact.' Maggie smiled shyly. 'Do you really think I'm good in bed?'

Stella smiled back. 'Yes I do, and I'd like us to be in bed together right now.'

'I can't at the moment but perhaps we can find time to do that again before we all go home?' said Maggie, smiling again and patting Stella's arm fondly.

Stella leant forward as if to kiss her. Maggie swayed backwards, aware that people in the bar could see them through the room's ceiling-to-floor windows.

'Not here, not now, Stella. It's far too public.'

Stella looked downcast. She smiled disconsolately at Maggie, slowly stood up, put down her glass and walked away in the direction of University Boulevard.

Maggie breathed a sigh of relief and went back into the bar.

*

A few minutes later, Rob asked her what she and Stella had spoken about.

'Oh nothing much. There's someone she wants to go out with and she was asking my advice, that's all.'

'Who does she want to go out with? It's not like the Ice Queen to actively fancy someone.'

'Oh you wouldn't know them – someone I used to be in a French tutorial with earlier in the year.'

'Well, wonders will never cease! Do you want another drink?'

Chapter 21: *You Wear It Well*

March, the present day

The morning after I'd met JJ in the pub I briefly flirted with the idea of going round to his house again to see how he was, but truthfully I couldn't stand the thought of spending any more time with him. The previous evening had been so utterly depressing. I put aside a niggling feeling of guilt and instead hung around my hotel room for a while, jotting down a few ideas for my novel before checking out and driving the few miles to where I had arranged to see Angela.

Angela Stewart, as she had been at university, had always been a very quiet, somewhat introverted person; very much a contrast to the strong characters of Toby and Rufus and, to a lesser extent, Maggie and Tina. We had agreed to meet up during the daytime because she wanted to be at home with her husband Richard in the evening – he had recently come out of hospital following a major operation for prostate cancer. So we decided to meet at, of all places, a garden centre café near to the village where she lived.

I had first met Angie when we had both signed up to work on *Ariel* at the Introductory Week's Societies Fair in our first week at university (the term "Freshers' Week" was, at that point in the 1970s, only used in America as far as I'm aware, certainly not at the University of the North). At the time, while she was quite physically attractive in an unassuming mouse-like sort of way, I thought her personality was a bit nondescript. As I got to know her though I realised she had hidden depths, and she turned out to be a very good writer and reporter for the university newspaper. She ended up being in overall charge of attracting advertising, which helped to pay for the newspaper's weekly publication. It was the advertising industry that she went on to work in after obtaining her marketing degree and I believe her career had been quite successful before her retirement some years ago. I had only met with her on a few occasions since university: at Tina and Nick's wedding, at her own wedding to Richard and then again at the funeral of Fiona's husband. In retrospect I wished I'd kept in more frequent contact as I'd always got along with her very well, but there's never enough time to do everything is there? Times wingéd chariot, and all that!

It won't surprise you, knowing my habit of arriving early to places, that I got to the café a little before she did and was sitting having a pot of tea and an Eccles cake when she turned up looking a little flustered.

'So sorry I'm late,' she said, as I stood up and gave her a little kiss on her cheek.

'You're not really. I'm always early.'

She smiled.

I got the formalities over with pretty quickly. I asked how she was, got her (rather lengthy) medical report about Richard, as well as a quick review of her family and how her son, daughter and assorted grandchildren were faring. I then went on to inform her about my circumstances, showed her pictures of my grandkids on my phone and all that palaver (necessary when we oldies get together of course but, as far as I'm concerned, always somewhat on the tedious side).

By the time we got down to the nitty-gritty of our meeting we were on to our second pot of tea and I had succumbed to another cake – a jam doughnut this time – that, for some reason I couldn't fathom, reminded me of Maggie.

Angie was genuinely sorry to hear about Maggie dying (I had pre-warned her in a phone call) and together we recalled some of the funny incidents that had taken place in the days when we were all working together on *Ariel*. We ended up laughing about them and I felt pleased that we hadn't got too morose about Maggie's death. In a way I think it was a bit of a relief for her to talk about someone else rather than continuously worrying about her husband's condition, something that had obviously occupied her thoughts for the preceding few months.

On the subject of the university reunion she was understandably non-committal, but I reassured her that, as it was some way in the future and Richard would no doubt make a complete recovery, they would both be welcome to come along to it. I told her that everyone would be very pleased to see them. That seemed to cheer her up a good deal. She then related the (actually quite long-winded and one that I had heard before) story of how she and Richard had met at the advertising agency she had worked for after leaving the University of the North. Nodding and smiling in all the right places as she did so, I took some time to look her up and down and assess how the passage of time had altered the young woman I had first met back in 1970. She was more confident now of course (actually I remembered how she had grown more assured about her ability during our time on the newspaper) and the ravages of time, while not leaving her alone entirely, had been relatively kind to her. She had kept her light brown hair (though I assumed it now originated from a regular trip to her hairdresser rather than being entirely down to nature) and she still had her small but neat figure and delicate facial features. While never coming into the "totally beautiful" category like Stella or Tina, Angela had always been attractive and still retained the vestiges of those good looks.

Now, I know what you're thinking! As I seemed to have slept with a large number of my female university friends you will want to know whether I ever became romantically linked to Angie? Well, perhaps surprisingly, the answer is no. It's not that I didn't fancy her, I did (as you know, my taste in girls at the time was pretty expansive and inclusive), but as it turned out the opportunity never arose; after only a week into our first year she was going out on a steady basis with a fellow marketing student called Chris. They seemed inseparable and stayed together for almost all of their university time together, and it wasn't until around exam time in our final year that they broke up. Apparently, he had got back together with an ex-girlfriend back in his hometown. I remember that Angie was absolutely heartbroken at the time and I had to comfort her in the *Ariel* office one day when she broke down in tears. I could have taken my chance then to offer her some other kind of comfort but even I couldn't do that to the poor girl. Besides, I was at the time obsessed with what I should do after university and Toby, I seem to remember, soon offered his consoling hand (and various other bits of his anatomy) in helping Angie recover from being dumped. Toby never missed a trick if he could possibly help it. And then tragically, Chris died soon afterwards in a road accident and Angela was completely and absolutely distraught. She straightaway left for her parents' home, not even waiting to receive her final exam results, and it was a while before I, or anyone else, saw her again. She attended Tina and Nick's wedding reception and I had a brief chat with her then. At that stage she seemed to have finally come to terms with everything that had happened, but I did notice that Toby kept well away from her; their little romance obviously had been only a temporary and utterly non-memorable blip in both of their lives.

Back in the garden centre café, I eventually got around to broaching the subject of Maggie and myself and our possible engagement. Angela had a bit of a think and then surprised me with her definite take on the subject.

'Yes,' she said. 'I remember that quite clearly. It was just before Chris died in that hit-and-run accident. I'm pretty certain that you two got engaged in the last week of term, after the exams were all over.'

'How can you be certain?'

She blushed a little, obviously at the picture that had just come into her head. 'I remember that Toby told me one night in bed.'

'Really?'

'Yes, I remember it quite distinctly. Chris, who I'd been going out with since the first year, had dumped me after sitting his last exam – just a few days before he died – and Toby had caught me very much on the rebound. In all honesty I didn't like him all that much, but our little relationship – we slept together a few times – helped me get over Chris and cope with the shock of his death. So, in a way, it was very useful and therapeutic. I'm sure Toby didn't actually think our fling would last and of course neither did I but it enabled me to get a few things in perspective and it taught me not to get too gooey-eyed about men and fall in love with every bloke that liked me.'

'So what did Toby say exactly?'

'I don't remember his exact words but the general gist was that at the party that most people, including Chris, had gone to, you had got extremely drunk, and to cheer Maggie up a bit and get back in her good books you had decided to ask her to get engaged.'

'Really? Are you sure it was Toby that told you?'

'Yes! I didn't go to bed with anyone else at that time!'

'No. Sorry... I wasn't suggesting...'

'I know. Only joking. Can I ask you something, Rob?'

'Yeah, sure.'

'Why are you so concerned about it all?'

It was a good question. Why *was* I so intent on discovering what had actually happened between Maggie and me so long ago? Why didn't I just let it go, forget about it and ignore the rather taciturn Mrs Sarah Webb along with Maggie's final letter? Well, I did think about it. In retrospect it might have saved me a great deal of hassle and heartache if I'd done just that, but I knew deep down that I had to know the complete truth. Perhaps it was just the writer in me wanted to discover the end of the story. And, of course, there was the question of Toby and why he had misled me in such a way. Had he, like me, forgotten about Maggie and me

199

getting engaged? Or, if not, did he have ulterior motives?

After Angie and I had parted, saying that we hoped to meet again at the reunion in a year or so, I watched her still-trim figure walk to her car, and I again resisted my first impulse to phone Toby straightaway and confront him with what I'd heard. I decided it would be best to wait and mull over what I now knew. Perhaps if I left things for a while everything would become a little clearer. Sadly for me, things didn't get better – they got a whole lot worse!

Chapter 22: *Reach Out I'll Be There*

Thursday, June 1973

'Right – it's time we all moved on to another bar I think. There's lots more beer to be drunk and we're just the people to do it.'

Toby had decided a change of scenery was needed, and as self-designated group leader he led the by now fairly well inebriated gaggle of friends out of Coniston Bar and on towards Grasmere Bar further down University Boulevard.

'You all right?' said Toby to Angela, who walked beside him.

'Yeah, sort of,' she replied.

'What's the problem? You look a bit on the miserable side. Tell your uncle Toby what's the matter.'

A tear had formed in one of Angela's eyes and rolled down her small, pale, freckled cheek. 'I thought everyone knew. It's Chris – we broke up on Tuesday.'

'Really? You've been together for ages.'

'Yeah, ever since the first week of our first year.'

Angela screwed her eyes up against the bright June sunshine, causing more tears to roll down both sides of her face.

Toby put his arm around her and pulled her into him. 'Do not fear, Toby is here! I'll look after you. To tell you the truth I never really liked Chris anyway. Always thought he was a bit of a twat and now I know he was. You can do much better than him.'

Angela gave a little laugh that was almost a sob. 'Thanks, Toby,' she said.

*

Just behind Toby and Angela, Maggie and Rob were sauntering along holding hands, swinging their arms and occasionally smiling at each other.

'Have you heard about Tim's party this Saturday?' said Rob.

'Who's Tim?' asked Maggie.

'Oh, you know, that lecturer in the history department I like? He's got a big old house in Burnside. Do you remember, we went to the village pub there once?'

'Oh yeah, right. That sounds great.'

'Yeah. He's going to clear out his cellar for dancing apparently – put lights up and stuff – and he's getting loads of drinks in.'

'That'll be nice. How do we get there?'

'Not sure yet; I'll work on that one. We obviously

need someone with a car.'

'It'd certainly help.'

'Oh, by the way, do you know why Stella walked off earlier? Seemed a bit odd.'

'Erm... I think she didn't fancy sitting with a big crowd of people. You know what she's like.'

'Yeah, certainly do. She always does things her own way. Bit anti-social though considering that the exams are all over, and she probably won't see most of us again once we've all left.'

'Yeah. She also said she had a bit of a headache and was going for a lie down. I thought I might pop round and check on her later. Take her a couple of aspirin or something.'

'Okay,' said Rob looking at Maggie, a half-inquiring look on his face. 'I'm sure she'll appreciate that.'

*

The group of friends entered Grasmere Bar and, after deciding it was Nick's round, found a table in the relatively uncrowded room. The warm June weather had persuaded many of the students at the university to look for more open-air venues in which to do their post-examination relaxing. Many were spending the afternoon and early evening frequenting local pub beer gardens or were picnicking and drinking in the extensive verdant grounds of the campus. Rob's friends, however, were inveterate occupiers of indoor bar areas, and this particular end of term was going to be no exception.

'Tina, when is Nick going home for the funeral?' asked Liz.

'Tomorrow I think. He's going to spend the weekend with his mum and dad so he's coming back on Monday,' replied Tina.

'What's that about a funeral?' said Rob.

'Oh, it's Nick – he's off home to go to his aunt's funeral. She died about a week ago,' said Tina.

'Oh, that's a shame,' said Rob.

'How old was she?' asked Maggie, who sat beside Rob and leaned across to speak to Tina.

'Not sure. In her sixties, I think. Nick was very fond of her. She used to send him a postal order for his birthday every year.'

'He's going to miss all the weekend fun then,' said Rob.

'Well, it's more important for him to be at the funeral,' said Tina.

'Yeah, of course it is,' said Rob and Maggie in unison.

'Okay, children, here you are. Get stuck in.'

Nick had returned from the bar and had carefully put a large tray of newly filled glasses on the table. Everyone cheered, grabbing their respective drinks. Soon the friends were singing along with another one of Michael's more risqué songs. For most in the group this time was one of the happiest they had ever experienced, free as they were from the worry of exams and, for a brief while anyway, unconcerned by what the near future might hold. Only Angela, feeling sadly sober, found it difficult to hold a smile for any length of time, although she tried hard to join in with the drunken fun and enjoyment everyone else seemed to be having. Rob noticed that Toby had laid his hand on Angie's jeans-covered thigh and she hadn't brushed it away.

'Er… what time are you going round to see Stella tonight?' said Rob to Maggie.

'Don't know really. Later perhaps – when I feel like it. Why?'

'Just wondered. I thought we could spend this evening together because I was planning to go drinking with Toby tomorrow night – just him and me – a last hurrah before we leave.'

'Oh, okay. I'll probably leave it till tomorrow to chat with Stella then.' Maggie looked thoughtful. 'Rob, do you think we'll keep in touch with everyone once we've all left?'

'Yeah, I think so. Hope so anyway. Why do you ask?'

'I don't know. It's just that there's a lot of people in this group – Toby, Rufus, Michael, JJ, Angela, whatever – and it might be quite difficult to keep in contact with them all when we've gone our separate ways.'

Rob was about to answer when Rufus interrupted him.

'Hey, you two look really serious. This is a time for

frolicsome fun and frivolity! You wouldn't expect me to talk about politics and the imminent workers' revolution all night would you?'

'You're always talking about the imminent workers' revolution, Rufe! Sometimes you sound as if you actually believe it too,' said Toby.

'You cut me to the quick, Tobias! Isn't it your round by the way?' said Rufus.

'Ah! Certainly looks that way. Same again for everyone?'

Everyone said yes.

'Angie, can you give me a hand with the glasses?' said Toby.

'Sure,' said Angela.

*

'Toby and Angie seem to be getting quite pally,' whispered Maggie to Rob.

'Yeah, it's his knight-in-shining-armour routine,' said Rob.

'I was really surprised when Angie and Chris split up. They seemed like a permanent fixture after all those years together.'

'Yeah. He started going out again with an old girlfriend back where he lives apparently.'

'Yeah, she told me. Shame really. I quite liked Chris,' said Maggie.

'Well, you know, these things happen,' said Rob.

'Will it happen to us?'

Rob looked shocked. 'What? Of course not. Why would you say that?' said Rob.

'Well, you haven't told me what you're doing after the summer holidays. You *still* haven't posted your application for the journalism course at Cardiff even though I have. It'll be too late soon.'

'No, there's plenty of time yet. I've almost finished the application form. Just one or two bits and pieces to finish off and I'll post it off on Monday.'

'Well, I've sent mine off already.'

'I know. You told me before.'

'Rob, it is quite important!'

Maggie looked exasperated and Rob grabbed her hand and squeezed it.

'Don't worry. It'll all sort itself out.' He leant towards her and gave her a kiss.

'Hey! Cut that out you two. No sex in here please! Today is all about drinking and not all that canoodling malarkey!' said Rufus, holding up his beer glass.

'Okay, sir!' said Maggie, smiling broadly and saluting. However, she had a strange sense of unease and wished more than anything that she could talk to Rob in private, away from this big group of noisily drunk people. Inwardly she shrugged. Oh well, plenty of time for that, she thought, as she drank some of her lager before joining in with singing along to another of Michael's bawdy rugby songs, which seemed to be something about caviar and a virgin sturgeon.

Chapter 23: *God Only Knows*

March, the present day

As I continue to think back to my time at university, I realise that I have learned a number of irrefutable, if somewhat belated, truths. For example, I've come to the conclusion that most of the things that happened at the time, things that appeared so very important back then, now seem incredibly banal and naïve. Relationships with others that were so all-consuming, albeit for a relatively short time, now appear shallow, almost to the point of farce. Above all perhaps, my place in the world and the ideas I had in those days, things that appeared so central and germane, today seem almost pathetically peripheral and inchoate. Well, I suppose that's the way of the world. When you are young everything seems fresh and laced with potential, but when you are elderly, as I am now, things often seem bland, uninteresting and, at times, downright tedious. I am fast coming to the conclusion that the reason why very old people seldom seem to fear death has got nothing to do with feelings of resignation and inevitability. Rather, it is because those people have seen it all before and the world that at one time seemed so promising, vibrant and redolent with hope for them, in the end turned out to be dull, tired and turgid.

I've wittered on in this narrative before about memory and the tricks it can play. It now seems, almost beyond all doubt, that Maggie and I did get engaged to be married and that I proposed to her at the party at a lecturer's house just before the end of our final term. It also transpires that soon afterwards I broke off our engagement via a quick telephone call. The fact that I cannot remember doing any of this is, of course, worrying in itself, but it is the realisation that I treated Maggie in such a downright despicable and cowardly way that will haunt me for the rest of my days, and believe me, when you are in prison those haunted days go by very slowly indeed.

Another aspect of this failure of my memory in regard to important aspects of my life (like asking someone to marry me!) is the rather annoying trait I seem to have developed for remembering little and seemingly unimportant memory snippets that happened at the time and which, for no apparent reason, have flooded back into my mind; memories that have no relation to anything very important. Let me give you an example. One day, I think in 1973, I was sitting in my room working at my desk when someone came to visit me (annoyingly I can't remember who it actually was).

We proceeded to have a conversation (again I can't remember what it was about – possibly something to do with *Ariel*) and just before she or he left they made a comment about the small tube of toothpaste that lay on my study/bedroom sink along with my toothbrush.

'You shouldn't buy such a small tube,' they said. 'It's a false economy.' (Possibly they were studying economics and were showing off a technical term they'd learnt recently).

Sounding more than a little smug I replied, 'Oh I must tell my mum the next time she *gives* me one then.'

My mum, who never had much spare money, used to "help me out" while I was at university by sending me useful items through the post, and that particular little tube of toothpaste had been one of them. On another occasion she sent me a vacuum-pack of bacon by registered post! (Bacon sandwiches were a real treat when you were a poverty-stricken student back in the early 1970s!).

As I have just related that story, I have suddenly realised why indeed I have remembered such an insignificant little detail that took place so very long ago. It was almost certainly because it related to my mum, who did so much to help my brother and me get on in life, albeit in a very unplanned and understated way. Of course I didn't appreciate her helpful gestures at the time; like everything else back then it was something I just took for granted. I actually kept some of the letters she wrote to me at university (she was a frequent letter-writer) and occasionally I re-read them with, of course, inevitable tears in my eyes. They were good letters in fact – full of clichés and spelling mistakes certainly, but they very much reflected her innately caring nature. I wish now I had made my thanks for everything she did for me much more obvious. It's too late now of course. Regrets eh? Unlike Frank Sinatra I've had more than a few and I now look back on those missed opportunities with a huge amount of sadness.

Anyway, returning to the main narrative. After leaving Angie and the garden centre café I drove north to where I was due to meet with Liz. Again, she hadn't suggested I could stay at her place so I had gone online and booked a room at a guesthouse (that for some reason was named Rookery Nook) in the Yorkshire town of Ilkley where she lived.

I arrived quite late on so after checking in I found a nice-looking pub and spent the rest of the evening dining on some very good pub fish and chips along with, as usual, some extremely good local ale. I'd been to Ilkley a few times in the past and had always enjoyed the feel of the place and it's proximity to its nearby moor, the setting of the famous *On Ilkla Moor Baht'at*, which was a song that had, over the years, become the unofficial national anthem of Yorkshire. I'd found myself humming it as I drove into the town passing the sign that said: Welcome to Ilkley.

Back in my guesthouse room lying in bed, I tried to do a little reading but found that my mind was too full of the revelations I had learned as a result of my trips around the country so far. In the end I gave up, turned off my bedside lamp and snuggled down for sleep. I must have dropped off very quickly for I soon found myself in the midst of another one of my strangely worrying dreams. This time there was no sign of hunting dogs, horses, Toby or Fiona, but I did find myself in a decidedly Kafkaesque world where I was lying in a hospital room hooked up to tubes and a drip, having no memory of why I was there or what was wrong with me. Every so often people I vaguely recognised would pass by the open door to my room but I couldn't pin down who they actually were. I called out to them and asked if they could tell me what I was doing in this hospital but they either ignored me or said they'd go and find out but never returned. I was so affected by the nightmare that when I woke up and it was still dark outside I turned on the bedside light, grabbed my notebook and wrote down the details of the dream. I'm not sure why I did – it wasn't the sort of thing I would normally do – but thinking about it later I suppose I thought the dream might offer some sort of clue about things that had happened to me in the distant past. A vain hope I suppose.

*

The next day after a very large and delicious Yorkshire breakfast at the guesthouse, I spent some time looking around the town and re-acquainting myself with the place and its attractive Victorian architecture. I'd arranged to meet Liz for lunch at one o'clock and so I had a few hours to while away strolling around, visiting the toy museum and sitting by the picturesque River Wharfe. I sat for quite a while wrapped up warmly against a cold northerly wind, contemplating matters and feeling generally uneasy.

Eventually it was time to meet Liz at the town's renowned Bettys Tea Rooms, a place I'd enjoyed on a number of previous occasions while in Ilkley. I'd also visited its sister restaurant when I'd been in York. As usual I turned up early and thought I might have to sit at my table alone for a while, but Liz, her hair badly dishevelled by the wind, arrived almost immediately, also early. We greeted each other with pecks on the cheek and soon fell into a pleasant conversation about the usual things. I'd met Liz on a number of occasions over the years and so we were more familiar with each other than most of those I had met on my recent travels. Inevitably, as we swapped the usual stories of holidays and grandchildren, my mind went back to the occasion in our first year at the University of the North when we had ended up in bed together. Unlike the cloudy memories I had about many of my encounters with people at the time, I actually remembered a great deal about our little "love" affair.

It happened quite early on and was my first university romance, if you could call it that. Like most such occasions at the time it started at a disco. I'd been determined to get to know Tina and Liz from the moment I first saw them. Both were extremely attractive, and once we had got talking and we started hitting it off, they both seemed to enjoy my company. Tina ended up talking to Nick (that may have been their first night together actually) while I spent much of the evening dancing, drinking and chatting to Liz. After the disco had finished I walked her back to the room she shared with Tina, only to find a handwritten notice pinned on the door saying: Sex in progress. Do not enter! We smiled at each other, walked the short distance to my room and, of course, after a few passionate kisses, fell into bed.

We slept together on a number of other occasions after that first time but, and I cannot recall the exact circumstances why, we eventually moved on from each other, parting quite amicably as far as I recall (for what that's worth!).

Liz still looked pretty good after all these years, despite her light brown hair now being mainly grey. A while ago she had been treated for breast cancer and had gone through all the chemotherapy but now seemed to be totally cured and looked as healthy as anyone pushing seventy years old was likely to look.

She had always been a quiet but very supportive person while at university, particularly in her friendship with Tina, and had eventually settled down into a long and successful marriage, I was pleased to say. How much she remembered about our sexual encounters of so long ago I did not know, and I wasn't about to introduce the topic myself into our conversation.

As we ate our way through one of the famed Bettys Tea Room afternoon teas we eventually got on to the subject of Maggie. Like everyone else I'd spoken to, Liz expressed her sadness about her death and we exchanged one or two memories of Maggie from our university days; memories that thankfully made both of us smile. I then turned the conversation around to the subject of our engagement and Liz was also able to confirm that she too could remember hearing about that news at the time. According to her she had spoken to me about what had happened, a memory that was not in my head in any form at all, but given the Swiss cheese-sized holes in my ability to recall certain aspects of my life at the time, that wasn't at all surprising. She told me that both she and Tina had given Maggie advice as far as her relationship with me was concerned. She had been pleased at the time when Maggie and I had seemingly got through any difficulties we had and appeared to be prepared to make a go of things once we had left the confines of the university.

'I remember feeling surprised when I heard that you two had split up in the summer,' said Liz.

'I have to admit that we didn't actually see each other in the summer holidays. Apparently I rang her up to break off the engagement quite early on, although to be perfectly honest I don't remember having that conversation. I never saw her again. I feel quite bad about it all now of course.'

'Well, I suppose we all make mistakes in our lives,' Liz said, somewhat wistfully.

'True, some perhaps more than others though,' I replied, while absent-mindedly smearing jam on a scone.

And then Liz surprised me. 'Do you think you and I should have stayed together?'

I almost spat out the large piece of scone that I had just popped into my mouth. To give me time to think, I chewed the cake rather more than I would normally have done while trying to look thoughtful and indicating to Liz that I had a full mouth. When I finally answered I decided to duck her question completely by asking her an inane one back. 'What exactly do you mean?' I said.

'Well, when we were in the first year we went out together for a few months. We even used the L word occasionally.'

'The L word?' I said, somewhat disingenuously.

'Love,' she replied.

'We did? When would that have been? I'm afraid I've no memory of it.'

'When we were in bed. On more than one occasion, actually.'

'Really? I'm sorry I can't remember saying it. I'm sure that I must have meant it at the time but…'

'No, actually, I don't think you did, Rob. I did though. I was head over heels in love with you at the time and was completely devastated when you dumped me.'

'I didn't realise,' I said.

'No, I don't suppose you did, but it was a bit of an eye-opener for me. It was the first time I realised that men will say pretty much anything to get you into bed and keep you coming back for more until they eventually get bored with you.'

I looked at Liz. It was obvious that she still felt the hurt I had caused her all those years ago (another one!). Her face was suddenly full of regret and resentment.

'I'm sorry,' I said. It sounded pathetically inadequate but it was all I could think to say.

'It's all water under the bridge now of course but I just wanted to make you realise that what at the time must have seemed very unimportant to you was actually quite meaningful as far as I was concerned.'

'I'm truly sorry,' I said again, this time hopefully sounding more sincere.

'Do you know Maggie once told me that she knew you and I had slept together? I passed it off as unimportant, saying that it hadn't meant anything. The conversation we had took place when you and she were going out and she got quite angry with me, I seem to remember and I had to calm her down. Looking back I wonder if she realised that I was not being all that accurate and whether, speaking frankly, she had seen you for what you really were at that time: a serial philanderer and a liar.'

To say I was shocked would have been an understatement. Liz, as far as I was concerned, was one of my oldest and dearest friends and here she was throwing insults at me (albeit no doubt very well-deserved ones). I looked around the tearoom by way of some sort of displacement activity, looking at the people at nearby tables and noting what they were eating and how they were dressed. One couple was wearing muddy walking boots and shorts; not the sort of clothes you'd expect people to wear in such plush surroundings I thought. I pushed my plate to one side. Despite the stand in front of me being still full of delicious-looking mini cakes, I suddenly didn't feel like eating any more. This meeting had, all of a sudden, developed into my most difficult encounter of them all.

Liz could see I was shocked. She almost looked as though she was feeling sorry for me but then she smiled and said, 'Well I suppose none of that matters very much anymore does it, Rob?'

'No, I suppose not,' I replied, feeling shaken. 'It just makes me sad to think I have made people unhappy: Maggie, you… and others I guess. I suppose that at the time it was all happening I believed that my behaviour towards other people wasn't really very important as deep down they must have realised that I was a really good person. That's what I thought at the time – mistakenly of course. I now know that I went about seriously hurting people and mistreating them without giving them any sort of thought, and now I feel inordinately bad about it all.'

'It's all a long time ago now, Rob. Don't get too depressed by your memories,' said Liz with a lot more understanding than I actually deserved. She smiled at me and patted my hands that were resting on the table top in a reassuring way that seemed to belie her plain speaking of a few moments ago.

Liz, thankfully, changed the subject, and we spoke about some of the others we knew at university. She was interested in hearing about those I had met up with on my travels around the country. She was particularly saddened to hear about the state that JJ was now in and told me that she would write to him as soon as she got back home. I didn't spoil her plans by saying I would be very surprised if he was able to stay sober long enough to hold a pen and write back to her.

We sat in Bettys Tea Rooms for a good deal of time just chatting about other more inconsequential things including ruminating on the possible reasons why, famously, there was no apostrophe in Bettys. I was even able, eventually, to eat one or two of the delicious little cakes from the cake stand.

When Liz and I parted, with a hug and a kiss and a promise to meet again, I felt a mixture of emotions. It had been good to see her again but I felt extremely unsettled by some of the things she had said to me. Unsettled was quickly becoming my default state! I watched her walk away down the windy street, half expecting her to look back and give me a little wave, but she didn't.

*

Later on, when I was lying in bed reviewing the day in my head and thinking about what Liz and I had said that afternoon, I felt even more depressed than I had done before. Why had I been such a different person back then in my university days? Why had I been so selfish and self-absorbed? How could I hurt people so easily and not think about the consequences?

When we had said our goodbyes outside Bettys Tea Rooms, Liz had said she would look forward to seeing everyone at the reunion and she sounded as if she really meant it. The more I thought about it the less happy I was at the thought of any further meetings with my friends from university, many of whom I had seemed to have dealt with in such offhand and horrible ways. It seemed that the person I had been back then I suddenly did not like anymore. How I wished I could go back in time and change those past events that now bothered me so much. Recently, as I have been languishing every day in my prison cell staring at the opposite wall, I have had that futile little thought many, many times: every single day!

Chapter 24: *It's Too Late*

Saturday, June 1973

'So, what's your name then?'

Stella had danced up closely to the tall, ruggedly good-looking man with the unfashionably short dark hair and, standing on her tiptoes, had spoken into his right ear.

'It's Trevor,' he said, putting his arm round Stella and cupping her towards him.

Fiona tapped Stella on the shoulder and gave her back the almost empty wine bottle. She looked annoyed at Stella's sudden and intimate intrusion. Stella stared at Fiona, took the wine bottle and moved even closer to the tall man.

'I'm Stella,' she said smiling, before throwing her arms around him and planting a kiss on his mouth. Trevor seemed delighted and joined in with the kiss enthusiastically. As far as he was concerned this was his lucky evening. Not only had he been dancing with a woman who was extremely posh-sounding, very nice-looking and who had the most voluptuous figure and magnificently large breasts, but now a slender, very sexy, blonde beauty was also making advances towards him. This was one night he definitely would not be describing in detail to his girlfriend when he saw her back in his hometown in a few days' time. As far as she was concerned he had been spending tonight enjoying a few quiet and relaxing drinks in the company of his male friends in one of the university bars.

'Would you like to go upstairs? I think there's a bedroom still free,' she shouted into Trevor's ear before delicately nibbling his ear lobe.

'Er, okay then,' he replied, and shrugged to Fiona as if to say: "what can a man do?"

Stella led Trevor by the hand across the cellar and up the steps to the hallway. A furious Fiona followed them, anger in her eyes, fists clenched tightly. As they stepped on to the stairs she grabbed Stella by the shoulder, squeezing hard and turning her around.

'Ow!' shouted Stella. 'That hurt.'

'It was meant to. What the hell do you think you're doing, Stella?'

'What I'm doing,' said Stella, rubbing her shoulder and grimacing, 'is taking Trevor upstairs to have sex with him. Any objections?'

Fiona, for once in her life, was left speechless. Trevor smiled at Fiona weakly and half considered inviting her to the bedroom too. He had never had a threesome and this evening his good luck was such that she might just agree. However, before he could speak Fiona leapt at Stella with a murderous look in her eyes and pulled her away from Trevor whose hand she had been clinging to. Fiona then grabbed Stella by her hair and forced her to the floor. Those individuals scattered about the hallway, who were in various states of intoxication, brought about by the evening's copious consumption of alcohol and marijuana, were unsure about what they should do. To some the sight of two women having a fight was a welcome bit of excitement during an otherwise spaced-out evening while others vaguely thought that someone should do something to stop the scuffle before any real damage was done to the participants. In the end it was Trevor who decided to act and grabbed Fiona, pulling her away from the prone Stella who had been screaming with pain as Fiona had tugged on her long hair and gouged at her face.

'That's enough,' he said with uncharacteristic authority, while realising his chances of a memorable sexual experience tonight were waning quickly. He held on tightly to Fiona until he felt her anger cool.

Red-faced, Fiona looked down at the figure of Stella who lay on the floor, sobbing quietly. 'You know, Stella, I've always had a lot of time for you but what you did tonight was the most despicable thing anyone has ever done to me!' She shook herself free from Trevor's grasp, gave one last scornful glance at Stella and turned to the tall man she had met for the first time the previous evening and who she had been very keen to get to know as they had danced together in the cellar. 'You can have her! You deserve each other!' she shouted, before disappearing down the cellar steps and hoping that she didn't look too foolish to those who watched with mouths agape.

Trevor helped Stella up. She was still crying. He held her close to him and stroked her long hair. He noticed that there were a number of scratches on the side of her face along with some bright ribbons of blood where Fiona's long nails had dug into her cheek as she had grabbed handfuls of her hair. Trevor stood comforting the small sobbing woman and wondered whether it would be a good idea to lead her back up the stairs toward one of the bedrooms (hope still sprang eternal inside his jeans).

'Do you still want to go upstairs?' he asked tentatively.

Stella looked up at him. She dried her eyes with her sleeve and nodded with resignation. Trevor smiled at her and felt relieved as he led her up the staircase. This was turning out to be a really interesting evening, he thought.

*

Back in the cellar Fiona looked around for people she knew. She hadn't felt quite so furious for a long time and needed to talk to someone with a friendly face. She couldn't see anyone she knew particularly well apart from Althea, who was dancing close to someone wearing a black leather waistcoat, her hands resting on his shoulders in a very friendly fashion. In view of what had just happened to her she didn't want to intrude on them. Instead she turned around, went up the stone cellar steps and out into the back garden where there were a number of people standing around chatting, smoking and drinking. Fiona took a packet of cigarettes out of her shoulder bag and lit one. She was doubly annoyed now as she had promised herself that she wouldn't smoke tonight as part of her medium-term strategy to give up the habit for good. She knew it wasn't healthy for her, and the horses back at home didn't like the smell of tobacco on her breath. Her own horse, Champion, was the greatest love of her life and there were few privations she would not be prepared to suffer for his sake. She now missed him more than she had ever done before.

As she puffed out a long stream of smoke she noticed Tina and Liz, paper cups in hand, standing talking together next to a rather dilapidated rose trellis that stood against the back of the house.

'Hello, you two,' she said, hoping that her face was back to its normal pallor.

'Hi,' answered Tina. 'What's happened to your face?'

'What's wrong with it?' said Fiona.

'You've got some blood on your forehead,' said Liz.

'Really?' replied Fiona, touching her forehead and

then looking at her fingers. 'Oh, it's probably not mine actually.'

Fiona's recounting of the recent events with Stella was as accurate as she could make it, believing that, as she was totally in the right, the facts needed no further embellishment.

Tina and Liz listened intently and with some sympathy as Fiona told the story of her encounter with Stella. Neither had ever seen Fiona so animated before; in the three years both had known her she had always been as restrained and measured a person as it was possible to be as a young undergraduate at university.

'I wonder why Stella did that?' pondered Tina. 'It's a bit out of character, isn't it?'

Liz nodded.

'I have no idea. She seemed to be drunk or high or both, as well as having it in for me personally, and I don't know why. We've always got on well together – right from the start of the first year when we shared a room.'

'This Trevor – have you known him long?'

'No, not really. I started chatting to him in the campus café yesterday and asked him if he fancied coming to this party. I came with him in his car. Hoped I might leave with him too.' Fiona sniffed and tried hard not to blub (as she would have put it).

Liz put out a consoling hand.

'Well, tonight does seem to be turning out to be a bit of a fraught one,' said Tina.

'Why's that?' said Fiona, taking a deep drag of her cigarette and feeling grateful to have stifled a sob.

'Oh, we were talking to Maggie earlier; she was in a real state. She went off to have it out with Rob in the pub. Men, eh!' said Tina.

'Hmm, women as well I'm afraid. You can't trust some of them either!' replied Fiona, the first flicker of a smile showing on her blood-smeared face.

*

A little later, upstairs in one of the bedrooms, Stella was putting her clothes back on. Trevor was lying on the bed and had already begun to feel guilty about what had just happened. He had cheated on his girlfriend twice before in the three years he had been a student at the University of the North and on both occasions he had decided not to tell her. He had reasoned that it was best she didn't know as it would only upset her. He didn't think this very quick sexual encounter with this rather beautiful and strange girl called Stella meant very much in the great scheme of things. To be honest, although she was extremely attractive, she also seemed a bit unbalanced and far too complicated for him. He certainly didn't want such a casual and meaningless event to spoil his relationship with his girlfriend who he had known since they were at school together. She was already collecting things for her bottom drawer in the expectation that as soon as he got his well-paid degree-level job they would "get married in that really lovely old church on the other side of town." He pulled up a sheet to cover his nakedness and was very pleased when Stella left the room without saying another word and closed the door behind her.

Chapter 25: *Paint It, Black*

March, the present day

A number of years ago, during one of our many post-university meetings, Toby told me that the human soul has been assessed as weighing twenty-one grams. This apparently was the conclusion reached by an American scientist (I'm not sure if Toby told me his name) who early in the twentieth century had weighed a number of terminally ill people (presumably they were volunteers) just before and just after their deaths. The scientist found that each one of the expired individuals weighed exactly twenty-one grams less than they had while they were alive and so he concluded that their now departed souls must have weighed exactly that amount. Like most of Toby's "interesting facts" I took this with a large pinch of salt, but as I have grown older that little factoid has stayed with me and has seemed more and more interesting; understandably I suppose. If it is indeed possible to identify a "soul" as something that leaves the body at the exact point of death then that does seem to imply that it must go somewhere else after it flies away from its human host. I have to say I've never been particularly religious or spiritual to any great degree but as I approach my seventies I find myself contemplating my eventual demise and whether there is any truth in all this afterlife business. Being in the place where I now find myself has only made my speculations more pertinent. Thinking time is the one thing you have plenty of when you're in prison.

*

I reached Toby's house in Skipton fairly late in the afternoon. I'd been there many times in the past and he had always seemed pleased to see me. It was never very long before we had adjourned to one of his local pubs, where everyone seemed to know him, and where we drank vast amounts of beer while chatting about cricket, football, politics and the general state of the world. This time, however, it all seemed very different. For one thing he didn't appear to be overly grateful to see me. He had been expecting me of course; I'd had a telephone conversation with him the day before after I'd met with Liz. Then, he had seemed to be happy that I was going to travel up to his place but now it was almost as though he expected our actual meeting to go badly, and that's exactly how things turned out.

Once we had arrived at the inevitable nearby pub where Toby had a quick bit of banter with a group of his usual drinking buddies and I brought back from the bar two pints of bitter, I gave him a run down on the conversations I'd had with Liz, Angela, Tina, Nick and the rest of those I'd seen recently in relation to the proposed university reunion. It was then that I noticed Toby had a strange look in his eyes; one I hadn't witnessed before. For the first time since I had met him all those years ago, I thought that perhaps there was a hint of incipient madness in them. He sat back in his chair cradling his pint glass and smiled malevolently at me somewhat in the fashion of a James Bond villain. Instead of launching into our usual conversation about the state of the England cricket team or some other sports-related topic, he looked at me across the pub table and spoke with a definite sneer in his voice.

'You know, Rob, you always give me the impression that you really believe your university days were the best and most important time of your life. Well, let me tell you how wrong you are. It wasn't the greatest time of our lives when we had boundless freedom that enabled us to *find ourselves*, whatever the hell that means. It was simply a relatively short span of time when the only things we were really interested in were drinking ourselves stupid and trying to get our leg over as often as possible. If we were lucky we occasionally found time in between to go to lectures and read a few books just as long as they didn't get in the way of those other things. So take off those rose-tinted spectacles of yours and just see those times for what they were: a

231

monumental doss for three years that served no one any real useful purpose.'

To say I was dumbfounded by Toby's out-of-the-blue tirade would have been an understatement.

'What about all the friends we made? That was something positive, surely?' I said, trying not to sound whiney.

'Really? And what was so important about them? Weren't they just a collection of people that by accident were there at the same time as we were and who we got to know for a brief amount of time? How many of those friends did we keep in touch with and see regularly after we left university?'

'Well, some – a few I suppose.'

'And how important were they in your life?'

'Some were – *are*,' I replied. 'And anyway, if you feel that way why bother suggesting we try to organise a reunion at all then? It was your idea after all.'

'You think it was because I wanted to see a lot of clapped-out old folks who never meant that much to me in the first place? No, I floated the whole idea in order to shake you up and set you on your quest to find out the truth about you and Maggie.'

'Sorry, I don't follow?'

'No, I didn't think you would get it. You were never the brightest were you, despite all those supposedly *clever* books you've written.'

'I'm sorry, Toby, but I'm finding your attitude a bit odd and also somewhat offensive.'

I knew that Toby was drunk (he had obviously been drinking before I arrived) but he was usually in that state. This was the first time in the last fifty or so years that I had ever heard him take this tone and disparage our friendship and that of the others we had spent our time with at university.

'Toby, are you all right?' I continued, concerned that something awful had happened to cause this strange attitude of his.

'Oh, I'm fine thanks, never better. Just ready to pass on a few home truths to you.' He picked up his pint and drank most of it in one go.

'What do you mean? Such as?'

Toby wiped his mouth with the back of his hand. 'I asked you to contact some of our old acquaintances from university so that you would begin to realise the truth about those days.'

'I still don't know what you mean.'

'No, I don't expect you do.'

'Toby, what's this all about? Is it some sort of joke?'

He didn't answer; he just shrugged, finished his beer and got up slowly out of his seat, groaning as he did so, and walked to the bar to get another couple of pints. At least he was still buying beer for me!

He soon returned with the drinks, put the two pint glasses on the table and sat down again. I looked at him quizzically.

'So what's the problem, Toby? Why are you being so… well, strange?'

He chuckled and shook his head. 'Do you know what Rob? The joke is that you always thought I was your friend when in reality I've always resented you; resented your arrogance and your smarminess. All those times you elbowed me aside while you went after some woman or other. Do you remember the girl from the BBC you got off with after spoiling things for me? Pushing me aside with your so-called smart comments. I could have got off with her if it hadn't been for you.'

(I was too gobsmacked to reply at this point!)

'And what of those other times when you went about saying things about me? Dishing the dirt, undermining me, telling everyone that I'd done this or that, or I'd let you down over an *Ariel* article I was too late with?'

I quickly brought to mind the incident he was talking about. It was one of the rare events that had stuck in my mind and had taken place in our final year when I was the editor of *Ariel*. Toby was contributing the occasional feature on newly released records or groups and other things connected with the music industry, which he knew a fair bit about. His writing was consistently very good and pithy but sometimes it was a bit of a struggle to get the promised articles off him in time for publication and that would cause last minute problems I then had to deal with. On the occasion he was referring to he had promised me a piece on the tour of the US by Led Zeppelin, a group that was probably the most popular in the world at the time. I waited until the very last minute I could prior to publication but he still hadn't shown up with it. So I went looking for him, checking out all the bars, and eventually found him in Windermere Bar, the furthest one from the *Ariel* office. Despite it being quite early on in the evening Toby was obviously already pretty well pissed as he sat with three or four of his other drinking cronies. When I asked him about the article he pointed to his head and said something like "it's all up here". I remember replying that in that case he needed to go along to the office right away and type it up so that we could publish on time. He refused and asked me if I wanted a pint saying that he would "pop along later" and do it. I stormed off, calling him a few choice names and sorted out that week's newspaper, getting someone (I forget who) to write a quick puff piece on whatever was the number one record at the time (something by Slade I think).

'Toby,' I said, 'that was one occasion when you let me down badly. You had promised to write something and failed to produce it in time. I think I was entitled to be a bit miffed to be perfectly honest.'

'And did you also feel entitled to show me up in front of my friends as we were having a quiet drink?'

To be frank I don't think Toby had ever had a "quiet" drink during his whole time at university. His attitude to drinking was simply to guzzle as much beer as possible and be as loud and raucous as he could. As you can already gather from this memoir, I wasn't that far behind him in that regard for much of the time, but there were occasions when I took other aspects of my university life fairly seriously too.

I drank some of my beer and shook my head. That seemed to encourage Toby to carry on his tirade against me. He dredged up a lot of stuff that I'd mostly forgotten about. His main gripe seemed to be about some of the women in our friendship group who he accused me of sleeping around with, while at the same time disrespecting him and preventing him doing the same sort of thing. I looked mystified and asked him who exactly he was referring to.

'Well, there was Tina to start with.'

'What about Tina?'

'Well you slept with her and badmouthed me so she wouldn't do the same with me.'

'Hang on, Toby,' I said. 'I never slept with Tina. If you remember, she was with Nick from the first year and I was never going to get off with anyone a friend was going out with.' I realised as I said this that I was bending the truth somewhat!

'That's not what Liz told me,' he scoffed.

'Really? Well, whatever she said she wasn't telling the truth.'

I was amazed at that revelation. Having met with Liz recently I felt a bit ill-used by her if what Toby was saying was actually true.

'Of course Liz was another of those who you tried to prevent me getting off with.'

'What are you talking about?' I said, more confused than ever.

'You slept with her a few times – or are you going to deny that too?'

'Yes, I did sleep with Liz. I liked her. We stayed friends afterwards.'

'And when you were with her you tried your best to make sure she wouldn't want to sleep with me.'

I shook my head again. 'Why would I do that? That's crazy! It's not what happened.'

'More of your lies!' hissed Toby. 'Liz told me that you said I was unreliable, and that you thought I was the person responsible for taking money from the *Ariel* cashbox and because of that you wouldn't let me be in the office alone – you made sure you were always there too.'

That brought me up short. I suddenly felt very guilty and probably looked it too. It brought back a memory that I had buried long ago. Liz and I were in bed; we had just had sex and were lying there smoking. The sex had been good and I was starting to think that going out with her on a long-term basis might be quite a good idea. At the time I was feeling guilty about taking the money from the petty cashbox in the *Ariel* office and I suppose I was thinking that it would make me appear less likely to have taken it if I could suggest that someone else was responsible for the missing money. Toby did have a bit of a reputation for being a little unreliable even so early on in his time at the University of the North and a number of people had commented on his frequent "piss artist" activities. He was an obvious suspect, I had told

Liz, laying it on all a bit thickly, I suppose. I regretted saying it now of course and certainly didn't expect it to go any further than Liz but you know, people being people and all that. After I had broken up with Liz she then hooked up with Toby, so I suppose it was inevitable she would tell him.

'Toby, I did say that to Liz. I apologise profusely for it. I'm sorry.'

'Bit late for that now,' said Toby, sniffing and finishing his pint before standing up with his usual groan. 'I've had enough beer. I'm going home. You can come if you want to.'

I never thought I would hear Toby say that he'd had enough beer. To be honest I was staggered. I should have driven home at that point but I'd left all my stuff in his spare room on the understanding that I was going to stay overnight. In any case I'd already had too much beer to safely drive anywhere. As it was, I soon caught up with his lumbering figure and we walked to his house in silence. It had started to rain.

Chapter 26: *The Tears of a Clown*

Saturday, June 1973

Stella closed the bedroom door and went into the bathroom. She sat on the toilet, peed and then stood up and checked her face in the medicine cabinet mirror. She touched the scratch marks left by Fiona's nails. They felt sore and looked red so she patted them with some cold water and then dried her face with a towel that was hanging next to the sink. She decided that she was reasonably satisfied with how she looked and left the bathroom and headed downstairs and into the kitchen. She needed a drink. The tussle with Fiona as well as the quick sex with Trevor had sobered her up and she wanted to feel drunk again.

There were still a number of wine bottles on the kitchen table so she picked one up and poured some white wine into a lone paper cup. It looked as though someone else had already used it but she shrugged and drank the whole cupful in one go.

As she filled up the paper cup again a gentle tap on

her shoulder made her turn around.

'Hi, Stella. How's it going with you?' said Althea.

'I'm all right,' said Stella after a moment's hesitation.

'Wow! What happened to your face?'

Stella touched the side of her face with her fingertips. 'Nothing really,' she said, looking up at the tall American. 'Bit of an accident with someone's nails. Not something to worry about. Want some wine?'

'Yeah, sure. I'm going outside for some fresh air. You coming?'

'Okay,' replied Stella, quickly draining her cup and grabbing the wine bottle.

*

It was now dark. A cool wind had blown up and in the back garden Althea folded her arms in an attempt to keep herself warm. Fiona, Tina and Liz stood nearby and all three glared at Stella. Althea gave them a little wave but they didn't acknowledge her.

'What's bugging them?' said Althea.

'They're mad at me I think. Fiona and I got into a little argument earlier on. Very stupid behaviour from a very stupid person.'

'Your face? Did she do that?'

'Yes, she did. She's always been nasty and vindictive.'

'Really? I'm surprised. I always thought Fiona was

the calm and collected type. Nothing really seems to upset her, in my experience.'

'Well you obviously don't know her very well,' said Stella. She then took a large swig from the wine bottle before passing it to Althea and then took out a cigarette from the packet in her bag and lit it.

Althea drank from the bottle. 'Why was she upset with you?'

Stella paused for thought and blew out some smoke in a long sigh. 'Apparently she's the jealous type. Didn't like it very much when I asked the guy she was dancing with if he wanted to shag me.'

'Does shag mean what I think it means?'

'Yeah. She took exception to me asking him. The fact that he agreed so quickly to go upstairs with me didn't say much for her chances anyway.' Stella grabbed the wine bottle from Althea and drank from it.

Althea looked at Stella, her eyes wide with surprise. 'Er, Stella, that really doesn't sound very fair. I saw Fiona arrive with that tall guy. I think she really liked him. Wouldn't it be a good idea for you to go and apologise to her? You are friends after all.'

Stella pointed to her face. 'She did this! She's no friend of mine. She's a bitch!' A scowling Stella announced the last word loudly, causing Fiona, Tina and Liz to look over at her.

'Oh come on, Stella. It's time to forgive and forget.' Althea attempted to take the wine bottle from Stella just as she was about to have another drink from it. 'I think you may have had enough, Stella.'

Stella looked angrily at Althea. Small tears were running down her cheeks; they stung when they rolled down over the scratches. She clung tightly on to the bottle. 'Who exactly do you think you are? Perhaps if you were white you might have something useful to say that I'd be interested in listening to!'

Althea looked askance at Stella. In all the time she had been in Britain, over the last year, no one had ever mentioned her skin colour apart from those times when she had occasionally heard people in the street referring to her as coloured. She had thought many times that the best thing about most people in this country was their innate fairness and ability to see her as an individual and not as a member of a particular race. Just lately she had even begun to consider coming back to live in the UK on a permanent basis at some point in the future. She didn't know Stella that well but had certainly never considered that she was the sort to make such an obvious racial slur.

'I'm going to pretend I didn't hear that, Stella, and just put it down to the fact that you've been drinking too much.'

Stella brandished the wine bottle and drank some more from it before staggering back a little. 'Typical black American: self-righteous as always! I've met plenty of your sort before. I was at school in Washington DC for a while. The blacks there thought that the world owed them a living all because some of their ancestors had been slaves at some time in the distant past and all they ever spoke about were their so-called civil rights! Totally pathetic!'

By now Stella was shouting and the people who were present in the garden were looking over at her, some shaking their heads. Tina restrained Fiona who was all for marching over to where Stella was and continuing their argument from earlier.

'I'm sorry, Stella,' said Althea, 'but I can't listen to any more of this. I think you're being deliberately offensive and I don't know why you're doing it. We've always got on well together before tonight but if this is the real you then I don't want anything to do with you ever again.' Althea walked away and went to join Fiona, Tina and Liz.

Stella watched her as she went, took another mouthful of white wine from the bottle and, jangling her keys in her hand, staggered off down the path toward where her car was parked.

'Please tell me she's not going to drive in that state,' said Liz.

Fiona and Althea both shrugged.

'Can't say that I'm too bothered,' said Fiona. 'I'm certainly not going to run after her and stop her.'

'But she might kill herself – or someone else,' said Liz.

'I'll go,' said Tina.

'I'll come with you,' said Liz.

The two young women ran up the path. Althea and

Fiona looked at each other. Neither was keen to follow.

'What do you think caused Stella to act that way?' said Althea.

'I haven't the faintest idea. And I wouldn't care if she did kill herself. She would have it coming anyway,' replied Fiona. 'Shall we go and have a dance?'

'That sounds like a very good idea,' said Althea.

The two girls smiled at each other, linked arms and walked inside.

*

Tina and Liz soon caught up with Stella who stopped occasionally to drink from her wine bottle.

'Stella, you can't get in your car!' said Tina.

'Why not?' Stella had stopped and flung the last of her cigarette on the ground. She turned and faced the two women.

'Because you're not fit to drive. You're too drunk!' said Tina.

Liz nodded her agreement.

Stella smiled and drank some more of the wine. 'You know, there are a lot of people giving me advice tonight. Why are you worried about what I do anyway?'

'Because you might hurt yourself, or other people! You really shouldn't drive,' said Tina.

'No, you shouldn't,' said Liz.

Stella looked at the two girls. She smiled. On such a beautiful face, Tina thought, Stella's smile looked surprisingly stark and ugly.

'Please!' said Liz.

Stella put her wine bottle on the ground before taking out another cigarette and lighting it. Her hand was shaking a little; the emotion of the night was getting to her, she realised.

'Do you want a cigarette?' said Stella, proffering the packet to the other two. Both shook their heads.

'Shall we go back to the house then?' said Tina.

'Why?'

'So we can chat and straighten things out between you and Fiona.'

Stella scoffed and smiled again. 'You're always the sensible one, aren't you? Sensible Tina and her hanger-on, lovable Liz! Always ready to say and do the right thing.'

Tina forced a smile. 'Come on, Stella, let's go and patch things up.'

'Patch things up? Is that what you're going to do with your drug dealing boyfriend when you see him?'

Tina looked bemused. 'What do you mean, Stella?'

Stella waggled her hand at Tina. Ash fell from her cigarette and floated to the ground. 'Oh so innocent is our Tina! What I mean is; are you going to be telling Nick about your little fling with Rob last night when he comes back?'

'Nothing happened between Rob and me last night,' said Tina.

'Really? That's not what I heard.

Tina looked at Liz. Liz shook her head.

'Well, Stella, whatever you heard from whoever it was, is completely untrue. Rob and I went for a drink and that was all.'

'So you didn't take Rob back to your room then?'

'No... yes, we did go back to my room but nothing happened! Who told you about that anyway?'

Stella waggled her finger and smiled. 'Ah, well that would be telling wouldn't it?'

Tina looked at Liz again who shook her head more vehemently while mouthing, 'No.'

'No, don't worry, it wasn't your little friend. But no doubt you'll guess who it was eventually, so I'll tell you: it was Toby who told me.'

'Toby?' Tina looked puzzled. 'How did he find...? Of course: Rob!'

Stella chuckled despite the tears that were now running down her face stinging her scratches again.

'Boys will always brag about their conquests. Let's hope that no one tells Nick when he comes back on Monday,' said Stella, her smile looking even crueller and more malevolent by the second.

Tina glared at her. 'If you do that, Stella, I swear I will...'

'What, Tina? What will you do?'

Tina looked back at Stella. She had never felt quite so angry and at the same time so frightened in her life before.

'Come on, Liz. If Stella wants to kill herself in her

246

car she's welcome to do it,' said Tina.

Stella watched the two women walk off. She picked up her wine bottle and drank the last dregs from it before throwing the bottle into a nearby hedge. She wiped her tears away, found her keys and headed off towards her car.

Chapter 27: *Rainy Days and Mondays*

March, the present day

By the time we got to Toby's house we were soaked through. Although it had only been a short walk, the rain shower was so heavy that even my underpants were wet and uncomfortable, so I stood in front of a radiator in an attempt to dry off while Toby went upstairs to get changed. I thought about changing into my spare pair of jeans but decided not to. As soon as I was partially dry and felt sober enough to drive I was going to leave and let Toby stew in his own juice. I could imagine him ringing me up tomorrow and offering his abject apologies. I was sure that once he'd sobered up he would feel extremely embarrassed when he remembered what he had said to me in the pub.

Toby's house was deathly quiet; just a few floorboard creaks as he moved about upstairs. It was always this way, at least for the past few years since his marriage had broken down. In his present mood it was very likely he would blame me for that too! In fact he had been married twice, although neither of his marriages had resulted in any children. His first wife, Wendy, had tragically died in a car crash many years ago. They were both still in their twenties when it happened. Of course everyone had felt devastated for Toby at the time and we were all pleased when a short time afterwards he had met someone else and re-married. He and his new wife, Roberta, seemed to get along really well for a couple of years but then the cracks began to show and they eventually separated and later got divorced, Roberta blaming the mental cruelty Toby had inflicted on her. Most of his friends, including myself, had been somewhat sceptical and believed that she had exaggerated the extent to which he had mistreated her in order to get a better divorce settlement. Since then, over the last twenty years I suppose, Toby had been living alone, a state of affairs that until today seemed to suit him fine. He had said to me on more than one occasion that he was much better on his own, and was happy that he could come and go as he pleased and drink as much as he wanted without a wife to act as his external conscience.

Toby eventually came downstairs. 'Do you want a beer? I'm having one,' he said, seemingly forgetting that not long before he had said that he'd had enough.

'No thanks,' I replied.

'Please yourself.' He went to the kitchen and took a can of lager out of the fridge.

'Actually, Toby, I think I should go soon. I'm just

going to sober up a bit then I'm going to drive home.'

For a moment he looked surprised, as though again he had forgotten the conversation we'd had in the pub. He then smiled and sat down in an armchair, staring at me as I stood with my backside close to the hot radiator. He was drinking the lager straight from the can, something I'd never seen him do before.

'Okay,' he said. 'But do you want to hear a few more home truths before you run off?'

I had decided that whatever Toby was going to say I would remain totally calm and not get angry. 'No, Toby, I do not. I don't know what's bought all this on but I don't intend to hang around here with you any longer than I need to.'

'Pity,' he said. 'I think you might be interested in what I've got to say.'

'No, I don't think I would be. I'm finding your whole attitude completely obnoxious and I'm just hoping that what you're saying isn't some indication that you are ill in some way.'

Toby laughed. 'Actually, Rob, what I've said to you today is the truth – the plain unmitigated truth – and if you don't want to face up to the fact that you've been deceiving yourself for so many years then that's your lookout. But you'll regret it.'

'What the hell are you talking about, Toby? This doesn't sound like you anymore.'

'Well, Rob, on that point you are totally correct. I don't sound like myself. For too long I've been playing second fiddle to you and pretending to be someone I'm not. It's about time you learned the real truth about things.'

'The real truth? What do you mean by that?'

Toby smiled, picked up his beer and stood up, making his usual groaning noise as he did so. He took a couple of steps towards me, looking more aggressive than I had ever seen him before. I wasn't exactly worried about being confronted by him in such a way but it was the first time in all the years I had known him that he appeared so belligerent towards me. He raised his arm and pointed his finger at me, the lager can still held in his other hand.

'I'll tell you what the real truth is, but you're not going to like it.'

I couldn't think what it was he wanted to say to me. I assumed that it was going to be the same kind of insane rubbish and gobbledygook he had been spouting in the pub. I felt for my car keys in my pocket, jangled them together and prepared to leave right away.

'I'm not bothered about what you want to say to me, Toby. I'm leaving. I just need to pick my bag up from upstairs and I'll be…'

'Maggie and I… we had a relationship after you finished with her.'

'What?'

'I went to see Maggie after you broke up with her and we were together for a while. I suggested moving in with her but she hadn't got over you, for some reason I couldn't understand. She wouldn't stop talking about you: about how wonderful you were, despite the fact that you had unceremoniously dumped her over the phone. In the end I couldn't stand hearing about you ad nauseum so we split up.'

My mouth must have been gaping wide open in surprise. 'You and Maggie? Why didn't you say anything?'

'Why should I have done? The point is that even though you weren't around, and didn't want to be around, she was still in love with you. In the end I never really had a chance, even though I'd always loved her and never stopped loving her. It was all so bloody unfair!' He was shouting by this stage.

'Toby, I didn't realise. You should have told me.'

'And what good would that have done? You didn't want Maggie any longer but you wouldn't have wanted me to have her either. That's what you were like, and if you don't know that then you're deluding yourself.'

I started to feel real anger then. 'Don't keep telling me what I would and would not have done. Despite knowing each other for over fifty years you obviously don't understand anything about me and I certainly don't recognise the person I've been speaking to today. What I thought about Maggie and what happened between the two of us was *our* business and was nothing to do with you. As far as you and her getting together, that just sounds like a mad fantasy on your part.'

Toby smiled at me again. It was a smile that seemed

to tell me that he knew something that I didn't. I was about to be proved correct in that assumption. He made a scoffing noise and took a swig of his beer before putting the can down on a coffee table.

'Maggie and I were only together for a short time then she decided that she was, as she put it, still in love with you, and was hopeful that you might come back to her. So she told me to go. As you can imagine, or perhaps you can't, I was devastated. I'd always liked... *loved* Maggie from the moment we first met her and then I had to put up with you going with her, sleeping with her and cheating on her in your usual fashion. And despite all of that she still preferred you to me!' (Toby was almost crying when he said this). 'It was so incredibly unfair. After I left Maggie, I went on a huge bender and was continually drunk for the rest of the summer. I only stopped because I was starting work, otherwise I would have just carried on.'

Toby, at this point, looked sadder than I had ever seen him. I almost felt like giving him a hug or something, but before I could move towards him he told me something absolutely devastating and stopped me right there in my tracks.

'And then one day I got a phone call from Maggie. I'd started work in York by that time and I was trying hard to forget all about her so I was surprised to hear from her. She told me that she was pregnant and that without doubt I was the father. When I'd got over the initial shock I told her that we should bring up the child together and give it a proper home. She refused and said she didn't want that sort of future and would look after the child on her own and...'

'Hang on!' I interrupted Toby. 'Are you saying that you are the father of Sarah Webb?'

'Yes, Rob, I am,' answered Toby, almost triumphantly. 'Little Sarah! I only saw her a few times when she was a child. Maggie referred to me as Uncle Toby when I met her! She was a nice kid. Very chatty and sweet.' Toby smiled at the memory.

'Then she doesn't know?'

'She didn't then but she does now. I went to see her after she'd met with you and explained everything. She hated you before; she hates you even more now!' Toby looked aggressive again – tearful *and* aggressive – not a good combination as I was to discover. I was still trying to comprehend what he had just told me when he got back into full tirade mode.

'You stole her from me, Rob!'

'What?'

'You stole Maggie from me first and then you stole Sarah from me! I could have had a proper relationship with my daughter if it hadn't been for Maggie being so stupidly besotted with you. You stole everything from me – without even a second thought. You stole my happiness!'

Toby had been advancing towards me as he spoke, and I only realised I had been backing away when I bumped into the armchair behind me and almost fell over. Toby was scary; the look on his face was something I'd never seen before on anyone. He was acting as though he was in another world, one in which he was a victim and I was the heartless oppressor who had been intent on always ruining his life. How I wished I'd never come to visit him. All I could think of was leaving his house as quickly as possible. I tried to move towards the door but Toby was blocking my way. And then he raised both arms and shoved me. That made me angry.

It's never a good look when two old blokes start fighting. Not that ours was an actual fight with fists flying (neither of us were up to that really) but we did push and shove and started to grapple and grab each other as if we were in some sort of awkward, surreal dance. It was comical in a way and I wouldn't have been surprised if we had both ended up laughing together. Sadly, however, that didn't happen and when he tried to grab me round the throat I was really annoyed and I pushed back really hard – far harder than I should have done. Toby staggered and then fell backwards over a footstool (he always had a cluttered house) and the inertia caused by his great weight made him lose his balance completely. It was such bad luck for him really (and me for that matter) that he hit the back of his head with quite a bit of force on the prominent edge of his fireplace, which was one of those overly ornate and solid ones. There was a muffled but sickening clunk as he did so. Then he just lay there not moving or even groaning. I froze. The whole thing looked like the scene of a crime in one of my Sheldon Heath novels.

At first I thought he was joking just to frighten me. His eyes were open and staring at me. I went over to him and bent down. My mouth must have been wide open in shock. Years ago my mum would say to my brother and me not to make faces because if the wind changed we'd be stuck like that forever. That mad, incongruous thought raced unbidden through my mind as I shut my gaping mouth and looked down on the unmoving figure of Toby.

I said his name in panic several times; each one louder than the last. I shook him and then I noticed the blood seeping into the carpet and making a large pool under his head. It was dark, almost black. I checked his pulse. There wasn't one... nothing that I could find anyway. If I had been thinking logically I would have immediately phoned for an ambulance and then administered CPR or something until the paramedics arrived, but my mind was in total turmoil. All I wanted to do was get out of Toby's house; to leave and drive away. Totally idiotic of course! You would think with all the murder story scenarios I had written about over the years I would have known what to do but unfortunately, when it happens in the real world, panic tends to set in. What I did, quite stupidly of course, was to leave Toby where he was, grab my bag from the spare bedroom, get in my car and drive away.

I was in a complete daze as I travelled home. I

couldn't remember any part of the long journey; I did it completely on autopilot.

*

It didn't take long for the police to come to see me.

They called at my house the next day and took me away for questioning after telling me I was under arrest for the murder of Tobias Barker. Jenny was shocked of course; I had avoided all her questions and hadn't told her anything about what had happened at Toby's house. I was taken to the local police station where I was questioned about the events of the previous day (I made sure that my lawyer was present) and I told them how Toby's death had been a complete accident. In spite of that, I was, a few hours later, charged with the manslaughter of Toby along with leaving the scene of a crime. I was refused bail before the trial and afterwards, as you already know, I ended up in prison after receiving a sentence of seven years.

And so here I am. It could be worse I suppose but not much. The newspapers had a field day of course: *Famous Crime Writer Jailed for Death of Best Friend*, and that sort of thing. Even though the vast majority of people had absolutely no idea who I was, I was still front-page news in all the tabloids, alongside the announcement of the latest contestants for *Strictly Come Dancing*. Ironically, I actually sold quite a few books on the strength of those headlines!

I don't get many visitors in prison. Jenny came on one occasion, mainly to sort out the divorce details and get my signature on some papers. My brother visited me a few times. Jess, my daughter, has never been to see me; she hasn't even responded to my letters. That makes me sad even though I can see her point. Even my agent and publisher have not been in touch. And what of my university friends – the ones I had hoped would be attending the reunion (the whole thing now aborted of course)? Well, none of them have ever contacted me and I don't suppose they ever will, or that I will see any of them again. Perhaps Toby was right in the end. Those friends we made all those years ago, including the few I'd kept in touch with, were not real friends but just casual acquaintances that we got to know by accident rather than design. Now they probably consider my actions to be beyond the pale and very likely believe my incarceration to be totally deserved!

Time goes by very slowly in prison. I try to get on with my writing, but for much of the time I sit here thinking about what has happened to me and how I could have done things differently. I look at the cell walls quite a lot, they could do with a lick of paint to be honest. I'd happily do it myself if they'd let me! It would be nice to have something active like that to do; I used to quite enjoy DIY. Exercise time is limited of course. A bit of walking around the prison exercise yard is the best that I can hope for. I avoid the prison gym and try not to speak to any of the other inmates as they all look pretty scary! The prison guards (I have not yet descended to calling them screws) are okay on the whole and are polite enough to me; I suppose because they don't see me as any sort of threat. By the way, I decided not to appeal against my conviction. My solicitor said that I could almost certainly get a reduction in my sentence, which she regarded as very harsh, but I said no after giving it a bit of thought. I guess in the end part of me considered that I actually deserved it all, not just for the death of Toby – which I maintain was a complete accident – but for the things he said about me, many of which I have decided were fundamentally correct. Looking back I think I would have to agree with his analysis that I was a reprehensible person on so many occasions in my life. I cheated, I deceived, I lied and I was totally blasé about other people's feelings. I looked after myself and disregarded others, even those I was supposedly very close to. If only Toby had said something earlier, much earlier, I may have tried to do something to change things. But in retrospect I probably would have just fallen out with him at an earlier stage.

And what of Maggie and Sarah, her daughter? How do I feel about them now? That's the saddest thing of all. Why I ever finished with Maggie in the first place is a mystery to me now. Looking back, our relationship seemed to have everything. More than anything it appears that she was in love with me, and how many times does that happen in a person's life? The fact that it was a struggle for me to remember my time with Maggie in any great detail is an indication that I was so full of myself; so focused on my own desires and needs that I ignored her love for me and failed to change my attitude towards her. I must have thought that someone better would come along and take her place. In that I was sadly mistaken.

And so now I am alone, completely alone in the world, where no one at all cares about me. And that, without doubt, is my real and, quite frankly, well-deserved punishment.

Chapter 28: *Time Has Come Today*

Sunday, June 1973

Stella had a hangover. It was the grandmother of all hangovers; it felt as though someone had hit her over the head with a large block of concrete. She had taken two aspirin tablets as soon as she had crept shakily from her bed and now sat in her room waiting for them to work, her head cradled in her hands. She listened to her heartbeat drumming unremittingly inside her skull.

She had no idea how she had managed to drive back from the party in the early hours of the morning. Stella had little memory of the journey apart from hitting a deer that ran out across the road in front of her car. It had happened too quickly for her to avoid, even if she had been completely sober. She had stopped her car and, with trepidation, slowly walked back the few yards to where the deer lay bleeding and twitching its life away at the side of the road. She looked into the glassy eye of the poor animal knowing there was nothing she could do. Sobbing, she staggered back to the car and drove to the university. She cried all the way.

Luckily Stella didn't meet anyone as she made her way back to her bedroom in The Tower. The lift was as slow and as noisily clanky as ever. By the time she reached her room she needed to dash to the toilet where she vomited copiously. She was there for a long time, on her knees, retching away until there was nothing else in her stomach to bring up.

Gradually she began to recall vaguely, sketchily, what she had said and done at the party. She moaned out loud as the very process of thinking seemed to make her head hurt even more. She remembered swallowing a couple of "uppers" that she'd got from Nick a few days before and then driving to the party. She remembered drinking a half bottle of vodka she had brought with her and then a large amount of wine. She remembered having sex with a man who was very tall. What was his name? Had she even asked him? She recalled her fight with Fiona and touched the scratches on her face, which still felt sore. She remembered shouting at someone angrily, pushing people away, and she remembered talking to Maggie and being rejected by her after she had told her the truth about Rob. She remembered crying about it all. She groaned at these memories and felt nauseous again; her stomach and throat still felt scoured and raw. She lay down on her bed again, closed her eyes and, against all the odds, fell soundly asleep.

*

Fiona woke up feeling disgruntled about something and then remembered what had happened the night before. The horrible things Stella had said and done! Fiona couldn't understand why she had been like that; they had always got along so well before. In their first year, when they shared a room, they used to lie in their respective beds and talk for hours on end about their hopes, dreams and plans for the future. They were good friends (or so Fiona had thought). And then out of the blue, last night, Stella had acted so awfully, taking Trevor to bed without a thought for her feelings!

Fiona had been hopeful about Trevor. He was handsome and tall (she liked tall men!). He was smartly turned out with clean jeans and a nice haircut. She would never have said it out loud but she didn't really like long hair on men as, in her view, they weren't capable of looking after it. Invariably it would end up greasy and dirty and smelling like Champion's stable at home. Trevor had short hair, well trimmed like a soldier's. Secretly she liked soldiers and hoped that she would meet one in the future, fall in love with him and get married. She fantasised about having men from his regiment (preferably a Guards' regiment) form a parade of honour as she and her handsome new husband came smiling out of the church.

She sighed. What should she do about Stella? Should she ignore her or go to her room and have it out with her? She would have to think long and hard about what to do. Instinctively Fiona felt that she should give Stella a good telling off and demand to know why she had acted that way when they were supposed to be friends. To be honest she would like to dig her nails into Stella's face again. She remembered doing that during their fight last night. It had felt satisfying and the memory made her smile. Now she had an uncontrollable desire to grab Stella round the neck and throttle her!

When should she confront her? Now? Later? Perhaps this evening? Yes, late in the day when there was no else about would be best. That would give her time to work out a plan of action and decide what she would say and do to Stella George in order to get her back for the things she had done last night. Fiona smiled.

*

Tina sat in the kitchen staring out of the window. She had just opened it to try and get rid of the rank smell that lingered there. One of the girls must have burnt something the day before and it still smelled smoky. The kitchen area was usually kept quite clean even though ten girls used it. They tended to wash up after themselves and even occasionally wiped down the surfaces. Tina was quite good at drawing up rotas for organising that sort of thing. She was glad that it was not like the state of the kitchens on the boys' floors. They were always unbelievably dirty with rubbish left lying around and sinks full of plates with congealed food stuck to them. She hated having to use Nick's kitchen in The Tower. And the toilet… that was just too awful to even think about!

Tina nibbled on some toast. Someone had used her last bit of butter from the fridge so she was forced to eat it dry. She didn't like it much but thought she had better get something in her stomach after the excesses of last night when she had ended up being extremely drunk. She hadn't been sick but it was a close run thing as she had lain in her bed with the room swirling and spiralling madly about her. After letting Stella drive off in her car last night, she, Liz, Althea and Fiona had gone back into the house and spent the rest of the evening dancing, drinking wine and gin and talking about what a cow Stella had been.

She didn't know where Stella was now – back in her room presumably – but actually she didn't care. Stella could go to hell as far as she was concerned.

She wished Nick was with her so she could hold him and be comforted by him. What would she do if Stella carried out her threat tomorrow to tell Nick about her thing with Rob? Nothing really had happened of course but Nick might not see it that way. He could be very jealous at times; she'd noticed that about him over the three years they had been together. And why the hell did Toby say anything to Stella anyway? Toby was supposed to be her friend so why had he been spreading rumours like that? Rumours – that's all they were. When Nick came back from his aunt's funeral on Monday she would meet him, whisk him straight off to her room where they would make love and have a nice cuddle and she would mention that she'd had a bit of a snog with Rob. No! That wouldn't do! Nick would then want to see Rob and have it out with him. She remembered the disagreement between Nick and Toby outside a pub last year. She couldn't remember what the argument was about now (some trivial boys' thing no doubt!) but Nick had been angry. She hadn't seen him like that before. He had murder in his eyes and would have given Toby a serious injury if others hadn't quickly restrained him. No, she couldn't tell him about Friday night with Rob. She would just have to hope that Stella didn't go through with her threat. It was stupid. Surely Stella would never do it? But she might! What should she do?

Tina stood up, dropped the last bit of her dry toast in the pedal bin, and went back to her room to lie down, play her *Let It Be* LP and think.

*

Liz lay in her bed going over the events of the night before. She felt lonely. She had hoped that she would have been spending the evening and night with Donald, but after kindly agreeing to drop her and Tina at the party he had to drive to his home near Ayr because his dad had been taken ill. Luckily they were all able to cadge a lift back to the campus in the van of someone she vaguely knew. She, Tina, Althea and Fiona had sat on the floor in the back, giggling drunkenly while they were tossed about from side to side.

Liz's head was sore. She wasn't really sure if it was from all the wine she had drunk or whether it was from the way she had bumped her head while being thrown around in the back of the van. She suspected it was the former. She remembered there was a bottle of gin as well. Where had that come from? She groaned as she lifted her head off the pillow. She should really get up and make some coffee and perhaps force down some food too. She lay back down again; her head didn't hurt so much when she kept still and horizontal. Perhaps she should bite the bullet? Get up and go for a walk to clear her head? Maybe later, when she felt a little better.

She thought about Stella's actions last night. What had brought that on? She had been so horrible to everyone. Over the years Liz had always quite admired Stella. She liked her independent attitude and her aloofness. But she hadn't liked the way Stella had treated her friends Fiona and Tina last night – Tina especially. Liz valued her friendship with Tina more than anything else. In the last few years their relationship had been a constant source of help, encouragement and stability for Liz. There was a time in the early part of her first year when she had believed that she wouldn't be able to cope with being at university. She missed her home; she had felt less than confident about the work she was expected to do and thought that she wasn't anywhere near as clever as all those around her. Tina had helped her come to grips with everything. She had been wonderful, a true friend! Liz's friends back at home in Manchester were nothing like Tina; she had been more reliable, more sensitive, more faithful than anyone Liz had ever met before. Under different circumstances they might even have… no, she mustn't think about that… it would drive her mad! She knew she would never be able to cope if she let those sorts of thoughts develop any further so she stifled them there and then. In any case, Tina and Nick were happy together – she could tell. After university they would almost certainly get married. They were meant to be together. And here was Stella trying to drive them apart for some reason. Liz had not seen the malicious side of Stella before but it was well in evidence last night. Why? Was she jealous of Tina? Did she fancy Nick herself? Fiona had told her last night about Stella stealing her boyfriend from under her nose and taking him upstairs to a bedroom. She had never seen Fiona look so upset and angry. She looked as though she could kill Stella, given half a chance.

Liz closed her eyes and thought hard, despite the pounding ache at the back of her eyes. She didn't want Tina to be affected by the actions of Stella. She would do anything to protect her friend – to protect Tina. But what could she do to help? She should do something. Nick would be back tomorrow and she knew that Tina was concerned about what Stella was planning to say to him. If Nick believed Stella and ended his relationship with Tina, Liz knew that it would totally devastate her friend. She would be so lost and upset and would probably never get over the rejection.

Liz decided what she was going to do. She would go to see Stella and talk to her. She would remain calm and considered. She would implore Stella not to say anything to Nick. She was sure that Stella would understand and be reasonable. She was probably already regretting the things she had said and done last night. When would be the best time to see Stella? It would probably be a good idea to wait until this evening; give Stella time to reflect upon her actions. Yes, that would be best. Liz would make Stella a nice mug of hot chocolate and take it to her in her room where she would almost certainly be spending most of the day, not wanting to bump into Fiona. Then she and Stella could have a quiet talk. Liz was sure that she could make Stella see sense. She would convince her how wrong it would be to break up Tina and Nick. Despite her headache Liz smiled and cuddled down into her blankets.

*

Angela freed her arm from under Toby. He had rolled on to it at some point during the night and it had gone totally numb. She lay there waiting for the inevitable and somewhat painful tingling sensation that would occur in her arm once its blood supply was restored to normal. Angela's night in the single bed had been uncomfortable, and she had woken up every time Toby turned over or snored loudly. In retrospect she had made a mistake letting him into her room last night but she had felt very lonely, not having seen anyone for the whole evening. Toby and the others had gone off to the party but she had felt too miserable to even think about going. She had fantasised that Chris would call round and patch things up but she soon realised that was a vain and forlorn hope rather than an actual expectation so she had stayed in her room all evening, feeling depressed, and read her book.

And then Toby had turned up. It was about three o'clock in the morning when he had banged on her door. She was asleep and the loud knocking had interrupted her dream where she was kissing Chris. She had let Toby in. He was very drunk. He immediately started to get undressed. She supposed she should have asked him to leave at that point but deep down she wanted some company and didn't want to go back to sleep and have hopeful but pointless dreams about Chris again. So she let Toby into her bed where they had, as far as she was concerned, some very unsatisfying sex. Toby smelled strongly of beer and fell asleep soon afterwards but not before he had told her about the party and how he had spent most of the night in the pub getting drunk with Rufus. He also told her about Rob and Maggie getting engaged. That was a big surprise. She was happy for them but cried a little after Toby had fallen asleep. It should have been her and Chris announcing their engagement this week.

Later that day Angela would receive some terrible news about Chris; news that would haunt her dreams for many years afterwards. She would be in a state of shock, unable to believe what Toby had returned to her room to tell her. She would then spend another night with him, being held tightly as she sobbed and sobbed, convinced that her own life had also come to an end.

*

Michael had got up early for his usual morning run around the campus perimeter road, after which he had jogged down to the university gym for a bit of a workout. He felt that he needed it. During the last few days he had consumed far more beer than he usually did and had even been drinking shorts of whisky, rum and gin. It had caused him to have an extremely painful headache and had also upset his stomach and digestive system in general. He felt heavy and bloated and was sure he had put on weight; something he wasn't happy with. So he had vowed that for the rest of the term, what was left of it, he would be much more sensible and only drink orange juice or lemonade. Alcohol didn't really suit him anyway, as his body constantly reminded him.

Thank goodness he hadn't been persuaded to go to last night's party. According to Maggie, who he had briefly met in The Square when coming back from the gym, the whole evening had been a totally fraught one, with lots of drinking and with people falling out left, right and centre. Maggie had seemed very pleased though. She had a positive aura about her and her eyes were sparkling. Michael was always glad to see her looking happy. Since being told by Rob to keep away, he hadn't seen very much of her. When he and Maggie did meet up it had to be done surreptitiously, which seemed strange although in some way it was oddly exciting.

After seeing Maggie in The Square he had bought a Sunday paper and taken it back to his room to have a relaxed read of it. He had just started to flick through the Observer magazine when someone knocked gently on his door. Springing up and opening it, he was surprised to see Maggie again, who furtively looked from side to side before coming inside and sitting down on the bed. She was obviously dying to tell him something.

'I couldn't tell you in The Square earlier – in the open. It didn't feel right,' she said, before telling Michael about Rob's proposal.

She told him how the evening had started off badly. Rob had seemed to ignore her before turning up late, having preferred to get pissed with Toby and Rufus in a pub. Then Stella had turned up unexpectedly and told her that Rob was no good for her and that they should be in a proper relationship instead of meeting up in bed on the nights that Rob was doing something else.

'But it was never really serious between you and Stella, was it?'

'No, definitely not. It was just a bit of fun really. Rob thinks it only happened the one time but Stella was saying that we ought to carry on and take it to the next level.'

'So what was her reaction when you said no?'

'Well, that's just it: she's threatened to go and see Rob and tell him about us and tell him that she loves me more than he does.'

'Ah, that doesn't sound good. How will Rob react if she tells him?'

'I'm not quite sure. Very badly probably. It could finish us.' At which point Maggie started to cry and Michael held her, pulling her close as she sobbed into his shoulder.

'Don't worry. I'll go and see Stella and ask her not to say anything to Rob.'

'Would you do that?' said Maggie, between sobs.

'Yes, of course.'

'Oh and best not mention to anyone about me and Rob getting engaged. Rob wants to make a proper announcement at some time.'

'Okay, will do. My lips are sealed forever or until you tell me otherwise.'

After that Maggie seemed to calm down a little and dried her eyes. The happiness she had displayed earlier had now dissipated a little. Michael hoped that it would soon come back. Above all else he wanted Maggie to be happy. The world seemed to be a much better place when she was smiling. He would keep his promise about not telling anyone about the engagement; he would not break his sacred promise to Maggie ever.

Maggie left his room soon afterwards, saying she needed to get back to Rob's and then go to see Jane in the medical centre. Michael sat down and thought. When would be the best time to confront Stella? He didn't know her that well and it would take him a while to pluck up the courage to see her. Later today would probably be the best time. Everyone else would doubtless go to one of the bars and start drinking again but he couldn't imagine Stella would want to do that. Yes, he would get her on her own and appeal to her to leave Maggie and Rob alone. He was determined that Maggie would be happy again, and removing the threat of Stella opening her mouth to Rob would definitely do that. Michael opened the *Observer* magazine again and smiled to himself. He knew what he had to do.

*

Althea had taken a walk to the café next to the university library and had ordered a black coffee. Today was going to be busy; she needed to sort out final arrangements for her trip back to the States. The coffee shop was quiet and virtually empty on this Sunday morning as she sat at a table near the window and checked over her various travel documents.

After satisfying herself that everything was in order she sat back, sipped her coffee and looked out at The

Square through the floor-to-ceiling windows. She had enjoyed her time at the University of the North over the past year and she would certainly miss the place. She had enjoyed the studying, the area, most of the people she had met and had also made a few good friends who she hoped she would be able to keep in touch with in the future. In a way it was a shame that the party last night had gone so badly wrong. She still could not believe the things Stella had said to her. Overt racism coming from someone she thought she knew and liked was a huge shock to her. Thankfully she was able to enjoy herself afterwards with Fiona, Tina and Liz; enjoy herself by getting very drunk in fact! She thought back to all the drink they had consumed during the evening (she had never tried gin before). The journey home had been crazy, all wedged in the back of some guy's box truck being bounced around and laughing! She had been very drunk and had woken up still wearing her clothes. Considering how much alcohol she had consumed last night she hadn't felt too bad this morning, although she didn't want to risk eating anything just yet, fearing that her insides might react badly to anything apart from coffee.

So what should her attitude be if she ran into Stella today? It was quite likely she would at some point as she lived in the room next to hers. Maybe she should knock on the door and confront her right away? Ask her to explain her comments from last night and why she had been such a jerk? Surely Stella couldn't have meant those things she had said? Then again it seemed as though she did. You can never really tell what people are thinking deep down and alcohol sometimes causes people to vocalise those deep-seated thoughts. If that was the case then she didn't really want anything to do with Stella ever again. But hey, everyone deserves a second chance, don't they? Althea found herself nodding and quickly looked around to see if anyone had noticed. Okay, that's what she would do. She would give Stella most of today to think about what she had said last night and then she would confront her later on; give her that second chance. Althea was ninety-five per cent sure that Stella would jump at the opportunity to recant her hurtful remarks and apologise profusely. No one could have too many friends, and Althea wasn't one to dismiss someone completely over a few nasty words uttered after they had got themselves very drunk. Althea felt happier now she had decided what to do. She finished her coffee and smiled.

*

Rufus had been very drunk by the time he had got back to the university. He had cadged a lift with someone he vaguely knew, and while they had driven along had carried on drinking from a bottle of single malt whisky he had found in the house. On arriving at the campus, not wanting to go to bed, he made his way instead to the room of a girl called Sheila who, like him, was a member of the International Marxist Collective and who he had ended up in bed with on two occasions the previous year. She had been all right, he remembered, if not quite as adventurous in the bedroom department as he would have wished. He would have preferred to have spent the night with June, the beautifully voluptuous barmaid in the pub where he had spent most of the evening, but that was not to be as in the end she refused to accompany him to the party due to her boyfriend not being very keen on the idea. How very bourgeois of her, Rufus had concluded.

Finding Sheila's room with some difficulty (he had to admit to himself that he felt very drunk indeed) he hammered on the locked door and in a loud voice demanded she let him in. The person in the next room, an American exchange student called Wayne, opened his door and shouted:

'Hey, cool it, buddy. People are trying to sleep!'

After a few more futile bangs on the door, as well as some entreaties to allow him to enter delivered in a stage whisper, Rufus decided that Sheila wasn't in and so made his rather frustrated way back to his own room. What a disappointment, he mused, as he fell into bed. Saturday night and no sex in sight was his last conscious thought before he fell into an immediate, deep and snore-provoking sleep.

In the morning, after a shower, he had wandered down to one of the campus refectories where he had coffee and a bacon sandwich. Luckily he didn't see any of his comrades from the IMC as he had told everyone in the group last year that he had become a militant vegetarian. He didn't have a hangover. The fact that he'd never suffered from that particular malady was something he was immensely proud of and made everyone else he knew aware of whenever possible. 'I have an iron constitution,' he would tell people. He remembered Sheila had been very impressed by that piece of information, as he had winked at her in a meaningful way before guiding her to his bedroom. Sheila wasn't the best-looking female in the IMC but she was certainly very willing and had a tidy body with breasts that, if not quite as outstanding as June's, were very passable indeed.

Brooding about his lack of sex the night before, Rufus, drunk again, would turn up at Sheila's room late that very evening and knock loudly on her door demanding she let him enter and making various offers that made him (in his own ultra-confident intoxicated mind) absolutely irresistible. To save time, his drunken brain had also advised him to take off all of his clothes so that he would be ready for action as soon as she opened the door. When Sheila eventually peered out of her room she was somewhat surprised to find a naked, already fully primed Rufus standing there. Keeping her face straight with great difficulty, Sheila had to explain that Jeff, the IMC's minute secretary, was already ensconced in her bed and so Rufus would have to go away. Rufus, somewhat downhearted and disappointed again, would slowly put his clothes back on and try to work out the best place on campus where he could find some late-night fun. He smiled as he decided what he would do.

*

On Saturday night Jack Barber had not been at the party but instead had spent the evening playing chess with a friend from the student mountaineering society. He had got up on Sunday morning and had gone for an early morning run, briefly acknowledging Michael as they passed each other on the university's perimeter road.

Later in the day he met up with another couple of friends from the university's rugby union club at a pub in a nearby village where he had a very nice Sunday lunch. It was just after finishing his roast beef and Yorkshire pudding that he heard the shocking news of the death of Chris Archer in a road accident that had taken place the previous night. He had known Chris via the rugby club and had often seen him and Angela together. He had noted how sad Angie had looked the other night during their end of exams drinking extravaganza. Maggie had told him that Chris and she had recently broken up and Angela, by all accounts, had been utterly devastated. God only knew what she must be feeling now. At the time Jack thought about going over to have a quiet word with Angela but he had noticed that Toby seemed to be taking on the role of comforter-in-chief fairly avidly.

JJ had admired Angie from afar for a while. In his opinion she was just the sort of person he would like to settle down with eventually: nice-looking with kind eyes, quiet but with hidden depths and obviously very intelligent. He felt sorry that she had broken up with Chris and couldn't begin to imagine what her state of mind must be like now that her recently estranged boyfriend had been tragically killed in some stupid road accident. Jack's rugby club friend knew only sketchy details about the tragedy but according to him, Chris had been hitching back from a party out in the wilds late at night when he had been hit by some kind of vehicle that had then driven off. Chris had been left, bleeding his life out, in a roadside ditch. It sounded like a very unpleasant death and for the rest of the day Jack felt sad and wondered if there was anything concrete he could do to make the situation any easier for Angela.

*

Jane was lying in her medical centre bed reading a book when Maggie dropped in to see her just after noon.

'I'm not allowed to get too close to you. The nurse was very clear about that,' said Maggie, pulling a sad face.

'It's lovely to see you,' said a smiling Jane. 'It gets so boring on my own.'

Maggie smiled in a consoling way. 'I've brought you

some grapes!' She placed a brown paper bag on Jane's bedside cabinet.

Both young women laughed at the grown-upness of the gesture. Maggie was glad she could brighten up Jane's day somewhat.

'We haven't had lunch yet. I'm starving. How did the party go last night?' said Jane, taking a grape from the bag and popping it into her mouth.

'Hmm, a bit mixed to tell the truth,' said Maggie who then went on to relate some of the events of the previous evening.

'How awful! Why was Stella acting like that?'

'No one knows really,' said Maggie, aware that she was probably blushing a little. She didn't know for certain if she had been the one to set off Stella's rampage at the party but she feared she might have been.

'Have you seen Stella today?'

'No. I don't think anyone has. She seems to be hiding away in her room. I'm going to talk to her later, hopefully.'

'Oh – have you heard the news about a student dying in a hit and run last night?'

'What? No! That's awful. Was it anyone we knew?'

'I don't know. One of the nurses was telling me about it earlier but she didn't know a name – just that it was a man. Terrible.'

'Yeah, absolutely tragic. I'll see if I can find out more and let you know later.'

'Thanks,' said Jane, as she put another grape into her

mouth.

'Something else happened last night,' said Maggie, switching from sad to happy as a big smile suddenly beamed across her face.

'Oh? What? Have a grape by the way.'

'Thanks,' said Maggie, reaching for one. 'It's some good news about Rob and me. We've got engaged!'

'What? Oh wow, that's great! Tell me about what happened.'

Maggie told Jane about what had taken place between herself and Rob. Jane was pleased that her friend was so animated and looked so happy. She'd had some reservations about Rob over the past few months. Some people she knew had alluded to the number of times he had supposedly cheated on Maggie but she had not said anything to her friend. She was pleased that everything now looked set fair between the two of them and hoped that it would be plain sailing for Maggie from now on.

'I'm really pleased for you, Maggie! Will I be invited to your wedding?' said Jane with a chuckle.

'Of course you will. How could I leave one of my best friends out? It may be some time before it happens though. We have to get next year in Cardiff sorted out and then get jobs so it'll be a couple of years at least.'

'Well I hope it all works out for you, but I'm going to miss you,' said Jane, who felt on the verge of tears.

Maggie smiled and, in spite of what she had been told by the nurse, stepped forward and held Jane's hand, squeezing it lovingly.

*

Nick sat with his mum and dad at the dining room table in the house he still described as home. He too had just enjoyed a plate of roast beef, Yorkshire pudding and roast potatoes and was now getting stuck into a bowl of apple crumble and custard. His mum was a good cook and every time he had one of her Sunday roast lunches he realised how much he missed her cooking.

Yesterday's funeral had gone pretty well, as much as any funeral can. His mum had been very upset of course; his Aunt Nora was her sister after all. Nick, however, would be glad to get back to the university; there was only a limited amount of time he could be at home before he became restless. He would have to spend some time at his mum and dad's in the summer but was hoping that he and Tina could go away on an extended holiday, somewhere in France preferably, before he started his postgraduate degree course at Oxford.

His mum especially had been so proud when he won his place at the University of the North and she was beside herself with excitement now that he was going to Oxford. He supposed that she had told everyone in the local area.

Tomorrow he would catch an early train and would

hopefully be back on campus by the afternoon. He was looking forward to getting his exam results next week although two lecturers in the chemistry department had already told him that he would almost certainly get a First. He felt as though he deserved one. He had worked really hard over the previous three years after very early on setting his mind on a First Class degree. Now he could relax a bit before starting at Oxford. He might even try some of the drugs that he'd been dealing over the past three years in order to supplement his grant; just the cannabis though, not any of the other harder sorts he'd sold – the Benzedrine pills and other amphetamines, and certainly not the LSD. He didn't want to mess too much with his own head. That sort of thing was okay for those who bought the stuff from him; they didn't seem to care too much about their own health so why should he worry about them? He had been a little uneasy earlier in the week when Stella George had buttonholed him in The Square and asked for a couple of bennies. She had said something then that had worried him slightly; something about what would happen if the police found out about his little "cottage industry" as she put it. He was so taken aback by her comment that he had said she could have the uppers for free – something he had never done before. Still, he was sure that Stella didn't actually mean anything by her throwaway comment. Hopefully not anyway.

He would be really pleased to see Tina again even though he'd only been away from her for a couple of days. His parents had half hinted that she should have attended the funeral too but he had decided that wouldn't have been a good idea. He'd already had to field lots of questions from various relatives about what he planned to do in the future. To throw Tina into the family mix at this stage would have been far too complicated. He would announce his engagement to Tina in his own good time once they were firmly placed on their respective career paths. Tina was set on getting a job in social work and he felt he had to support her ambition despite thinking that she was probably mad to want to spend her time dealing with the problems of dysfunctional families and various low-lives. She would certainly be good at it; he was in no doubt about that. She was very adept at the sympathy and the empathy aspects of life, but as far as he could see there was very little financial reward in social work and he would have much preferred it if Tina had gone into a career where the wages were much higher; she had the brains after all. In fact it was her intellect, as well as her undisputed beauty, that had attracted him to her in the first place. He saw himself in a few years' time with a top job in a major pharmaceutical company. He would be on a big salary and would no doubt be required to attend many social functions as well as entertain other high-ups, and having a beautiful wife who could hold her own in general discussions would be an undoubted plus point in his favour. Indeed, he saw his future career laid out neatly in front of him with plenty of money, a large house, membership to a local golf club, a couple of status-rich cars and eventually two or three children attending some prestigious private school. He hoped that Tina wouldn't baulk at fee-paying schools (she did have some curious left-wing ideas about equality and so-called social justice at times) but he was sure that when the time came to make such decisions she would see sense.

Nick leaned back in his chair, feeling nicely full and satisfied.

'Want some more crumble?' said his mother.

'No thanks, Mum, I'm totally stuffed. That was great. I've really missed your Sunday lunches.'

'Well, I hope you have been eating well. What's Tina's cooking like?' Nick's mum always looked and sounded slightly disparaging when she mentioned his girlfriend's name.

'It's very good, but of course she doesn't get much chance to cook while she's at university.'

'Hmm,' said his mum, as she stood up and began to clear the table.

Nick watched her stack the pudding bowls and collect cutlery. It occurred to him he'd never really thought about Tina's culinary skills before. Before they got engaged, he would have to ensure that she could in fact cook to an acceptable standard.

It was with that thought that Nick suddenly decided that he wouldn't wait until tomorrow to return to the campus but instead would catch a train this afternoon, aiming to be back at university by early evening. It would also give him a chance to have a word with Stella George and ask her what she meant by her police comment the other day. *Best to be on the safe side*, he thought.

'Dad,' he said to his rather sleepy-looking father who was sitting on the opposite side of the dining table. 'Could you give me a lift to the station this afternoon?'

*

Toby sat in Grasmere Bar with a half-finished pint of bitter on the table in front of him. He looked into the distance as he munched on the pork pie he'd bought from the only campus grocery shop that stayed open on a Sunday. Normally he liked to seek out someone he knew at lunchtime and sit and have a natter and a few convivial pints with them. However, on this day he wanted to be on his own and think things through. Soon, perhaps after he'd had another pint or two, he would have to go and see Angela and break some very bad news to her. He dreaded having to do it. He was quite fond of Angela and didn't want to upset her, but upset her he would have to. It was only fair. He had no idea how she would react. Would she push him away and retreat into her shell? Or would she cling to him even though he had been the harbinger of dreadful news? He hoped it would be the latter.

Yes, he definitely liked Angela; he had enjoyed last

night in bed with her (at least the parts he could remember). He hoped that he would be able to spend tonight with her too although that was wholly dependent on how she greeted the terrible news he would soon have to impart to her; the news that a boyfriend she'd been with for three years up until a few days ago had been killed in a hit-and-run road accident, having been seemingly run over by a car as he tried to hitch home from last night's party. Toby hadn't seen Chris at the party but that wasn't surprising as he hadn't actually been at the house for most of the time, preferring to sit in the village pub with Rufus and get absolutely legless. They'd walked up to the party after the pub closed and had spent the rest of the evening topping up on drink and trying to chat up various girls. He had seen a few other people he knew but apart from Rob, Rufus and some anonymous females, he hadn't really spoken to anyone at length.

But today, on his way to the bar (he had told Angela that he had to meet with someone about a job reference he needed), he'd bumped into one of his acquaintances who'd told him the news that Chris, a mutual friend, had been killed in a road accident in the early hours. Police were searching for the driver who had not stopped but they had little to go on, as there didn't appear to be any witnesses to the incident.

Toby finished his beer and half considered getting another before shrugging and leaving the bar. On a whim he decided to walk through the car park on the way back to Angela's room in The Tower. He had heard about how Stella had decided to drive off in her car, despite being hardly capable of walking in a straight line and so wanted to check out the state of her car just to set his mind at rest.

After a brief search he found Stella's gold-coloured Hillman Avenger. It was last year's model, no doubt bought for her by her mother and father to ensure that she wouldn't be reliant on public transport as most of her fellow students would be. Toby walked round to the front of the car and examined its passenger side wing. There were the unmistakable signs that the car had been involved in a recent accident. The dent in the bodywork was not all that obvious at first but the smear of blood, still sticky when he touched it, provided all the proof he needed that Stella had hit someone last evening. Toby looked up and tried to work out the best way to use this item of damning evidence to his advantage. In spite of everything that had happened recently he couldn't help smiling.

*

Maggie was desperate for some tea. Her throat felt dried out and sandpaper-rough from all the cigarettes she had smoked the night before and her head felt delicate from the sustained bout of drinking. She had squeezed out of Rob's bed, slipped on her knickers and put on his t-shirt, both of which were lying on the floor where they had left them, and padded to the kitchen in her bare feet. She noticed with distaste how grubby and sticky the floor felt. She looked in the fridge and saw that the carton of milk she had put in there yesterday had already disappeared. She puffed out her cheek in annoyance; she would have to pop out to the campus shop to get some. She went back to Rob's room. She smiled at him, now sprawled across the single bed snoring peacefully, and slipped on her jeans and shoes.

Walking to the shop she met Michael coming back from the gym. She briefly mentioned the party of the previous evening and told him that she was only out of bed to fetch some milk for her tea. She promised to call round to see him later once she felt more human.

Back in the kitchen she made tea for herself and Rob and half wondered whether she should wash up some of the dirty plates and cutlery that lay festering in the sink. She shrugged and decided it wasn't her job, but would certainly suggest to Rob that it was something he might want to do at some point during the day. He would almost certainly say he was far too busy to do such things. She smiled at the thought – she knew him so well.

While she was waiting for the tea to brew (she liked it strong) she looked out of the smudged and dirty windows at the misty scene out towards the town of Flitborough and the nearby lake. The mist would soon burn off; it was going to be a warm day. Perhaps she and Rob could go for a walk later and begin to make some plans for the future now that he had asked her to marry him. She still felt excited and had done right from the moment she had woken up wedged against the wall by Rob's body. Last night had started badly certainly, but by the end of the evening she had felt so happy she could have burst. She smiled and looked at her ring that was now officially her engagement ring. Then she frowned. What if Stella tried to see Rob today to tell him that she was in love with her? What could she do? How could she stop her? After her cup of tea she would go and see Michael and ask him what he thought about the situation. He would know what to do; he normally did. After that she would need to go and see Jane in the medical centre. She would take her some grapes; Jane would find that quite funny. Maggie smiled to herself at the thought.

She took the teabags out of the cups and dropped them into the swing bin, which was full of empty beer cans and bottles. She added milk to the two cups as well as some sugar (two for Rob, one for her) and carefully carried them back to Rob's room. As she did so she thought of the ways she could persuade Rob to go for a nice long walk in the countryside instead of sitting in a bar all day drinking beer. However, she didn't feel too confident about her chances of achieving that particular objective.

*

Rob woke up to Maggie shaking him.

'I've made you a nice cup of tea,' she said, as Rob sat up and rubbed his eyes to make them less bleary.

'Oh, thanks,' he said.

Maggie sat down on the bed. She reached over to Rob and smoothed down some of his hair that was sticking up on the back of his head. Rob took a large slurp of his tea.

'That's really good,' he said.

'I thought it might be nice to go for a bit of a walk today – get some fresh air,' said Maggie.

'What? Hmm, yeah, that sounds good. I've just got a few *Ariel* jobs to do first. I need to make sure everything's in order and then I said I'd meet up with Dave Horner who's taking over as editor next year.'

'Where are you meeting him?'

'We said we'd see each other at twelve-thirty in Grasmere Bar. Why?'

'Just asking,' said Maggie. 'Try not to drink too much and we can go for our walk after you've spoken to him.'

'Okay, I'll make a big effort not to but I will need a "hair-of-the-dog". After last night I've got a bit of a hangover to be honest.'

Maggie nodded and then smiled. 'It was so lovely when you proposed last night,' she said. Maggie again looked at her ring, now on her wedding finger, and touched it gently.

'Oh, yeah – it was okay,' said Rob, drinking some

more of his tea and blushing slightly.

'Only okay! I think it merits a few better words than okay,' said Maggie.

Rob drank the rest of his tea before putting the mug down and reaching out to Maggie, pulling her back to him so she lay on top of him in the bed.

'I think I can do better than words,' he said, kissing her and sliding his hand under her t-shirt.

Maggie sighed with pleasure.

Rob's mind was in turmoil. He'd had some pretty alarming dreams last night and was vaguely hoping that Maggie might have forgotten about what he had said outside the pub. Some hope! She was obviously obsessed by the idea of their engagement. *Why did I say it*? He involuntarily groaned as he undid Maggie's jeans and started to slide them down, hoping that she thought it was a sign of passion rather than regret. *How the hell am I going to get out of this situation?* he thought, as he rolled over on top of her.

*

Stella stayed in her room for most of the day, only once sneaking out to go to the toilet, hoping that she wouldn't be seen by anyone else. By the afternoon she was hungry, her stomach feeling empty and rumbling, so she devoured most of the packet of Jaffa Cakes she had been keeping for when Maggie next came round. Maggie had said that she really loved them.

Stella decided, during the course of the long hours lying on her bed or gazing out of the window, that she would stay in her room until the evening, quickly pack her suitcase and then drive to her parents' home in Hampshire. She would have to leave a lot of stuff behind, most of her books for example, but that was better than bumping into anyone she knew as she ferried boxes from her room to her car, having to keep apologising for her words and actions last night. She would miss Maggie more than anything else she could imagine but had finally decided that leaving today would be the least worst thing she could do.

She had briefly considered but then dismissed the idea of going round and talking to all those she'd had dealings with the night before (those she could recall in any case). She could say she was sorry for the things she had said and done and hope that they forgave her. But what about Maggie? What could she say to her that would put matters right again? She was in love with Maggie and she wanted everyone to know it but just saying that would put most people against her. And what about Fiona? It was unlikely that she would ever forgive her for what had happened at the party. Fiona simply wasn't the sort to do that; she would definitely want her pound of flesh and they might end up coming to blows again.

Early in the afternoon, while she lay on her bed, someone knocked on Stella's door. Surprised, she sat up and momentarily thought about seeing who it was but then rejected the idea. She still couldn't face anyone. She decided that it was probably Althea Stokes whose room was next to hers. She couldn't remember exactly what she'd said to Althea, who was someone she had always liked and admired. Whatever it was she doubted it would have been anything too pleasant. Last night she had been obsessed with Maggie and nothing else seemed to have any importance at all. If she couldn't have Maggie, quite frankly, she wasn't bothered about anything or anyone else.

Maggie! Should she go and see her now and bite the bullet? Stella got up from her bed and walked toward the door. She had her hand on the door handle before withdrawing it and going back to her bed and perching on the end of it. Maggie would probably be with Rob. Would she have the nerve if both were together to then declare her love for Maggie and say that she didn't think she could live without her? Maggie would probably never forgive her if she said that in front of Rob. Stella lay down again and quietly sobbed. She would have liked to cry out, to howl loudly at how fate had treated her so unfairly. The more she thought about life without Maggie the more despairing she felt. When she drove away from the campus later on she would never see Maggie again, and she doubted she would ever be able to get over the loss. She would go home to her parents and she would have to pretend that everything was perfectly fine and that she was happily looking forward to the future. Her parents would no doubt be intent on fixing her up with some young, eligible army officer from the Grenadier Guards or some other elite regiment her father had close connections to in Aldershot. She would hate every minute of the plans they would carefully lay out for her. How could she tell her mother and father that the last thing she wanted was some vacuous, over-privileged, self-satisfied young man drooling over her? How could she tell them that all she wanted was Maggie and no one else? And how could she tell them that Maggie didn't want her and therefore her life, for all intents and purposes, was now over? Stella sobbed and sobbed and eventually fell asleep again.

When she awoke, she got up slowly from her bed and went over to the sink. She looked at her reflection in the mirror. Her face looked blotchy and red; the scratches on her face were still bright pink. It was time to go, she decided.

She took down her suitcase from on top of the wardrobe and quickly threw some of her clothes into it. She fitted as many into the case as possible before slamming it shut. She would have to leave most of her winter clothes behind including the black maxi-length coat that she loved, but she only wanted to make the one journey to her car. Almost as an afterthought she grabbed the chunky knit jumper that was also hanging up in the wardrobe and slung it over her shoulder. It was already gone eight o'clock in the evening and she might need it once the sun had gone down.

She gently opened her door and peered out into the corridor. No one about; they'd probably all be in one of the campus bars by now. She locked her door. She would have to send in her keys by post as she wasn't going to risk bumping into anyone by going over to the university reception desk. She pressed the button for the lift and luckily, when it opened after much clanking and squeaking, there was no one in it. Stella breathed a sigh of relief and pressed the "G" button. The lobby at the foot of The Tower was deserted and Stella was again pleased that she didn't have to say anything to anyone about where she was going with her suitcase.

At her car she unlocked the boot and put her case into it. She slipped on her jumper; already there was a bit of an unseasonable chill in the air and the heater didn't work very well, despite it being a relatively new car. She looked up at the university accommodation block; she would miss it. A small tear ran down her cheek. She was just about to open the car door when she heard a voice from behind calling her name. It was a voice she recognised.

Chapter 29: *Walk on the Wild Side*

Today.

As you know, I didn't mean to kill Toby; it was a complete accident. Obviously if I had my time over again I wouldn't have pushed him with such force that he fell backwards and struck his head against the sharp corner of his fireplace. The blow apparently caused an acute subdural hematoma in his brain and poor Toby would have died later that evening while still lying unattended on the floor of his sitting room. His cleaner discovered his body early the following day.

I totally regret what happened, of course, despite all the things he had said to me that day. He was, after all, my oldest friend. Occasionally, here in my prison cell, I find myself smiling at the things he used to say, his jokes and his "interesting facts". He once explained to me the origin of the term "red herring" which I, as a member of the crime writing fraternity found particularly interesting. Red herrings, he had informed me, were fish smoked in a special way which were not only actually a deep red colour but were also so strongly smelling that criminals being pursued would sometimes drop them on the ground in order to confuse any dogs that were being used to track them.

I certainly miss going with him to football and cricket matches. It used to be great fun in a quiet, contemplative, boozy sort of way. The annoying thing is that if I hadn't pushed Toby he would probably have died soon anyway; he hadn't looked after himself at all and a heart attack or stroke couldn't have been too far away. But in the end, it was all down to me – it was my fault – and I can't escape that. So here I am in my cell, which I also can't escape from. Life is a real bugger at times, isn't it?

I remember I once went out with a girl because I simply adored the smell of her (I was at school in the sixth form at the time). She seemed to smell deliciously of marzipan, roses and cut grass in the rain all at the same time. I was completely smitten and loved to sit next to her and luxuriate in her wonderful aroma. And then one day I was walking though the ground floor of a big department store looking for an up escalator (you know the sort of place where they have lots of counters selling all kinds of make-up and perfumes). Suddenly I smelled her and turned around expecting to see her standing right behind me. And then I realised the scent was coming from one of the perfumes that was being sprayed onto some woman's hand. I forget what the perfume was called now; no doubt it would have had some sort of outlandish name. That was when I realised that people weren't always exactly what they seemed. My young, naïve and very unworldly self had been head-over-heels attracted to a person because of the artificial scent she had sprayed on herself! It was an obvious and salutary lesson that very belatedly taught me not to rely on such superficialities. Well, you might be thinking, that lesson just reflected my general gullibility and lack of knowledge at the time. That's true of course but it did mean that, like the rock group The Who, I was never fooled again; everything I did subsequently (most things anyway) I tried to do with great deliberation and planning. And look where it got me!

Well, as I come to the final section of my brief memoir, I can now reflect on why I decided to work on it in the first place. The simple answer is that I need to write every day to keep some semblance of sanity, as writing is, for me I suppose, a therapy as well as a compulsion. Also, in all honesty, it's the only thing I have been able to think about since entering the depressing portals of HMP Dartmoor – a category C prison (not exactly the move to the South West of England I had envisaged during my travels around the country!). It was of course inevitable that one day I would write my autobiography, my ego, I would be the first to admit, being about the size of a small planet. But I didn't ever think I would be doing so in such circumstances. My single occupancy cell in the prison's

D-wing is classed as solitary confinement, which I asked to be put in as soon as I arrived at this hell on earth. The thought of having to share a prison cell with one or maybe even two murderous criminal low-lifes was my main area of concern when I was on my way to the prison after being sentenced. I simply requested to be put on my own away from the other prisoners because I felt that my life would be in danger otherwise. As a writer of crime fiction who was well aware of all the various strategies used by criminals, and as a friend of many police officers who had provided me with all sorts of help and advice over the years, I didn't think the other inmates would look too favourably on me. Surprisingly, the prison authorities didn't ask too many questions and seemed quite happy to stick me in a cell on my own where I could get on with my writing. I'm even allowed to have a laptop, albeit one not connected to the Internet. It took me an awful lot of pleading about the state of my mental health to actually get it.

The unfortunate things that would eventually lead me to this pretty pass all happened so many years ago. As someone once said (I think it was Eugene O'Neill, but like I said I have no Internet to check facts these days): "there is no present or future – only the past, happening over and over again". It just seems so stupid and unfair that I could be found guilty of something that was a complete accident, something that was caused by a train of events that began so long ago when Toby and I were at university. I suppose if I had done things differently back in 1973 the future might not have turned out as it did. Who knows? But I was a different person back then – *literally* a different person to the one I now am. Toby once told me that the cells of the human body are completely replaced every seven years or so, the result being that no one is physically the same as they were in the past. But it's a lame argument I know. We are all victims of our past: Toby, Maggie, me, along with the rest of my friends and acquaintances from those days, a truth from which there is no escape. I suppose the ultimate lesson I have learned from all of this is that, in the end, life will always end up crushing you like an empty beer can. As I have already said, Jenny had started divorce proceedings while the trial was still going on, which was something I found quite hurtful to tell you the truth. She might have given me the benefit of the doubt and at least waited until I was actually found guilty. C'est la vie!

And what of Stella? How did she come to die? I imagine by now you have decided that it definitely wasn't suicide that carried the beautiful but misguided Stella to her early grave. So who was responsible? Who was the person that pushed Stella George off the kitchen balcony back in 1973? I did eventually work it all out and I could tell you straight off but it would be more fun to let you find out in another way. After all, one cannot have too much enjoyment in life (especially if you are the inmate of one of Her Majesty's prisons!). Maybe if my literary creation – the brilliant detective Sheldon

Heath – was a real person he would have been able to point his finger at the killer at a much earlier point, but unfortunately he is just a figment of my imagination. Shame really; if he were real I would have someone to commiserate with but I haven't, as yet, begun to have conversations with imaginary people sitting with me in my cell!

Right, let's have that bit of fun then, shall we? After all, I've got nothing better to do. Let my famous fictional character, Detective Chief Inspector Sheldon Heath, with his vast array of massive grey cells, explain it all to you. I'll do it in my usual style, the way all of my crime novels climax (and pretty much everyone else's too) by having the brilliant solver of criminal puzzles confront all of the suspects in the crucial, final denouement.

Let's imagine that he has gathered them together at their university reunion (a reunion that never happened in real life of course). In my slightly fevered imagination the reunion would not have taken place in one of the boringly sparse utilitarian rooms inside the functional and uninspiring sixties' buildings of the University of the North but rather in the plush, polished leather and Gothic Revival surroundings of a library in one of the ancient colleges of Oxford University. That way, I believe, the pictures in your mind's eye will be so much better.

Chapter 30: *Mama Weer All Crazee Now*

Never

Detective Chief Inspector Sheldon Heath sucked on his pipe; a cloud of fragrant tobacco smoke wafted into the air around him. He looked around at those present. His craggy yet handsome features were set in a mask of concentration, and despite the warmth of the oak-panelled room that was sustained by a large roaring log fire in the hearth, he still wore his fedora pulled down, slightly obscuring his left eye; his battered old raincoat, belted in the middle. (Yes, I know the inspector's appearance is something of a Chandleresque cliché but he is *my* character and that's how he's dressed in all of my stories. He also bears a remarkably strong facial resemblance to myself, of course!).

Gathered together in the library were the suspects in the case, all seated around the room on well-worn leather sofas or richly upholstered armchairs. All those present had dealings with the dead woman, Stella George, some fifty years ago during the events leading

304

up to her death, which until now had been classed as a straightforward suicide. Sheldon Heath revelled in solving these mysterious "cold cases"; those incidents that had seemingly baffled police officers at the time. Now it was once again his opportunity to demonstrate his great insight, perceptiveness and utter genius when it came to investigating and solving such crimes.

The inscrutable Scotland Yard detective made a point of staring at each individual in the room in turn, his piercing pale blue eyes seeming to reach into their very souls in order to pluck out the truth. One by one each of the well-dressed and now elderly people in the room were made to feel guiltily uncomfortable by DCI Heath's unremitting stare. All of the potential suspects found themselves looking around with feigned interest at the bookshelves in the room, crowded as they were with agéd leather-bound volumes, or peering at their feet, fervently studying their own shoes.

Chief Inspector Heath put his pipe down on the desk he had chosen to lean against to deliver his address. (Yes, I know that smoking indoors is not allowed anymore but in the universe in which this story takes place it still is.)

Sheldon Heath's voice was deep and mellifluous and tinged with a world-weariness borne out of the many murder investigations he had conducted over the years. But his delivery also had an edge to it that seemed to indicate to all those present that here was someone who was singularly determined to discover the truth and could be ignored only at their peril. After many hours investigating the death of Stella George he was now ready to reveal what had happened all those years ago.

Sheldon Heath looked intently at Fiona, who was sat bolt upright on a red leather wingback chair.

'Mrs Fiona Oakman, at the time of Stella George's death you were one of her many friends at the University of the North.'

Uncharacteristically Fiona seemed to visibly wither, like a piece of plastic melting on a bonfire, as the detective pointed at her with his trusty pipe (which he'd picked up again).

'At one time you shared a university study/bedroom with Miss George but because of an incident that happened on the day before her death you had fallen out with her and could no longer even bring yourself to converse with her.'

Fiona gave an almost imperceptible nod.

'According to my own investigations,' continued the detective, 'along with those made by police officers in 1973, you were at the party at a house in the village of Burnside, a house rented at the time by one of the lecturers at the university. Indeed, many of those individuals currently in this room also attended that same party.'

Fiona nodded, warily this time.

'It was at this particular party that Stella George joined you and a male friend by the name of Trevor Cook in the cellar of the house and started dancing with you both. Shortly afterwards, according to many witnesses at the time, a fight broke out between yourself and Miss George after which she disappeared with Mr Cook into one of the upstairs bedrooms.'

Under the inspector's glare Fiona looked somewhat abashed and blushed a little at the memory of something that had happened so long ago. She nodded again.

'According to witnesses you were furious at the way Stella George had humiliated you and vowed to punish her for what she had done. Is that correct?'

Fiona thought carefully before nodding again.

'Around the time of Miss George's death,' continued Inspector Heath, 'you were in your room of the tower block that stands at one of the corners of Queen's Plaza, known colloquially as The Square.'

Fiona nodded again, and against all of her natural instincts remained as silent as a snake carefully shedding its skin.

'It is therefore obvious that you had the opportunity to kill Miss George as you were in the immediate vicinity when the unfortunate young woman was pushed to her death from the balcony of the tower block where you both resided. You were, and still are might I say, tall and strong, and used to handling horses at your parents' stables. This would have enabled you to easily lift the slightly built Miss George over the low wall of the balcony and cause her to fall to her death below. But what would have been your motive? Would you have really been so angered by a simple, if somewhat traumatic, falling out between yourself and Miss George? That is something we will answer during the course of this evening, Mrs Oakman.'

Sheldon Heath's piercing gaze now fell on Rufus Munro who momentarily looked shaken by the experience of being stared at by the detective, before regaining his poise and composure and staring back at the Scotland Yard inspector. As a long-standing member of the House of Commons, and latterly of the House of Lords, he was not used to being easily intimidated by a mere plebeian law officer. As Inspector Heath began to speak Munro straightened his back and set his jowly jaw in what he hoped would give him a determined and Churchillian look.

'Moving on to you, Lord Munro of Camden,' began Sheldon Heath. 'It seems you were not able to remember exactly what you were doing on the night Stella George died.'

Rufus Munro began to speak in the same pompous manner he always adopted when addressing his fellow peers in the House of Lords, a place where he was used to being listened to on a very regular basis as an important party grandee, a doyen of New Labour and a former cabinet minister in the Blair Government. On this occasion, however, Inspector Heath simply held up his right hand, narrowed his eyes and by his sheer and formidable presence stopped His Lordship from uttering anything more than a single, saliva-soaked syllable.

'My investigations have revealed,' continued the

inspector, 'that on the evening in question you spent a great deal of time in one of the university bars, becoming extremely inebriated – for the second time in twenty-four hours it seems – before going to the room of a female student who you then proceeded to sexually harass in a particularly persistent manner.'

In response, His Lordship Rufus Munro, face purple with anger, spluttered a few words – "outrageous"; "intolerable" – but was soon returned to silence by the inspector who simply raised his hand again. To those present it seemed that DCI Sheldon Heath could have stopped a runaway train simply by holding up his hand and looking totally determined that he was going to carry out his task and not be interrupted by a mere rogue locomotive hurtling towards him.

'Just before the time that Stella George met her untimely death you were attempting, unsuccessfully I might add, to secure the sexual favours of a certain young woman by banging loudly on her bedroom door, taking off all of your clothes, brandishing your genitalia and shouting at the top of your voice, and I quote: "Look at what a big boy Comrade Rufus is!". No doubt, Lord Munro, when this story emerges, your credibility in the chamber of the House of Lords may take something of a nosedive.'

Despite the serious atmosphere in the library a number of its occupants smiled broadly for a moment while looking at the bright red face of Rufus Munro who now could not even splutter his objections.

'Of course,' continued Sheldon Heath, 'a sexual indiscretion some fifty years ago might today be seen as irrelevant and is liable to be overlooked by most. But what about murder? Would people, and the media in particular, be quite as understanding if it were discovered that you were responsible for the murder of an innocent young lady back in 1973? I think not. Did you, Lord Munro, having been unsuccessful in gaining access to the room of a young woman you were demanding to have sex with, put your clothes back on, walk to the university's tower block, go up to the tenth floor, demand sex from Miss George and then, when she refused, in your drunken state follow her to the kitchen balcony and callously throw her to her cruel death? We shall soon find out this evening, one way or the other.'

Heath's steely gaze now moved from the red face of Rufus Munro and shifted to Tina and Nick Rogers. 'And now on to you Mr and Mrs Rogers.'

Inspector Heath's icy stare transfixed Tina and Nick who, as a result, slid a little nearer each other on the large Chesterfield settee.

'You were a loving couple more or less right from the start of your university time together; a model couple in many ways, you have stayed together and have now been happily married for almost fifty years. But is that the complete picture? Were there hidden tensions below the surface of your relationship when you were at university that might have caused either of you to take the life of Stella George? I strongly believe there may have been. Mr Rogers says he was not on the campus when the death of Miss George took place, only arriving back at the university the following afternoon. But do we know that for a fact? Is it possible that he returned secretly, at an earlier time, in order to confront Miss George about something she had been threatening to tell the authorities?'

Nick Rogers looked impassive and shook his head as the inspector continued.

'Did the fact that you were a supplier of various illicit narcotic substances throughout your time at the University of the North have anything to do with the death of Miss George? Had she threatened to expose your drug dealing to the police and did this lead directly to her death?'

Nick's face had suddenly turned ashen as Inspector Heath finished talking and stared unwaveringly at him.

'And what about you Mrs Rogers? You were privy to the accusations that Miss George had been spreading around your friendship group regarding yourself and Mr Robert Cross. Is it possible that you were so incensed by what Stella George had been saying, and so worried that her accusations would get back to your then boyfriend, Mr Rogers, that you sought out Miss George? And seeing her standing on the balcony, marched up to her and, perhaps without saying a single word, grabbed her and in your anger summoned up the strength to hoist her off the balcony and onto the ground many feet below?'

Tina looked wide-eyed with shock and close to tears,

shaking her head vehemently before quickly looking around at the others in the room. 'No, no, I didn't do that! I couldn't do a thing like that! It wasn't me!'

Inspector Heath continued to stare at her, a little smile briefly playing across his mouth and eyes, before he transferred his gaze to Liz, who sat on the same sofa as Nick and Tina.

'Mrs Hutton, or Miss Elizabeth Pilling, as you were back in 1973, you had been at the same party as many of the others on that Saturday evening,' said DCI Heath.

'Yes,' said Liz, a worried look in her eyes.

'You witnessed some of the events unfold on that fateful evening.'

'Yes,' repeated Liz.

'What were your feelings towards Miss George at that time?'

'Er... well... she, er, Stella, from what I can remember, seemed to be very drunk – out of control really. Fiona and Althea both told me how they had been abused by her; one physically the other verbally.'

'What about her attitude to your friend, Tina?'

'Some of the things that Stella said had... upset her.'

'What things?'

'Umm... I find it difficult to remember everything that was said. It was so long ago.'

'Just in general then. Why were you so concerned about Mrs Rogers – Tina?'

Liz hesitated before she spoke again. She looked at Tina who sat next to her on the Chesterfield. 'I was

312

concerned about what Stella might say about Tina and Nick – Mr Rogers.'

'And what did you think Stella might say about them?'

'Well it's already been said, hasn't it? Tina was worried that Stella would tell Nick that she'd had a thing with Rob and also that she would inform the police that Nick had been… er, dealing drugs.'

'What do you think might have happened had Stella said these things about Tina, Nick and Robert Cross?'

'Well, I think it would have finished Tina and Nick's relationship. Tina would have been so upset. She was my best friend. I was worried that it would have made her unhappy for the rest of her life.'

'So what did you do to stop that happening?'

'I went to Stella's room and I knocked on the door. I waited but she didn't open it. I knew she was in there. I waited for quite a time before I went away.'

'Did you see her later?'

'Yes, I saw her in the car park later that day. She was about to get into her car and drive off. I spoke to her – I was nice to her – I suggested we went for a coffee. She hesitated at first but then agreed. She seemed sad. I thought I could get her to see Tina and apologise – put her mind at rest. She thought about it but then said that it would be best if she just left and didn't see anyone ever again.'

'So she didn't threaten to talk to Mr Rogers about Tina's relationship with Mr Cross?'

'At first she didn't, but then she said something about writing letters to everyone to explain why she had acted the way she did on the night before.'

'And those letters might have caused problems for a number of those individuals present here today?'

'I suppose so. Yes, they definitely would.'

'Did she leave after speaking to you?'

'I thought she would but later on I heard that she had gone to see Maggie again.'

The inspector suddenly switched his gaze to Maggie. 'And so we come to you, Miss Margaret Harman.'

(Yes, that's right! I have temporarily resurrected Maggie for this dramatic denouement.) DCI Heath looked accusingly at Maggie who sat up with her large eyes wide open, seemingly transfixed by the policeman's unwavering, basilisk glare. (By the way, in my mind's eye, as I write these words, I am imagining that Maggie looked exactly like she did on the last day I saw her back in June 1973. It was the only way I could actually visualise her.)

'Miss Harman,' continued Inspector Heath. 'According to a number of witnesses you had an argument with your then boyfriend, the aforesaid Robert Cross, at the previously mentioned party held on the Saturday evening, the day before the untimely death of Miss George.'

A miserable looking Maggie nodded resignedly.

'Later that evening it appears you managed to patch things up with Mr Cross, to the extent that the pair of you agreed to get engaged to be married.'

Maggie nodded and looked down at the ring on her finger. (Yes, I know the last time I mentioned the ring it was in my desk drawer in my study but this is fiction, remember, where all things are possible.)

'According to my investigations, Miss Harman, you were at the time, and again shortly afterwards, extremely worried that Stella George was ready to announce to the world at large that you and she had been involved in an on-going physical, and presumably loving, relationship unbeknown to your erstwhile fiancé. This, if it had happened, would undoubtedly have complicated your relationship with Mr Cross, and would have led, almost certainly, to its irrevocable breakdown.'

Maggie nodded and opened her mouth to say something before thinking better of it.

Inspector Heath continued. 'Did you then, as a result of what Miss George might have said to Mr Cross, meet with her at some point during the day and plead with her not to inform him that you and she had been lovers? When she steadfastly refused you returned late in the evening with murderous intent and, finding her standing on the kitchen balcony, grab her and unceremoniously pitched her off the balcony to her death?'

Maggie at this point shook her head, whispering, 'No,' under her breath as she wiped away a tear or two.

Inspector Heath continued to stare at her for a few long seconds as if trying to read her innermost thoughts, before turning to look at Michael who was sitting close to Maggie.

'Michael Key,' began the inspector, 'you were a close friend of Miss Harman's?'

Michael nodded.

'You were convinced that if Stella George confronted Mr Cross with the information that she and Miss Harman were lovers it would lead to Maggie being made unhappy in the extreme. As her friend – her special friend one might say – that was something that above all you did not want to happen?'

Michael nodded again and whispered, 'Yes.'

'As a result of this, Mr Key, you sought out Miss George and spoke to her. Can you tell me what occurred when you did?'

Michael gave a sigh and looked around the room. He realised that all eyes were now on him. 'I saw Stella in the coffee shop talking to Liz. I waited across The Square until Stella left and then followed her to the car park where she got into her car. She was about to leave but I ran and stood in front. She beckoned me to get in and so we sat in the car and talked for a long time.'

'And what was the outcome?'

'I convinced her not to leave.' Michael suddenly looked horrified. 'I wish I hadn't – she wouldn't have died later that day!'

'So she went back to her room at that point?

'Yes, I suppose so. She said she would go and think about things. She seemed confused by everything.'

'Did you follow her and continue the conversation in her room?'

'No. I thought about it, but I did not.'

'Did you go to her room later on that evening, and finding that she was still intent on informing Mr Cross about Miss Harman and herself, did you deal with the situation in the most final of ways and push Miss George off the kitchen balcony?'

Michael looked the inspector in the eye and shook his head. Sheldon Heath looked back at Michael for several seconds before shifting his stare in the direction of Althea.

'Mrs Althea Jones. Back in June 1973 you attended the party along with a number of your friends. At some point during that evening words were passed between yourself and Stella George, words that you found particularly unpleasant.'

Althea nodded.

'The comments that Miss George used on that occasion were, I believe, of a racist nature?'

Again Althea nodded.

'You, no doubt totally understandably, felt hurt and somewhat bewildered that someone you had previously regarded as a friend was addressing you with such abusive and racially loaded language. That being the case, did you see Stella George later the next day to ask her why she had spoken to you in that way? And not being given a satisfactory apology or explanation for her actions, did you visit her even later and, finding Miss

George standing on the balcony, push her to her death?'

This time Althea shook her head. 'No, I would never have done anything like that, no matter what Stella had done,' she said and stared back at the inspector with a look of defiance on her face.

However, Sheldon Heath didn't get the full benefit of her glare as his attention had quickly shifted to Jack Barber who sat slumped slightly on one end of a Chesterfield sofa. He was nursing a whisky glass that was now almost empty. He had been sipping it frequently while the inspector had been addressing the others.

'Mr Jack Barber, I believe that on the day following the party, a Sunday, someone had mentioned to you that they thought it highly likely that Stella George had been responsible for the death of one of your friends, a Mr Christopher Archer, on the previous evening in a hit-and-run road accident?'

Jack nodded and sipped his rapidly dwindling whisky.

'Am I also correct in thinking that the person who told you of these suspicions was Toby Barker?'

Jack nodded again, this time rather more reluctantly, before finishing his whisky, tipping his glass up to obtain the very last drop.

'Did Mr Barker explain to you why he had formed this opinion?'

JJ looked at his empty glass with genuine sadness in his eyes before replying to the inspector with a simple,

'Yes.'

'And please remind me what he said to you.'

'My recollection is that Toby said that he had looked at Stella's car and there was evidence on it that she had hit Chris Archer.'

'You later confirmed his hypothesis by examining the state of the vehicle yourself?'

Jack nodded again.

'What did you find?'

'A streak of blood and a dent in the front of the car. She had hit someone or something. There was no doubt about it; it was obvious,' said JJ slowly and deliberately.

'Thank you, Mr Barber. And so after presuming that Miss George was responsible for the death of Mr Archer and because your other friend, Angela Stewart, was beside herself with grief as a result, did you angrily visit the tenth floor of the tower block where Stella George resided? Did you knock on her door, intent on taking justice into your own hands? Finding her room empty did you then go into the kitchen and seeing Miss George on the balcony, without saying another word, did you approach her from behind and grab her, lifting her over the balcony's guard rail and causing her to plummet to her death below?'

Jack listened to the inspector, his mouth sagging open, before shaking his head and then looking wistfully again at his empty glass.

'And you, Mrs Knight, formerly Miss Angela Stewart.'

Sheldon Heath bought his by now familiar stare to bear on the petite figure of Angela who looked lost in a large, plush, leather armchair.

'Your relationship with Mr Archer had lasted for most of your time at university. Is that correct?' Angela nodded. 'That relationship had finished just a few days before Miss George's death. Is that also correct?'

Angela nodded again and looked sad as though Inspector Heath's words had brought back the tragic events of that time all over again and forced her to relive them.

'Mrs Knight, it seems unlikely to me that someone so small in stature would be able to lift another person, albeit one who was also slightly built such as Stella George, over the balcony's balustrade, consigning them to their death on the concrete and flagstones below.'

Angela sighed.

'However, Mrs Knight, it also occurs to me that you were in a very good position to enlist the help of someone else to do, as it were, the heavy lifting. There are two candidates it seems to me who might have been willing to provide you with assistance in dispatching Miss George, who you were convinced had been responsible for the death of your long-term boyfriend. One was Mr Barber, who we have just heard from, and the other was Mr Barker, with whom I believe you had embarked on a relationship soon after the breakdown of your previous love affair with Mr Archer.'

Angela looked across to Toby, who she had

deliberately decided not to sit next to, before nodding at the Detective Inspector.

'Did you, having been informed by either Mr Barker or Mr Barber of Stella George's supposed involvement in the death of your ex-boyfriend, decide that she herself deserved to die and ask one of them to accompany you to her room with the intent purpose of killing her?'

Angela looked horrified and shook her head as the inspector continued.

'Finding that she wasn't in her room, did you and your accomplice go to the kitchen area where you saw Miss George standing alone on the balcony? Did you then stand back and allow your male helper, either Mr Barker or Mr Barber, to march out on to the balcony and, without a single word, pick Stella George up and fling her to her death below?'

'No, no! That didn't happen!' half-sobbed, half-shouted Angela.

The inspector looked at her, as if trying to decide whether she was being truthful or not, before turning his attention to Toby (who, as you can see, I have also brought back from the dead especially for this scene).

Toby Barker looked defiant as Sheldon Heath turned his singular stare on him. (Toby looked like he did on the day he died. I considered at one point having him seated there lovingly clutching his can of lager to his chest.)

'Mr Barker,' said Inspector Heath, 'for many years you had been secretly in love with Miss Harman. Is that an accurate assessment?'

Toby looked across to Maggie, a quick smile passing over his lips, before he nodded to the inspector.

'Following her engagement to Mr Cross being called off, is it correct to say that you entered into a physical relationship with Miss Harman?'

'Yes,' said Toby in a clear, defiant voice.

'Is it fair to say that you would have done anything for her?'

Toby hesitated before nodding.

'I propose therefore that after Miss Harman had quite deliberately pushed Miss George to her death, it was you that she saw almost immediately afterwards and it was you who she confessed her crime to.'

Toby looked again at Maggie. She nodded to him almost imperceptivity, giving Toby permission to agree with Inspector Heath's statement. Toby looked at the inspector and answered, 'Yes.'

'And what exactly did she say to you?'

Toby hesitated slightly before shrugging and then answering the question. 'Maggie was distraught when she came to see me. She tapped on the door. I was in bed with Angela – Miss Stewart. It was late. I put on my jeans and went out into the corridor to speak with her. It took me a while to understand what she was saying; I'd had several drinks that evening, I believe. She said that she had spoken at length to Stella and again told her that their relationship was over. Stella wouldn't accept this apparently so Maggie went back later to speak to her again. She found her on the balcony. She went across to her and without saying anything lifted Stella over the balustrade. She said it all happened before she had time to think about it. It was instinctive, I remember her saying. She said if she had thought about it she wouldn't have done it.' Toby looked across to Maggie and smiled at her again.

'Did she say why she had carried out the deed?' said the inspector.

'Yes. She said that Stella had told her earlier that Rob had been unfaithful to her. She said he had slept with many other women during the year he was supposed to be going out with her.'

'And that made Miss Harman angry enough to kill Stella George?'

'No, that wasn't the reason at all. She already suspected what Rob was like – she was probably aware of his little dalliances – but she also knew that if Stella announced it to the world it would give Rob a reason to break off their engagement. Rob meant everything to her, unfortunately, and she couldn't stand the idea of losing him and was prepared to commit murder to stop that occurring.' Toby breathed a sigh of relief. After all those years he was pleased to be able to tell the truth about what had happened.

'However, it was all in vain, wasn't it? Because Mr Cross, soon afterwards, called off the engagement anyway,' said Inspector Heath.

'That's correct,' said Toby. 'He rang her up a few

days later when Maggie was at her parents' house and told her that they wouldn't be getting married after all. It was a short phone call apparently. Maggie was stunned by it.'

'And soon afterwards you were in a relationship with Miss Harman.'

'Yes. But she still was in love with Rob so I never had a chance.'

'How did that make you feel?'

'How do you think? I was devastated! It made me depressed for a long time. It was the worst thing that ever happened to me. From that moment onwards I hated Rob even more than I had done before.'

'Even though you kept in touch with him and saw him on a regular basis over many years?'

Toby scoffed and then nodded.

Sheldon Heath then switched his steely gaze to Maggie again. She looked so alone and vulnerable as she sat there.

'Miss Margaret Harman, Maggie. Can you tell me more about what happened on that Sunday in the June of 1973?'

Maggie puffed out her cheeks and began. 'I got up late that day; I was hungover from the party the night before. I made myself and Rob – Mr Cross – some tea. I had to pop to the shop to get some milk first as we'd run out. Then I took Rob his cup of tea and we… talked for a bit. Oh, I briefly spoke with Michael in The Square. He had been for a run I think.'

'You saw Michael again later I believe?'

'I did. I visited him because I wanted to tell him about Rob and me getting engaged.'

'According to his recollections he says that you were upset about what Stella George might tell Mr Cross later in the day.'

'It was a long time ago; I can't remember everything I said to him.'

Inspector Heath looked sceptical. 'After leaving Michael Key's room you then went back to Mr Cross's room?'

'Yes, I think so. He had gone back to sleep so I went to the shop again and bought some grapes and went to see my friend Jane in the medical centre. I remember that she was pleased that Rob and I were engaged. After I left her I went for a long walk on my own in the afternoon. Rob had gone to the bar even though he'd had a bad hangover all morning. It was nice in the outdoors – sunny, calming and quiet, with just the birds singing. When I got back in the early evening I felt nice and relaxed and so after a while I decided not to meet Rob in Grasmere Bar but instead went back to see Stella.'

Maggie paused, taking a deep breath before continuing.

'She was in her room. She was pleased to see me, I think. We sat and talked. I think at first she half expected me to say I was going to leave Rob and run away with her instead!' Maggie smiled at the memory, half wondering perhaps what her life might have turned out like if she had agreed to do that.

'And then what happened?' enquired the inspector.

'We chatted for a long while. She told me that she had planned to leave – to drive home – but then had changed her mind. She told me how awful she had felt about the party and what she had said to people. She also told me about driving back to the campus when she was so drunk she could hardly stand, and how she had hit a deer on the road and how that had sobered her up. I thought everything was going well and then she tried to kiss me. I pushed her away and shook my head. I told her we couldn't be close – couldn't be intimate again. I told her again that I was in love with Rob and that whatever she said wouldn't alter that. And then her attitude changed. She looked evil; full of anger and bitterness. She shouted at me. She said that if she couldn't have me then neither could Rob! She said she would go and see Rob in the morning and tell him all about me and her and how we were in love and it was she I really wanted all along, and that he was a cheating liar!'

'How did that make you feel?' asked Sheldon Heath.

'I cried at first and then felt angry. She was trying to spoil my future – my life, my happiness. I left her room and slammed the door. No doubt she was upset too. When I saw her later on the balcony she had tears in her eyes, but I was angry. I went down in the lift and stood for a while in the lobby of The Tower. Everywhere was deserted. It was late by then; we had talked for hours.

She had followed me down and we talked some more in the lobby. We smoked lots of cigarettes as we stood there. She tried and tried to persuade me to leave Rob; tried until she became pathetic really. I remember that a group of drunken lads got into the lift at one point. We both just glared at them and dared them to say anything to us.' Maggie gave a forlorn little chuckle as she thought back to the incident.

'And then what happened?' said Inspector Heath.

'She left and got into the lift.'

'And what did you do?'

'I was so worried. As far as I was concerned, she was still going to speak to Rob in the morning. I didn't know what he would say when he knew about Stella and me being together for so long but I was scared he'd call off our engagement and leave me. So I went back to her room.'

'Why did you do that?'

'I suppose I wanted to make one last attempt to ask her – to plead with her – not to tell Rob.' Maggie gave a little laugh as she realised that everything she had done on that night was pointless; Rob had broken up with her on the phone a few days later. 'I ran up the stairs; I was in too much of a hurry to use the lift – it was always so slow! Stella's door was open. She wasn't in her room so I went to the kitchen and saw her outside on the balcony. I stepped out onto the balcony. She heard me and turned around. She said something like "it's you". She had tears streaming down her cheeks. I suppose I should have felt sorry for her then – put my arm around her, comforted her in some way – but instead all of this anger welled up in me and I glared at her. At that moment I hated her. And so I grabbed her shoulder and her large belt buckle (if the police had bothered to take fingerprints…). I don't know how I managed to lift her as we were about the same size, but I did. It was the anger and the adrenaline I suppose. And I watched her as she fell. Her face looked back at me questioning. I had nightmares about her face for years afterwards! And then she hit the ground. There was no sound. You'd think there would be wouldn't you? She just lay there. I went to Rob's room then. He had just gone to bed, drunk of course. I told him I'd been for a walk and then spent the night reading. He believed me – always did I think. He was incredibly gullible really. He never really understood me; always thought that I'd be bothered about the other women he'd been with. I wasn't though – not really. I thought once we were married I'd have him all to myself and we'd have a couple of kids and everything would be perfect. Just goes to show!' Maggie laughed quietly to herself.

The inspector looked up and nodded and a uniformed police officer, who had been standing by the door, approached her. Maggie stood up and the officer put his hand gently on her shoulder.

Inspector Heath looked at her and spoke. 'Miss Margaret Harman, you are under arrest for the murder of Miss Stella George on the 24th June 1973. You do

not have to say anything but it may harm your defence
if you do not mention, when questioned, something that
you later rely on in court.'

Chapter 31: *The End*

Today

So there it is. An already deceased Maggie charged with the murder of Stella that took place almost fifty years ago! I suppose part of me had suspected Maggie was guilty from quite an early stage; maybe even on the night Stella died when she came to my room really late appearing quite nervous. I'm not going to pretend it was one of the reasons why I decided to finish with her (you know me better than that) but it may be another reason why it has been so hard for me to remember all of the details from those times; it was almost as if my brain refused to believe what had happened was actually possible. However, that is probably me just re-writing history (like everyone else does I suspect).

Toby knew what Maggie had done; I realised that later. If he hadn't died that day in his house, I'm sure he would have told me. In fact I think he was about to when I pushed him away and he fell. I presume that Maggie had admitted her guilt to him when they were together and he had protected her all through the years. Quite chivalrous of him really, I doubt I would have done the same. But I suppose he not only wanted to protect Maggie, who he loved, but his daughter too of course.

I actually think of Toby a lot. How hard it must have been for him to have a daughter – one who called him Uncle Toby – and not be able to tell her, or anyone else, the truth. When I eventually suspected that it was Maggie who had thrown Stella off the balcony, I briefly considered telling the police before dismissing the idea. What good would it have served really? Although my one meeting with Maggie's daughter, Sarah Webb, hadn't endeared her to me, I didn't want her to be any more upset than she already was. After all, she had lost both her mother and father in the space of a few months; sadness enough for anyone, I guess. I know what you're thinking – that sounds uncharacteristically noble of me – but over the years I have changed, and I believe I am now a much better person than I once was. Well, that's my opinion anyway. You'll have to draw your own conclusions.

In any case, the death of Stella took place so long ago. Does it really matter anymore? Does anyone actually care now about things that took place nigh on fifty years ago? Pretty soon all of the players in those events will be dead, and all of those memories, the good along with the bad, will fade away with them. Even my somewhat disjoined recollections from that time will die along with me and, of course, the world will not notice one tiny jot. And so it goes!

In the end, does the past really matter? Things happened and people played their part. They eventually moved on and changed; sometimes for the better, sometimes for the worse. The things that happen to us, both good and ill, which seem so incredibly important at the time, get forgotten. In the long run, everyone becomes dust and their memories blow away in the wind. Life, as someone once said, will always disappoint you in the final analysis.

In spite of all those depressing thoughts, however, I do find myself thinking of those times and the people involved in them: JJ, Tina, Liz, Nick, Angela, Rufus, Jane, Althea, Michael, Fiona and, of course, Toby and Maggie. For a few short years our lives and our actions were intertwined and seemed so vitally important but, as Toby quite rightly said, how many of those individuals did I actively keep in touch with or see on a regular basis? As you now know very few of them in fact. Is that the same for everyone? Do we simply meet too many people during the course of our lives? Too many to care about in any meaningful way? Too many to form extended friendships with over a long period of time?

The days here in prison are long and mind numbing. Time goes by so very slowly. One day my sentence will come to an end, either when I am allowed to walk out of here under my own steam or when I am carried out in a long wooden box. Sadly, I am getting to the stage where

I'm hoping that each one of these interminable days will turn out to be my last and one morning I just won't wake up and have to face another one of them.

Things fade of course – bodies as well as memories – and as someone else once said (it may have been John Maynard Keynes): "in the long run we are all dead". That, I think, is as good a place as anywhere to leave things. So here's to our next life! Perhaps we can all make a better fist of it then.

Dedications and Acknowledgments

This book is dedicated to all the friends I made during my time at The University of Lancaster between 1970 and 1973. They include Alan, Bill, Carol, Cathy, Colin, Diana, Gill, Heather, Jerry, John, Ken, Malcolm, Martin, Nan, Peter, Rick, Rod, Rosi, Sally and Steve – I remember them all with great affection and even still see a few of them to this day. I would like to reassure all those I knew back then that none of the (very fictional) characters in this book bears even the slightest resemblance to any real people, living or dead. My friends were all so very much nicer than any of the characters that populate the pages of this story and it was a pleasure knowing each and every one of them during those long ago, bygone times now fifty years in the past – a distance in time I find increasingly difficult to comprehend!

The University of the North is vaguely based on Lancaster University and a few of the incidents in the book actually did happen to me or other people. For example, the Wings concert at Lancaster in February

1972 took place pretty much as it is described in the story and I did cause an American to fall on the floor laughing due to me telling him (rather than her) what faggots were. However, the vast majority of the incidents and events in the story are pure invention - the result of my fevered and warped imagination. I am particularly pleased to say that at no time did anyone I know fall to their death from Bowland Tower, Lancaster University's high-rise block!

I would like to say a big thank you to my wife, Sue Coley, for her constant love, support and encouragement (and invaluable help as my first reader). I would also like to thank all those other good people who spent their valuable time reading parts (or all in some cases) of my manuscript at its various stages and for their many very helpful (and in some cases vital) suggestions about how to improve it: Andrew Coley, Anna Coley, Gill Langley, Heather Weatherhead, John Anderson, Ken Langley, Rosi Edwards and Tom Coley in particular. Their help and advice was absolutely, welcome, important and much needed and I am totally in their debt.

Finally I would like to express my thanks to Vicky Richards and the team at Cranthorpe Millner for their hard work, skill and patience. It has been really appreciated.

Author's Note

The song titles for each chapter all come from the period before 1973. It was an era of popular music that has, in my opinion, seldom been bettered. The list forms rather a good playlist:

Prologue: *Bad Moon Rising* – Creedence Clearwater Revival (1969)
1: *Something in the Air* – Thunderclap Newman (1969)
2: *Maggie May* – Rod Stewart (1971)
3: *Two of Us* – The Beatles (1970)
4: *Sunday Morning* – The Velvet Underground & Nico (1966)
5: *Meet on the Ledge* – Fairport Convention (1968)
6: *Will You Love Me Tomorrow?* – Carole King (1971)
7: *Who Knows Where the Time Goes?* – Fairport Convention (1968)
8: *Paranoid* – Black Sabbath (1970)
9: *Changes* – David Bowie (1972)
10: *In a Broken Dream* – Python Lee Jackson (1970)
11: *Gotta See Jane* – R. Dean Taylor (1968)

12: *Without You* – Nilsson (1971)

13: *American Pie* – Don McLean (1971)

14: *Days* – The Kinks (1968)

15: *You're So Vain* – Carly Simon (1972)

16: *All the Young Dudes* – Mott the Hoople (1972)

17: *Maybe I'm Amazed* – Paul McCartney (1970)

18: *A Thing Called Love* – Johnny Cash (1972)

19: *You Can't Always Get What You Want* – The Rolling Stones (1969)

20: *(If Paradise Is) Half As Nice* – Amen Corner (1969)

21: *You Wear It Well* – Rod Stewart (1972)

22: *Reach Out I'll Be There* – The Four Tops (1966)

23: *God Only Knows* – The Beach Boys (1966)

24: *It's Too Late* – Carole King (1971)

25: *Paint It, Black* – The Rolling Stones (1966)

26: *The Tears of a Clown* – Smokey Robinson & the Miracles (1970)

27: *Rainy Days and Mondays* – The Carpenters (1971)

28: *Time Has Come Today* – The Chambers Brothers (1967)

29: *Walk on the Wild Side* – Lou Reed (1972)

30: *Mama Weer All Crazee Now* – Slade (1972)

31: *The End* – The Beatles (1969)

BV - #0069 - 080223 - C0 - 197/132/19 - PB - 9781803781020 - Matt Lamination